THE DARK OBSESSION

N.A.Preedy

CONTENTS

Dedicated to all those who believed in me.

Also to all those who didn't and all those who will in the future.

Disowned and disgraced,
The wings from the sky,
Earths gift from the devil,
The devils gift from up high,
Fluttering footfalls of beings alike,
Grace holds no-one,
I must fight to have life,
The ones thought to be fallen,
Stand guard to protect me,
Illusions of what perfection is,
Cascades through the echos of time,
And leaves me on the floor,
With acceptance I find salvation,
In the wings I find peace,
And in life I find eternity.

N.A.Preedy

CHAPTER 1

"For never was a story of more woe than this of Juliet and her Romeo."

My body is ablaze with romance and lust for the kind of love I've just read about. This is at least my fourth time reading *Romeo and Juliet*, and I still can't get enough of it. I sigh and remind myself, *Rosa, remember they both died*. Damn university finishing. At least I wasn't alone all the time when I was still getting my degree. My fingers massage my temples.

As gracefully as possible, I rise to my feet from the comfy brown leather chair I was snuggled into at the town's ancient library. I hate to leave, but it's getting late. I glance at the beautiful, carved wooden beams high on the grey stone ceiling; the two dazzling glass chandeliers always catch my eye.

I place the book onto the shelf and drag my finger along the old wooden shelving, dust collecting on my fingertip. The shelves hold hundreds of classical books, some so old they look as though they'll fall apart. A gentle cough from across the warmly lit room startles me. Someone else is here. Keeping my head down, I take the book closest to my finger and sit on the still-warm chair. Peeking up, I notice a tall blonde man in a long black jacket eyeing the books opposite me. I glance at my own book. *Pride and Prejudice.*

"In vain, I have struggled. It will not do. My feelings will no longer be repressed. You must allow me to tell you how ardently I admire and love you." I can't help but speak out loud. After all, it is my favourite quote from the book.

"Pride and Prejudice. A classic," a smooth male voice says behind me.

Shit! My heart jumps out of my chest and into my hands as the book drops to the floor with a thud, sending a spiral of dust into the air off the dingy carpet.

"Sorry I startled you," the mysterious blonde man says in a gentle voice.

"It's okay," I reply coolly, not making eye contact with him, instead spying the mass of books that surround us.

He walks around to face me, picks up the book, and holds it out to me.

My eyes linger on his pale and bony hand. I avert my gaze as fast as I can, staring at my feet.

"I'm Dale. Pleasure to meet you." This time he speaks with a smooth but more confident voice.

"Rosa, I'm Rosa." I push the hair draping over my left eye behind my ear. "You like the classics?"

"I do. I'm a bit old-fashioned myself. Love relaxing with a book." Dale's tone is calm as he sits on the old leather chair opposite me. "Why are you here this late?"

"I could ask you the same," I blurt out quietly with a grin as I turn my attention to his face. His dark-brown eyes stand out against his pale skin and short white-blond hair. His lips are a dark shade of red, his jawline chiseled, and a single deep dimple dots his cheek on the side where his lips curve into a smile. *He's gorgeous*, I celebrate in my head whilst hiding behind my book.

"My father passed away recently, so I'm in town organising his estate, and the library has always been my happy place. I thought I'd try to escape for a couple of hours," he says in a low voice.

I watch his face, his eyes expectant, seemingly more self-conscious than ever. "Oh, uh. I'm sorry," I mutter.

"It's all right. I didn't really know him well."

I shuffle awkwardly. "Well, I recently graduated from university—criminal law. Now I have t-too much free time." I try to pretend I didn't stutter. The truth is I'm desperately lonely; right now, books are my only friends. All my real friends have relocated to jobs across seas or live in bigger cities. I've never been good at lying, but there's no need to tell anyone, especially a random stranger, about my life.

"Oh, uni. So, you're about twenty-three?" he asks, as if talking more to himself than to me.

I grin. "Exactly."

He smiles his one-sided dimpled smile and winks.

I laugh and fumble with my book, then drop it again with another loud thud. *Shit.* I know my cheeks must be bright pink by now, so I fake a yawn and lean down to gather my bag. "I'd best be off, important day tomorrow," I say through another suppressed yawn. I groan internally. It's unlike me to skip an opportunity to get to know a man.

"Take my number, please, and give me a call. Maybe we can meet up for coffee." He retrieves a card from his pocket and holds it out to me.

My insides squirm excitedly as I take the card. Our fingers touch for barely a second, sending a lightning bolt up my arm. I try hard to hide the smile that spreads across my lips. The card reads, *Dale Cartwright, Director, Author*. I shove it into my back pocket.

"Okay. I'll call you." I smile and stand, and he rises with me and grasps my hand to shake it. My fingers tingle with his warmth.

"Make sure you do—tomorrow."

I stare, astonished by his demanding tone. Smiling wearily, I nod, wave, and walk at the same time and catch my heel on the side of a chair, then trip awkwardly over my own feet. *I'm such a klutz!*

*****

I run up to the front door of my house, and relief fills me as I enter. Now that I am finally home and comfortable, the pale walls feel warm and cosy. I shrug off my coat and hang it on a hook. Should I really call Dale tomorrow? My mind is swimming with different scenarios. Does he like me? Or maybe he wants ideas from me. Could it be he's just bored on his trip back to our small town? I creep through the dark hallway in an effort not to wake my older brother Benjamin. I'm completely preoccupied as I pass the kitchen.

"Rosalie," I hear from the kitchen, the tone relieved.

I double back and turn towards the kitchen, the bright white light burning my eyes. I squint as I reply, "Benjamin, I'm just going to bed. Got a bit carried away at the library." I wink at him. "Met some ma ..." A wide grin spreads across my tired face.

His eyes widen, and I can almost hear the cogs turning in his brain as he approaches me. "Who? Are you meeting him again?" His eyes search my face, as if I held some deep, dark secret.

I laugh, punching his chest. "Don't think so, Ben. Important interview tomorrow though. I'd best sleep." I turn to walk up the stairs.

My brother's big blue eyes light up, his eyebrows furrowed at the news. But all he says is "Night."

I go straight to my room, not switching on any lights, drop my backpack, and fall straight onto my bed. Time check—1:50 a.m. I close my eyes, thinking about the fact that I have to be awake in only a few hours. Panic colours my dreams, a set of handcuffs and Dale's dark eyes.

*****

I awake in a hurry after sleeping in too late and scramble into the smartest clothes I can find: a black pencil skirt with a white shirt. Can't go wrong. *I need to do the laundry*, I repeat over and over, taking a red pen and scribbling, *DO LAUNDRY*, onto a yellow sticky note and slap it onto my mirror. I rub my eyes and stare at myself in the mirror, deciding how much work needs to be done. Mascara, definitely mascara. I brush on a heavy coat until my blue eyes pop against the black makeup. At least my eyes don't just blend into my pale skin now. My blonde waves are messy, but I haven't left myself enough time to do much about it, so I force a brush through the tangles and do my best to make it look organised. Much better, much more professional. Staring at myself, I search for the beauty in my face that others say they see, but I can never really embrace it. With a nod to myself to boost my confidence, I leave my room and half skip down the stairs.

I brush past Ben in the hallway. He's a lot taller than me, and his tan never seems to fade despite the almost constant clouds England has to offer. We have our similarities, but his light-brown hair is our biggest difference. He sings a beautiful melody as he ruffles my hair to acknowledge my existence. I don't have the time to linger and moan at him for messing up my hair, so I put it to the back of my mind to argue about when I get home. He's great to live with really, clean and caring. Our parents moved to London, but we enjoy our small town near the border of Scotland.

"Rose, I'll be going to meet my director now. I should be home before you are." Ben watches me rush down the hallway.

I grab my bag from the kitchen table and ensure my car keys are in there as I shoot for the door.

Before I can answer, he's singing loudly again.

"Great, you can tell me all about it later, then," I mumble. He never lets me forget his successful theatre career. I shout a goodbye and slam the door; his melody is silenced as I walk down the pavement outside my door and onto the street.

CHAPTER 2

I arrive at the building for my interview five minutes early. I'd hate to be late for my first-ever job interview. The building sticks out like a sore thumb in my small town; it's large and white with tinted black glass windows. Its ten floors stretch high above anything my town has to offer; our centre only consists of a few little boutiques, a library, and a coffeeshop. I could see it way before I arrived. I glance at a pink Post-it Note I had screwed up into my fist to triple check I have the right place, then, taking a deep breath, I enter the large revolving doors. My eyes widen as I behold the spectacular and clean entrance hall. Working for this law firm would be a dream; my specialty is criminology, but I'd take anything right now—too much time on my hands. I walk to the large black desk with white illuminating lights reading, ALCAZARS' LAWYERS, at the back of a spacious room. A young man, about my age, sits on a comfy black leather seat behind it, with black hair, dark eyes, and a dark suit.

"I'm here for my interview with Mr. Alcazar," I state as confidently as possible.

He grabs a piece of paper off the top of a pile, and his lips move as he reads; a single eyebrow lifts.

I clench my fists to control my shaking hands.

"Miss Lockwood. Yes, if you go to floor eight and report to the desk," he says with a twinkle in his eye and nods to his left where I see two lifts.

I walk over as elegantly as possible and press the large button on the side of the lift. With a ding, the doors open, and I step inside. A sweet lullaby is playing, which is definitely a failed attempt at making me feel calm. I bounce on the balls of my feet until the doors ding open, and I exit into a vast dark-coloured room with a star-lit ceiling. I saunter farther into the darkness, and the colossal room lights up all around me. In front of me is a very large, long desk with three stiff men in black suits sitting in the middle. I stumble as I enter, and all three men stand fast and graciously.

"Hello, Miss Lockwood. If you would please follow the desk to the left, you will come to Mr Alcazars' office," the one in the middle says with a deep voice.

I nod and stride to the only door I see. *What the hell is this place?* I knock on the door twice and stand readying myself, waiting for an answer.

"Come in," another deep voice calls out.

I turn the shiny silver knob and enter a room resembling nothing like the rest of the building. The walls are towering with books, a smart dark wood desk sits in the middle of the office, with a leather chair to one side and a two-seater leather sofa on the other. I do not yet see the owner of the voice, but as I scan the room, I notice a figure in front of the bookshelf to my left.

He steps forward, his hand out to shake mine.

I take a moment to look at him properly. Dark curly hair, large bright green eyes with black-rimmed square glasses, his cheekbones are strong. He has olive-coloured skin, his bright white and perfect teeth shine through his slightly parted lips. He smirks in my direction; his one hand is tucked into his pocket. He wears a light-blue suit with a purple tie.

I proffer my trembling hand and step towards him. His large hand wraps around mine. I involuntarily shiver at his icy touch, and with both of his smooth hands, he shakes.

"Nice to meet you, Miss Lockwood," he says with a soft voice. I note a slight Spanish accent. Still grasping my hand, his bright eyes lock onto mine. "Sit, please." He gestures for me to sit on the sofa.

I turn towards the sofa and slowly sit, looking up to his desk.

He comes forward and sits opposite me. His hands raise towards his eyes, and he removes his glasses. His eyes shine brighter than ever as he lays his glasses on the table and places his hands together. "I'll start off by saying I'm no longer looking for someone for the position in environmental law, but after seeing your resume, I couldn't help but ask for you to come in. I am looking for someone to join me in criminology as a partner, if you may. Someone who will help me with cases and ease the workload." His presence makes my stomach twist.

"So, an assistant ..." I blurt out.

He eyes me. "No, Miss Lockwood. I mean it when I say partner." He sighs. "We will work together. We'll work on cases and visit prisoners together. We will talk to our clients together, and in no way will I be asking you to get me a coffee—unless you're getting one for yourself." He reaches for his cup. "Anyway, I have many assistants already." I'm sure I notice his lip twitch into a smile. He takes a small sip from the cup and places it onto the table.

"I'm definitely interested." My heart is in my throat. As I contemplate working alongside Mr Alcazar himself, my stomach turns again.

"I loved your resume," he says while chuckling lightheartedly. "But I'd love you to tell me a little bit about yourself."

I swallow hard. "Uh, well ..."

"Confidently, please."

I take a deep breath. "I am passionate about doing what's right. I acknowledge I sometimes think with my emotions, and for me, that's not always a bad thing. I would love to be given a chance to work with you."

"What do you like to do on a day off?"

I clear my throat as I think. "I like to read and visit new places. I enjoy history."

"And your work hours are flexible?" He leans an elbow on the table.

"Yes, completely. I'm ready to work at any time." I hurry my words, sounding a little bit too enthusiastic.

"I want a trial with you."

That was quick. My heart hammers as I process what he said.

"Though I have a pointer, if I may?" He waits for my answering nod. "You should try to talk with more authority. You know our clients trust us to do what's right. I am sure that will come with time anyway."

"Okay, well, that's brilliant." I choke out, trying to sound more confident but obviously failing.

He flashes a white smile. "I expect you to be here at seven a.m. on Thursday, and we will give this a go. I'll email you any more details." He rises from his seat and walks around to me.

I rise in synchronisation with him.

He proffers his hand once more. "I will see you soon, then, Miss Lockwood." His cold hand grips mine again.

"Mr Alcazar." I nod and leave the room, trying not to look back. *Well, he's different.* I wander to the lift, no longer taking in my surroundings but recalling my encounter with the firm's owner. Struggling to suppress a goofy grin, I look to the floor, letting my hair falls across my face.

Rain hits my face as I step into the cold air. Damn this English weather. I don't have a jacket, so I shrug and sprint towards my car.

I jump into my black Mini Cooper and pull my phone from my pocket. A shiver runs through my body as I slam the car door and turn on the engine. Looking at my screen, I see two missed calls from my mother; she'll want to know what's happened at my interview. I make a mental note to call her later, then retrieve a card from inside my bag. *Dale Cartwright.* I take a deep breath, then dial his number into my phone. The call tone blares, and he answers on the second ring.

"Hello. Dale Cartwright speaking."

"Hello. It's Rosa from last night. You said for me to call you today," I speak clearly; talking on the phone is so much easier than in person.

"Ahh yes, coffee. Are you available now? I'm currently in the coffeeshop opposite the library."

"Oh, okay. Yes, sure, I'll be there in five minutes." I end the call.

Oh my god, oh my god. I flick on the car's headlights as I pull off through the heavy rain. Dark, cloudy skies cover the sun; it looks like a storm is coming.

CHAPTER 3

I pull up to a small, almost empty coffeeshop and park directly out front. How lucky, a quick escape if needed; I grin to myself. I clamber out of the car and straighten my black pencil skirt, pulling it farther up my thigh. After several heavy breaths, I enter and almost immediately spot a blonde figure sitting at the back of the cramped but cosy coffeeshop. Only one other couple is sitting near the front window. I stride to the table, not giving myself a chance to back out and run away.

He stands, smiling his dimpled smile, then walks around and pulls out my seat. I sit, and he returns to his seat. His eyes meet mine, and his beautiful smile grows.

My heartbeat rockets as I scan his handsome features. My eyes linger on his, as I fall deeper into them.

"Rosa, you look beautiful. Very smart."

"Thank you. I had an interview at Alcazars' Law." My cheeks burn crimson.

"How did it go?" He doesn't take his gaze off me as we speak.

"I've got a trial to work with Mr Alcazar himself in criminal law." A great smile splits across my face; it's nice to brag.

"Oh, so you majored in criminology? Very good. Congratulations." He grins as he places his hands on the table.

A young waitress comes up behind me and flips her writing pad, ready to take my order.

"Latte, please."

She nods and wanders off. Within a minute, she's back with my latte, too hot to drink.

I lean forward to blow gently into the boiling latte. I feel his eyes watching me. I take a scolding sip and refocus on the handsome man sitting opposite me. My stomach has not stopped turning since my interview, and it feels like it's doing constant somersaults.

He holds the conversation well. We laugh and talk about my brother. We discuss his work in writing. "It's nice, just writing what I want and getting paid for it." He smiles.

"It must be, but don't you ever run out of ideas?"

"Yes, but then I meet people like you. And just like that, I'm filled with imagination again."

I blush bright red, my hands wrapping around my coffee cup.

He orders more coffee, and shockingly, our conversation seems natural, like I've known him a long time. My laughter is more real now as he tells me a story about his experiences in university.

I hear a crack as glass sprays across the table, the waitress yelps, and Dale is out of his seat. A burning pain sears up my thigh as I realise what has happened, the pain of a thousand needles stabbing all at once. *Holy shit! holy shit!* I scream on the inside, but outside, I try to stay composed. My eyes well up with tears as my leg, if possible, burns with more force. I hear Dale shout a string of rude words at the waitress and ask for a cold, wet towel as he kneels by my side. Time seems to slow a little as he pushes the towel onto my burning leg.

"Don't touch it!" I shout at him a bit more aggressive than I hoped.

He completely ignores me, applying more pressure.

"Come, I live just behind here. I'll patch you up at mine." He speaks calmly but doesn't wait for a response, lifting me off the chair and letting me bear all my weight on him.

I can't focus on much, the pain pulling my mind into a frenzy.

"Just let me go home. I'm fine," I say between deep breaths.

"I can't. Look at you. Trust me, please."

He's breathing heavily as we approach a sizeable white house. The front garden is large, with bright green grass. An incredible pain sears up my thigh when I try to bare my weight on it. I let out a little moan and squeeze my eyes shut for a moment, letting the pain take over.

My head spins painfully as he moves me awkwardly onto a soft white sofa. As my eyes adjust, I discern a room with white shelves that cover almost every wall. Each shelf contains hundreds of sculptures of bones and books on medical science. A breeze blows across my face from the open window behind me. *What the hell type of room is this?* I face the window to see black and thunderous clouds. A flash sparks through the sky, and thunder replies with a loud, low grumble. Rain hammers across the vast lush green gardens outside.

"Thank you." Red creeps up my face; I can feel my cheeks burning hot.

He smiles and sits next to me.

I struggle to regard him through pain and embarrassment.

Dale shrugs off his wet jacket to reveal a bright white button-up shirt, with the sleeves rolled up, his top buttons undone. I can't help, even when I'm in pain, to spy his chest; he's so pale, and even with his slightly baggy shirt, I can see how muscular his figure is.

I readjust in my seat as he studies me.

"Don't be embarrassed. Rosa. It happens to the best of us." He strokes my burning red cheek. "If anything, I'm quite impressed you didn't scream." His dark, mysterious eyes peer into mine.

"I, well ..." I blush furiously.

His eyebrows furrow as he pulls his gaze away from mine. "Rosa, you were hurting. Don't hold back on me ... I want to know all about you. I want to know the real you ..."

He looks at me again, his eyes no longer locking onto mine but scanning my face. He stops on my lips. His hot hands cup my flushing cheeks. He nibbles his lip, and his eyes fill with longing.

My heart skips a beat as I process that he wants me.

"You are so beautiful, Rosa." His gaze flits from my eyes to my lips.

I hold my breath, frozen to the spot. We're close enough now that I can smell his alluring sweet scent mixed with what I think is cigarette smoke. I take a deep breath and embrace the smell that's heightening all my senses.

His dark eyes are shining. His hands fall as his lips falter into a weak smile. "Sorry, I have an uncontrollable desire to kiss you, though I don't want to be too forward with you. It's just ... you make me feel so ..." A defeated look crosses his face.

But I want him too. I want to feel his embrace, to taste his lips. "I, well, I actually have no objections," I whisper alluringly as I look down and tuck my hair behind my ear. I can feel him smiling.

Again, his hands cup my cheeks, this time a little rougher, as he pulls me in.

Losing all self-control, I wrap my arms around his neck.

His lips close in on mine, and his breathing hitches. Our lips lock and move together in perfect synchronisation.

My heart feels like it will explode, my body trembling with nerves.

His lips part from mine as he takes my hand and looks at me. "You are shaking, Rosa." The worry in his voice is evident. Concern washes over his bright eyes, his face, flustered, still breathing faster than normal.

"My leg still hurts. Plus, I'm a little nervous. It's been a while since I got intimate with anyone." My voice is shaking as I lower my head in embarrassment again.

He wraps his hand around my shoulder and clenches me into his chest. His heart beats fast and strong against my ear. "Don't be.

There's no rush," he says, quiet and smooth. He reaches behind him and retrieves a tube of cream and a bandage. "It's very red, but it's not blistering, so I think it'll heal quickly." He nods at my leg.

"That's good." My voice comes out as a squeak as his fingers move along my lower thigh where the burn starts.

"Cream?" he asks and waits for my nod.

He passes me his jacket to put across my body. I lie it across the middle of my skirt, then his fingers move to the hem of my skirt. He raises it, revealing more red and angry skin. His fingers stop when he reaches the top of my thigh where the last of the burns are.

I sit motionless, trying to stop my nervous body from shaking. I'm conflicted as the pain when he applies the cream makes me want to cry out, but somehow, it feels good. I grip his sturdy shoulder as his fingers reach the top of my leg. They move in circular motions for a moment, the cooling effect of the cream helping greatly. He stops much too soon.

"Stand up, and I can wrap this around it." He holds out a bandage.

My heart is in my throat as I step off the sofa, my skirt a pointless piece of fabric wrapped around my waist.

Dale wraps the fabric around my upper thigh, his fingers trembling.

"You do this well," I say breathlessly.

He chuckles as he finishes wrapping my leg. He stands and turns away as I yank down my skirt as fast as possible to cover the bandage.

"Come, let me show you my house." He smiles and proffers his hand.

I take a deep breath and hold his pale, strong hand. We leave the door and enter a large, brightly lit hallway. The rain pounds on the rooftops.

He tightens his grip on my hand as we pass a couple doors. I'm curious as to what is inside. He mentions his parents' old room and an office, then opens the third door down. We enter a large, square bedroom which contains a large bookcase, a desk with a laptop, two doors to the left of the room, and a grand double bed with red and black bedding. He walks farther inside and sits on the end of the bed.

I follow him.

"Bathroom and wardrobe." He appears preoccupied as he gestures towards the doors.

I notice a desk clock reading 17:30.

He puts a hand on my leg, and his eyes shine at me once more.

My heart rate quickens as his hand trails up and down my good thigh, the other continues to throb and I swallow back the pain.

"My room when I was a kid. I grew up in this house, so many fond memories here ..."

I put my hand on his before I stand. "I have to go, Dale. It's quite late already. My brother will be wondering where I am."

He rises too and holds out a hand again, and I take it. He guides me into him and kisses my head. "Can I see you again?" He finally looks back into my eyes, excitement rising through my body.

"I'm free all day tomorrow." I smile at him.

His smile breaks into a glorious grin. "Tomorrow ten a.m., meet me here? I will make us breakfast, and we can take a walk." He's smiling as he leads me out the bedroom and down the long hallway to a winding staircase. He releases my hand and nods towards the stair bannister for me to hold and smirks. "I noticed you can be a little clumsy."

I scowl, but he doesn't notice. We come to a large double front door, and he opens it. We step outside into the thrashing rain.

"The coffeeshop shop is just behind my house. I'll drive you; this rain is heavy."

"No, I'm fine. My car is just outside the shop. Besides, I like the rain," I lie. "See you tomorrow, then, Dale," I say slowly, secretly hoping for him to pull me back inside in a strong embrace and lead me to his bedroom.

Instead, he kisses my head once more. "Until tomorrow, beautiful."

I can't contain my smile.

A troubled look sweeps across his face.

I regard him with a questioning expression.

"I'm fine. I just ... well, never mind. We can talk tomorrow," he says and lets me go.

I turn and self-consciously walk out of his huge driveway, not noticing the rain's force. Instead, I notice two cars parked neatly in line—a large black Bentley and a neat white Jaguar. I wonder which one is his.

I arrive at the corner and see my car waiting for me. *Did I do something?* I glance back once more, wondering how I never paid more attention to this big house in the middle of the centre. Ensuring I am out of sight, I run towards my car, regretting not letting him drive me. The rain is getting heavier. I am absolutely drenched, and the thunderous wind is blustering. I shake my hair like a dog as I pull my car door open and crank the heating to full. A shiver rolls through my body as I pull off, leaving the town behind.

Of course, my brother is curious about where I have been, what's taken me so long, why am I so giggly, and why the hell I have a bandage wrapped around my leg.

"So, my interview went all right." I sigh, feigning sadness.

"Aww, what did they say?"

"That there are no positions left for environmental law. Luckily, Mr Alcazar himself was looking for someone to work for him, and it's me!" I squeal.

We discuss me getting a trial at Alcazars' Lawyers and how different the owner is from what everyone expects.

"What about your leg?" Ben frowns.

"Well, I met with Dale, and we were drinking coffee, and the waitress spilled some on my leg."

"Dale? You mean Dale Cartwright?" Benjamin's eyebrows cross with disapproval.

"How do you know?" I study Ben's reaction.

"He is the writer of our script for our next production. He comes in sometimes and does a bit of directing." He flashes a grim smile.

My cheeks heat up, which seems to be a common occurrence today. "Oh, so ... you see him a lot?"

"No, barely ever. He's always too busy. He's a bit old for you anyway, Rosa." His eyebrows crease.

"Yeah, it's not like that, really. We just met for coffee and had a chat." I concentrate on looking guilt free. "Nothing much happened."

Ben laughs. "Right, just be careful. He's got a reputation with the women."

I frown. "Oh, right. Lucky nothing is going on, then." I force a laugh.

"Grace is coming tonight, by the way." He smirks as he walks into the kitchen.

Dammit, not another girl. How does he do it? I stand and head for my bedroom. I set up my laptop on my bed, open Google, and type, *Dale Cartwright, author.* Under his picture are titles of different books he's written, mainly horror and a couple thrillers. I click to enlarge his picture, and a funny feeling forms in the pit of my stomach, like something is fluttering around. So many times, I have heard people talk about getting so-called butterflies, but now I really understand. I have never felt this way about any other man, never this feeling deep within.

I put on some gentle music and change into my baggy grey t-shirt. With a loud yawn, I stretch myself across my bed. What a day! I recount the interview, and my heart palpitates when I think of working with him.

DING. My phone illuminates; it's Dale. *"Hope you made it home safe."*

I can't help but grin as I text back, *"Yes, I'm fine. Thank you for helping me today."* I send it and sit still, studying my phone. My thigh burns as I turn onto my stomach.

"See you tomorrow, beauty."

I giggle and lean onto my hands. My eyes flutter to a close. I fall into a wonderfully colourful dream. His arms wrapped around me, his lips on mine, his strong hands locked onto my hair.

I slowly open my eyes, my body feeling electrical, replaying my dream of him. I chortle at myself when I realise my dream was about another man—a man I'd never have a chance with: my new boss, Mr Alcazar. My phone vibrates. My head snaps up, and my arm whips out to answer the phone.

"Sorry. Did I offend you?" Dale whispers through the phone. The panic in his voice touches my heart; although, I'm confused as to why he's calling me at three in the morning.

I snicker. "What? Offend me? How?"

29

"It's just you didn't reply to my last message."

"Sorry. I fell asleep. I'll see you tomorrow."

"Goodnight"

"Night." I put down the phone and wrap myself in my duvet. I lie back to collect my thoughts as I drift into a deep sleep.

*****

I wake early, a smile spreading across my face as I see the sun breaking through the light, fluffy clouds. I check my phone and realise I have an hour and a half before I'm meant to be at Dale's. The butterflies instantly swarm into my stomach. I search through my draws, my mind on which underwear to wear. No-one is seeing them, I remind myself, but still, I pick the black lacey ones. After showering, I spend fifteen minutes choosing the perfect outfit—an off-the-shoulder white top, with skinny light-blue jeans.

DING. My phone has a new message from Dale. *"See you soon, beautiful."*

My cheeks lift with my answering grin, and I head for the kitchen to see Benjamin and a pretty brunette sitting on the sofa.

"Rosa, this is Grace," Benjamin says as I pass the kitchen.

I avert my course and poke my head around the door. "Grace ..." I smile. "Have a nice night?"

She giggles and nods, then stands, holding Ben's hand. She's tall and slim. Her smooth brown hair falls to her lower back. My confidence is hit when she flashes me a smile. She's gorgeous.

"Yes. You have a lovely home." She glances at Benjamin. "Come, let's go upstairs." She giggles and pulls him towards the stairs.

Benjamin regards me apologetically before his teeth bite his lip through his grin. "Have a nice day, Rosa. Call me if you need me," he shouts as he disappears.

CHAPTER 4

I park next to the spotless Jaguar in front of Dale's house. After several deep breaths and a mild panic attack, I clamber out of the car and fiddle with my hair as I approach the front door. My hands tremble as I reach for a beautifully carved lion, the bell hiding just inside its mouth. I stare at my feet as I wait. *Why am I so nervous?* I shake my head in frustration.

I raise my hand in farewell as I leave him standing in the doorway. His confused expression as he turns around tugs at my heart.

The front door swings open, and Dale stands there, grinning, wearing baggy sweatpants and a tight white t-shirt, his hair tousled. His eyes widen as he beholds me. He bites his lip, grabs my hand, and pulls me into his home. Bright lights illuminate the cream-coloured hallway. He holds me for a moment in a tight embrace.

I instantly smell his sweet scent and take a deep breath.

He smiles as he leads me into a dining room. "Hungry?" He points to the circular white table where he has made omelettes, bacon, and toasted bread.

"Yeah, sure." I don't feel hungry, but I sit opposite him and nibble on the food whilst the butterflies in my stomach flutter furiously.

"As always, you look beautiful, Rosa." He smiles, then focuses on my face to see my response.

I take a deep breath and smile sweetly, suddenly becoming extra interested in my bacon.

"Sorry I'm not dressed up." He blushes. "I got a bit carried away trying to make decent omelettes."

"They are delicious," I say, my second lie this morning; the eggs were way too salty. I place my knife and fork down together, hoping he notices and doesn't mind I've left most of my food on my plate. I feel quite happy that I wasn't hungry to begin with.

"Come into the garden with me." He stands. "It's not exactly warm outside, but it is dry." He walks around to me and offers me his hand.

We walk hand-in-hand through two large glass double doors. A whisper of wind blows through the many trees as we enter a beautiful garden. A small black stone fountain of a fish sits neatly in the middle of a colourful Iris flower patch.

"Tell me about your family," I say, gaining confidence as we walk farther from his house and deeper into his territory.

I stare around in amazement at the quiet and serene garden. It's almost impossible to believe he was so close to the centre of the small town. The only giveaway is the gentle sound of cars—the wonders of the countryside.

"There's not much to tell, really. You tell me about yours." He shrugs with a smirk.

"I asked first. Besides, my family is not that interesting." I nudge him, grinning.

"No, I told you I wanted to know everything about you." He wraps his arm around me.

I lean into him, and his hand tightens on my shoulder. Though I'm not looking at him, I can feel his triumphant grin.

"My mom is an estate agent; she's always too busy with her work." I face him, and his concentration on my words surprises me. "My dad is a retired lawyer. I've spent a lot more time with him. They live in London, but my brother and I prefer it here."

"Do you miss them?"

"Sometimes, just depends, I guess. My mom is a handful." I laugh. "Missing someone, is there much point? All that heartache and sadness, all for an illusion, after all, they're still here and alive."

"Yesterday, I noticed you said you haven't been intimate for a while. How long?" He stops walking, his eyes focusing on mine.

I chuckle, my eyebrows rising as high as I can get them.

He smiles a deep-dimpled smile, his cheeks glowing pink.

"About one year, not too long. Well, it's long enough, but I asked you a question about your family." I frown. "Don't change the subject."

He sighs and runs his pale fingers through his shining hair. "My father was a brilliant cardiologist, but also a very violent man when he didn't get what he wanted. Nearing the end of his days, he became a drunk, but I'm pretty sure he was always a drunk. My mother was a beautiful, sweet woman. She had white-blond hair and light-blue eyes, always had so much love to give." He takes a deep breath, and with my hand, he directs me to a little wooden bench under a large willow tree.

The sun's weak heat splays across my cold face.

"My mother left when I was eight; she just disappeared." He shrugs and lowers his eyes to the ground.

The pain in his voice causes a hard lump to form in my throat. I put my hand on his shoulder, not muttering a word, because I know nothing I can say will make it better. "Come, let's walk some more."

He regards me with his dark eyes and shakes his head. "My father sent me to live with my aunt the day my mother left. I just remember him as tall and broad, dark hair with dark eyes. I got this house when he passed away." He flashes a grim smile. "I never saw him again, except in my dreams."

A shiver runs down my spine as I use his hand to tug him into standing.

He squeezes my hand. "Sorry. As a rule, I usually don't tell people about my life."

"It's good to talk."

We head back towards his house. The cool wind blusters, and the gentle bird's song vanishes.

"It's so quiet," I say with a sigh and lean into him; I lightly place my hands on his soft cheeks.

As we touch, I want nothing but his lips on mine, to taste his breath. I pull his face lower.

His eyebrows rise with surprise, eyes glowing with desire. He wraps his arms around my waist and pulls me closer so our bodies lock in a tight embrace. As our lips touch, his hand slides up my back to my neck. Our kiss becomes more urgent; the passion radiates from his body.

My racing heart beats so powerfully he surely must feel it thudding in my chest. I feel his lips curve into a smile against mine. I return the smile, unable to suppress it. I want one thing and can only think of that one thing: him. Our kiss comes to an end, but I crave more. I watch his flaming eyes as he steps backwards and grabs my hand to head for his house.

"Are you sure it's been a year? You seem perfectly up to scratch with your kissing." He grins and spies my hand loosely holding his.

I smirk. "Yes, but I practice with my pillow."

"Lucky pillow." He laughs as we enter his house, and he leads me to a large front room.

The first thing I see is a large colourful piece of art, featuring a lady in white lounging across a beautiful sofa, covering covers most of the light beige wall in front of me. A double brown leather sofa sits opposite a huge flatscreen TV. Two beautiful diamond lamps on either side of the room casts a shimmering light across the snow-white ceiling.

I sit on the sofa, while Dale disappears from the room, mentioning something about drinks, but I'm too distracted to hear. I finally have a little time to think; everything is moving so fast. I feel drawn to this beautiful blonde man who I barely know; I want to be in his arms—his smell, his touch, his thoughtful looks, which entice me, the butterflies whenever I think about him, his lips, those bright red soft lips that when touching mine make me feel so alive. At the same time, I recognise a feeling I've not felt before, like something telling me to stop, to slow down, or even run. I've been with men before but never have I felt like this. *I need to snap out of this! I need to slow this down. I don't want to rush.* My words echo in my head.

Dale coughs lightly to let me know his presence, snapping me from my thoughts.

"Do you like horror?" He sets two glasses and a bottle of wine onto the coffee table.

I nod and smile, still too preoccupied to answer. I watch him pour us each a glass of white wine. He hands me the wine, and I take a sip; I don't drink much, but wine is the only alcohol I enjoy. It's fruity and a little dry; it burns slightly as it runs down my throat. I shuffle aside, trying to put a gap between us. The magnetic force of the passion I feel tries to pull me back.

"How is it?" He puts his arm around my shoulder and squeezes it gently. He presses Play on *The Shining*.

I have never watched the movie through—horror bores me—but I recline into his arm, faking a look of excitement, and sip on my wine. "It's nice, fruity. What made you pick a horror?"

He glances at me and grins. "What better way to get you to cuddle me than a horror?"

The movie was uneventful, nothing I didn't expect. We sat and discussed different movies we watch, our favourite genres. Dale's favourite is horror; mine is a good crime thriller.

I sip on my fourth glass of wine. My head spins slightly, and my stomach churns whenever I move my head. I should have eaten the stupid omelette. I hold my breath when he tightens his hand on my shoulder and pulls me closer to him on the sofa. I look at him with blurred vision, then giggle childishly for no reason.

He smiles; his dimple deepens as his hands rest on my crimson cheeks. He steadies my face close to his and kisses my lips.

I inhale deeply, his glorious scent overwhelming me.

He places both hands on my waist, and his fingers move slowly up my sides. With his soft lips, he traces my jawline, lightly kissing when his lips fall to my neck.

I quiver and throw back my head, giving him space, and exhale a gentle sigh. Each kiss intoxicates me further. I grasp his hair as his lips travel around my neck, kissing and nibbling.

"You like this?" he whispers between each kiss, looking up to me.

I roll my eyes and smile. I place my fingers under his chin to bring his face level to mine. I fix my lips to his for a short moment before I recoil. "I have to go, Dale," I say softly.

He bites his bottom lip.

"I feel like we are rushing. I don't want to rush." I lower my gaze to my hands. "See me again next week?"

I want him; I want all of him. But if I want this to last, to be real, we must take it slower. I see the shock from my rejection in his eyes; he's momentarily lost for words.

He opens his mouth to speak several times before changing his mind. "Okay, I understand. It's Wednesday now. Maybe on Monday we can meet and talk?" The lack of confidence in his voice is evident.

I kiss his cheek as I rise from my seat.

"Just one thing, did I do something? Did I say too much?"

"No," I say hurriedly, not wanting him to think I dislike him. "I like you a lot, that's why I want us to move slower, give us time, a real fighting chance. I want to see you again." I head to the front door.

His stance is stiffer this time. His dark eyes watch me as I turn, and he follows. At the front door, he kisses my cheek and nods.

CHAPTER 5

Alone I sit on my sofa, my mind a blur as I argue with myself about why I've done what I did. I'm furious at myself for forcing time away when I want him so much, when I can't even stop thinking about him. Though I know this space between us will give us both time to think, I don't want to mess around anymore. I want a real relationship. I can't help but wonder why I feel so drawn to him. I never get attached like this; my own emotions scare me, and I ponder about what has made this situation any different from my other romantic interests. There must be a reason someone so handsome and sweet hangs around a library, picking up girls.

My train of thought crashes as my brother enters the front room.

"Rosa, some of the guys from my theatre group are coming tonight for a pre-production drink. You're welcome to sit with us, though I'm sure you won't want to sit around a load of guys. But Michael will be there." He winks, grinning, then focuses on my face. "What's up, Ro?"

"Ahh yeah, my childhood crush. Think he'll finally grant my deepest, darkest desires?" I laugh heartily. "Nothing, I'm fine," I say, surprised at how convincing I sound.

"Eww, Rose. If he does, he'll be answering to me." Ben's eyebrows cross fiercely.

"I think I'll pop down and say hello, but other than that, I'll be upstairs. What time?" I ask with a grin.

He chuckles and rolls his eyes then tells me to come down at around eight p.m.

I sit in my bedroom for what seems to be hours, preparing for my first day on trial with Mr Alcazar, unable to focus for more than a few minutes without thinking about Dale, then screwing my eyes up and refocusing on my work. The front door opens and closes several times before I decide to peek downstairs.

I halt outside the door to the room and glance through the gap. Nine men sit in a circle, completely covering the sofa and the chairs. The atmosphere is full of laughter and excitement. Three bottles of whiskey sit on the centre of the dining table, glasses are placed on every stable surface. I take a deep breath and open the door. Each smiling face turns to me, but nothing can contain the shock on my face when I see him staring in my direction.

Dale smirks in my direction, then resumes staring at his glass, as if it's the most interesting glass in the world.

"You've decided to grace us with your presence," Benjamin says with a huge grin.

"I, well ... yeah," I stutter back, unable to keep my eyes off his face.

Benjamin glances at Dale, who's still busy examining the glass. Ben's eyes light up, and his grin turns smug as he shoves a glass of whiskey into my hand. "This is Dale, our screenwriter," my brother says loudly, introducing us from across the room with a smirk.

My heart jolts as Dale stands and approaches me. His hair is brushed back, eyes shining more than ever. He is wearing a white shirt that clings to his muscular body and tight black jeans. I notice everyone's eyes are still on me and take a large gulp of whiskey. I hear Benjamin's and his friends' laughter.

"Nice to meet you, Rosa." He proffers his hand, flashing his dimpled smile, and winks as I take his hand. His grip is tight and warm, his touch intoxicating.

I can do nothing but stare at his face, still shocked to see him here with my brother and all of his friends.

He focuses on my lips and returns to his place in the centre of the group.

My stomach flips as I force a smile and sit next to my brother. My heart is hammering as I finish my first glass of whiskey. I mainly listen to the group of friends talk. I drink more than I usually do and laugh in all the right places. I notice Dale's eyes keep flitting toward me, even though he's talking to others; his body faces me, his left hand unconsciously pushing his hair from his eyes. My body craves his gentle touch, the taste of his experienced lips, and his irresistible smell.

I bite my lip and turn away, trying to distract myself by talking to my brother's closest friend and my childhood crush, Michael. Michael has always looked good with his dusty-blonde surfer style. We chat about when we were younger, about how much I've grown. I haven't seen him for years, since I started college and uni, when I had no boobs and braces. My face glows red at the thought.

"You had quite the crush on me when you were younger." Michael laughs, his voice is very low.

I laugh a bit louder than usual. "Yes, don't worry though. I'm over it."

"Are you sure? You're blushing quite a lot." Michael looks a bit disappointed when he stares at his hands.

"No, not entirely," I say, trying to make him feel a bit better.

Michael pinches my cheek. His eyes linger on mine until Benjamin flicks his nose, like a dog.

"Off limits, bro," Ben whispers to Michael.

I can't see Dale, but I can feel him watch me while Michael talks animatedly, drunkenly putting his arm around my shoulder.

My brother loudly exclaims that he'll officiate our wedding.

I scoff, "He wishes," and nod at a very drunk Michael.

I hear a cough and the chime of glass. My heart flutters when I turn to see Dale standing in the middle of the room, but before he can talk, I spring from my seat. "Toilet," I squeak as I exit the room, not looking back. I rush into the bathroom then close the door and taking a deep breath. *What is with me? It's just a man* ...

My vision is foggy from the whiskey. I feel dizzy and nauseated. I lean closer to the mirror to examine my eyes and brush back my hair. I regain my balance a little and turn to leave.

"Rosa." I hear him first, then his stunning face comes into view. He shuts the bathroom door behind him. "Is everything okay?"

I stumble backwards in shock; his handsome features stand out, and my heart leaps into my throat. "I didn't expect to see you tonight."

He takes my hands and pushes his fingers between mine.

Excitement surges through my body from deep inside to my fingertips.

He pushes me backwards, holds me against the wall, and brings my arms above my head, not taking his eyes off mine. His lips teasingly brush mine, then they reach my neck, kissing and biting, then back to my lips.

My body trembles with each touch. I try to move my hands so I can touch him, but his grip tightens.

He steps closer to me, his body right up against mine, and thrusts his hips, pressing harder against me.

I inhale sharply when we lock lips, his mouth forcing mine to open. I taste the whiskey on his breath. Each time his body pushes against mine, my lower stomach tingles. His soft tongue slips through my lips, and I break my hands free, wrapping them around his neck.

"I didn't expect to see you either," he whispers between kisses. He slides his hand into my shirt and caresses me.

I pull him as close as possible and playfully flick my tongue over his. I feel him smile against my lips, my hands now exploring his chest.

His lips travel to my neck and over my collarbone, weakening my body with each kiss. "Hold me," he says with a moan.

My shaking hand falls to his jeans button, and my heart flutters with excitement, passion surging through me.

His hands grip me tighter, our breathing accelerating as my fingers fumble on the zipper. He bites his lip and suppresses a groan, then puts his lips to my forehead with his eyes closed as I explore his body with my hands.

"Rosa, what are you doing in there?" We both jump at the sound of my brother's voice.

I yank my hand from Dale's jeans. "Sorry, was on my phone! One minute!"

Dale grins at me as he pushes back his hair.

As quick as I can, I straighten my hair in the mirror.

Dale puts his hands around my waist from behind. "I'll come up to you tonight when the guys have gone home. Let's talk," he whispers enticingly in my ear.

"No," I say quietly.

"Please ..."

I nod hesitantly, then turn to the door to leave. The front room is still full of chatter when I reenter, my face bright red and rosy. It dawns on me what the others might be thinking about me being in the bathroom for so long. Did they notice Dale's absence as well? I notice Benjamin staring at me as I sit between him and his best friend, Michael.

"Rosa, come on. Our playwriter, really," Michael says, disappointment etched across his face.

"What are you talking about?" I reply with a high-pitched voice that I hope will be convincing.

"Rosa, I don't even know what to say. I told you about him. Why can't you listen? I don't even want to know what went on in that bathroom. But don't come to me when he breaks your heart." Benjamin's turns away from me, his jaw set and eyes fixed on his glass.

Dale enters the room, straightening his shirt. His top button's undone, and his hair is a little scruffier.

My brother scowls in his direction. Michael accompanies him with his narrowing eyes. Benjamin says loudly, obviously wanting Dale to hear, "Smug sonofabi—"

"Just leave it," I retort, rising from my seat, and wave my goodbyes before marching off across the room.

CHAPTER 6

I slam my door much louder than I mean to. I can feel the heat rising up my face, anger and embarrassment washing over me. *What is the problem?* I ask myself repeatedly as I sit on my bed, breathing deeply. My brother has no control over me. I can do what I want.

I take off my clothes and throw them around my room. I yank my comfy t-shirt over my head and flop onto my bed. My little tantrum's steam is running out. My mind overflows with what's just happened—Dale's sudden advances, my battle between wanting him and wanting space. I look out my window at the almost pitch-black night. The moon shines dimly into my dark bedroom. I shake my head, trying to figure out my emotions. I startle at a gentle knock on my door and ignore it with hopes they will just leave.

"Rosa …" a gentle, eloquent voice says as my bedroom door opens. Dale enters and stands at the door, beholding me.

I huff irritation at Dale's forcefulness annoying me further. "We are not meant to be seeing each other, remember? Space." I don't look up, taking out my anger on him.

He closes the door and approaches. "I feel like I can't not see you. I'm drawn to you, baby. Can't you see what you do to me? I want you, Rosa."

My throat dries up as I hear his words; he actually wants me. I try to swallow when I think of my reply, but instead, I lift my gaze just enough so I can see him out of the corners of my eyes. I've never had someone say something like that to me before.

"I feel like I can't get enough of you. And you don't give me enough of you." His voice is louder, his eyes narrowing at me. His face is no longer soft and friendly but slightly mad.

"I-I don't want to r-rush." I push my hair in front of my face.

"If being passionate is a crime, then punish me. If wanting you is a sin, then please send me to Hell." He comes closer, and his gaze falls onto my t-shirt. His lip twitches into a smile.

"I have never wanted someone so much, and that scares me," I say, finally releasing my feelings but realising how vulnerable I sound. "I just feel like we need to take it easy or we'll just burn up."

"Did you enjoy what we did?"

"Huh?" I look at him, perplexed.

"In the bathroom ..." He grins.

"Yes." My cheeks redden.

A smile flickers across his lips. "So, why wait? I want to feel you. I want to feel everything, for your taste to be all over me. I don't know why, but I need to have you." He sits on the side of my bed, surveying what I am wearing. "Comfy," he whispers with a smirk.

I ignore his comment about my shirt. "It's all a bit sudden. I know I have strong emotions. I just haven't decided what they are yet. How did you get up here, anyway? With Benjamin—"

"I told him, 'It's between me and your sister.' He did object, but I told him to let you decide." Dale grins. "C'mon, let me taste you." He leans in, and his lips move softly against mine. "It's okay ... If you decide you don't want me, at least we'll still have this."

I grip his hand on impulse, half of me feeling bad for him and the other desperately wants to feel his love. I can no longer make excuses as to why I need to hold myself back if even he just wants some fun tonight.

He frowns at me as I guide his hand up my leg. He looks into my eyes, pulling back his hand. "I've been thinking of this moment since I first met you."

I kneel on the bed, lift my t-shirt over my head, and throw it onto the floor beside me.

His eyes light up, and he bites his lip as he takes hold of my waist.

My lips turn up seductively, and I climb onto him, pushing him backwards. "I want you inside me," I whisper into his ear.

His muscles flex as I lean into him, my body pushing hard against his.

I kiss him passionately and let out a soft sigh as he grabs every inch of me while I unbutton his shirt. I take the lead and tug his shirt lower as I kiss his pale, muscular chest. I feel his heart thumping when I trail my fingers down his hard abdomen, my lips caressing along his v-cut abs.

Dale breathes heavily and grasps my shoulders.

I feel a tingling deep in the pit of my stomach. I undo his button and pull down the zipper, teasing him, kissing and biting. His relaxed body tenses as I pull his jeans lower. I bite my lip as I watch him from beneath my eyelashes, then lean over him again, slowly pressing him against me. His fingers touch my naked chest, and I quiver. He thrusts his hips against me, and I release a small moan of pain, but he's too interested in trying to feel as much of me as possible. I glance at his eyes; they are dark, almost glowing in what small light is in my room.

The dull lamp in my room casts a dancing silhouette across the pale walls as our bodies entwine passionately. My body tingles and is alight with excitement. Together we move slowly, his hands around my waist, my teeth biting his shoulder.

He lifts me off him and lies me back, spreading my arms out and holding them against the bed. His hungry eyes explore my body. He bites my lip as a moan is about to escape me. His hands caress every piece of me that he can. I reach out to touch him, my fingers tingling as they touch his hard, sweating body. His teeth bite at the skin of my neck, sending a series of tremors down my spine. He grabs my hands and pushes them above my head and against the headboard. His body hardens as we both release ourselves—a beautiful release.

His pale skin shines with sweat in the dim light. I look at his beauty as I kiss his bicep. Neither of us can contain our grins, his perfect dimple deep in his cheek.

"Rosa!" I hear from behind my bedroom door.

Dale grabs his jeans off the floor and puts them on with haste.

I slide the blankets to my neck just in time as Benjamin lets himself into my room. He scans Dale sitting shirtless on the edge of my bed, then me covered with a blanket.

My cheeks burn with embarrassment

"Right, Dale. I think it's time you left." Benjamin's voice is low and threatening, resentment etched across his face. Benjamin, who's even taller and definitely broader than Dale, stares at the defiant man sitting as still as stone on the end of my bed.

"Is that not up to Rosa?" Dale's eyebrows cross as he rises. His pale face flushes with anger, and he doesn't take his dark eyes off Benjamin.

Benjamin steps closer to Dale, squaring his shoulders.

Dale's knuckles tense; each bone in his hands are pronounced under his pale white skin.

My skin prickles as I sense a fight. I jump from my bed, my blanket wrapped tight around my naked body, and stand between them. "Stop."

"Or, what?" Ben growls, not taking his gaze off Dale.

Dale laughs. "You've got problems, man."

"You, what?" Ben takes one small step, completely closing the gap between them.

"You best go, Dale. Let's meet after my work tomorrow," I say, my voice high and gentle.

Dale notices my concerned expression, and his eyes soften. He steps backwards from Ben and places a warm hand on my heated cheek. "Sorry, Rosa. Yes, call me when you're out. Good luck, beautiful." He leans in to kiss me but diverts when he sees the look Benjamin shoots at him. He pulls his shirt over his head and leaves, not looking back.

Benjamin scrutinizes me, disgust filling his eyes, and turns swiftly to the door.

"Ben," I shout after him, but he doesn't respond. I fall onto my bed and stare at the ceiling. My eyes burn with angry tears as my emotions hit me. I take deep breaths to calm my nerves.

What the hell has just happened? I let myself shudder as I imagine Dale's dangerously dark eyes. My skin remembers Dale—his soft touch, his beautiful pale body against mine. My body feels wronged, as if I have made a big mistake. I shrug it off and turn onto my side. My heart flutters like a thousand butterflies trapped in a glass cage. I remember the tension and the look my brother gave me. I close my eyes, letting a single tear carve a burning path down my cheek. A tear not of sadness, but of anger—anger for what has happened, because of a simple decision I have made. Benjamin's hate towards my decision to be with Dale. But most of all, anger at myself for feeling bad for Dale, for giving him my body so easily. It's just that I can't get enough of him, his smell, his taste. The way he moves, his smile.

Even his anger.

CHAPTER 7

I awake from a long night of disturbed sleep. Dreams of death plagued my slumber. My brother's lifeless body, spread across the kitchen floor, flashes before my eyes as I turn onto my back.

I blink several times before I can see clearly enough to check the time on my watch—4:45. I lie still for a moment, my body stiff. I try to remember more of my nightmare; nothing comes back to me. I take my phone from my bedside table. Squinting to see the screen ,I notice I have a single email that reads, "*7 a.m., Woodbury Town Police Station.*"

My heart jumps, and I sit upright much too fast, my head spinning. Straight on the job. I think in a panic that I have never done any work in this field. My body aches as I scramble from bed and hurry to the bathroom. The mirror shows brown rings around my eyes, my hair a mess, and, to my surprise, my neck boasts a large purple-red bite mark. I fiddle with my makeup, trying to cover the remains of last night. How unprofessional would I look with a giant love bite and brown eyebags on my first day? I scold myself, scribbling, *Need to be MORE Professional*, on a sticky note and slap it to my bathroom mirror.

After my morning routine of washing my hair, brushing my teeth, ensuring I look presentable, choosing the right pair of high heels, and grabbing my laptop and notepad, I rush through my bedroom door, wanting to be early. I creep down the hallway, hoping not to wake Benjamin, hoping to leave without problems, though, as I arrive at the kitchen, I see him sitting there, coffee in hand.

"Morning, Rosalie."

"Morning, Benjamin. Why are you up so early? It's six fifteen, you know." I flash a fake smile, awkwardly straightening my black skirt and pulling it down a little.

He readjusts in his chair, his eyes boring into mine. He gestures towards the chair opposite him.

I take my time to approach the table.

He does not speak till I sit. He opens his mouth several times before closing it again, lost for words. He breathes deeply and grabs my hand. "I'm sorry, Rosa. I was a dick." He drops my hand and takes a sip of his coffee. "I just don't like the guy. I know what he's like ..." He shook his head.

"Benjamin, there is absolutely no point in saying sorry, to then start back on the problem. I'm not a child anymore. I can't rely on you to protect me from everything." My voice gaining power with each word.

I study Benjamin as he furrows his eyebrows at me, his deep-blue eyes large and bright. I notice they are also ringed and dark around the edges. Our large kitchen is bright, the early mornings sunrays shine through the double glass doors that lead into the garden. The sun glitters against the light-blue-painted walls. I squint as I wait out this awkward conversation.

"I feel sick to my stomach thinking of you and him together. I don't like it, but for you, I'll take it." He narrows his gaze at me and walks to the coffeepot to pour a cup. He slides it across the table to me. He doesn't sit but heads to the kitchen door. "But one sign that something is not right, I'm there. Rosalie, I'm being serious."

"I'm just having some fun. Don't worry."

He glares at me and leaves the kitchen.

I sit in silence, my fingers wrapped around the hot cup. I contemplate the extreme hate between Ben and Dale. Surely this can't be because Benjamin is overprotective. I listen to the sweet songbirds singing a beautiful, joyful tune. I watch out the window; the fluffy white clouds pass across the red-tinged sky, the blustery wind swirling as the old, large oak tree's branches bend and groan. I pull my gaze from the window and onto the clock that hangs on the back wall—6:35. I jump to my feet and dash out the front door, grabbing my bag as I go.

The raging wind, matching my emotions, whip my face. The roaring fills the empty sleeping street as I jog to my car, my heart thumping hard enough that I feel it in my ears. My first day on trial, my first day working in criminology.

*****

I arrive at the police station with ten minutes to spare. I use this time to fiddle with my hair whilst I try to calm myself: deep breathing, slow breathing, classical music, and closing my eyes. At last, my heart flutters at a near-normal rate, though it still hammers against my ribs.

A beautiful black Mercedes parked neatly next to a police car is the first thing I see as I slide from my car. Green vines climb the walls of the large and outdated two-story police station. An unfashionably bright red door with a call box sits to the right side. I stand still to scan the building for Mr Alcazar. I notice a window adorned with vertical, thick, and rusty steel bars. I wonder what it is used for. Picturing a room full of guns and weaponry, I grin.

"Miss Lockwood, over here," a soft voice calls out from inside the bright red wooden door.

I do a pirouette on the spot and wobble clumsily. "Mr Alcazar." I nod towards him in acknowledgement, hoping he hasn't seen my blunder.

A shining toothy grin spreads across his face. His thick curls bounce as he strides towards me. His glasses sit neatly on his head. He proffers his hand, then grasps mine.

The handshake sends tingles up my arm. I shake it off as he points towards the outdated red door. I tremble with anticipation for my first day at work. I can't help but smile as we enter the building. My smile dissolves as quickly as it came, changing into a dropped jaw, when I see two long rows of continual, plain, and thick metal bars. My heart seems to fall into my belly as it grumbles.

"We are working with a family today. Don't worry, I'm just showing you around. This is a holding unit for people awaiting their trial. I need confidence from you today. This family have been through a lot. We're working very closely with the police on this, helping in any way possible. I want this solved quickly."

"Okay, Mr Alcazar. Sorry," I whisper as we pass the cells, their occupants not even acknowledging us.

A deep shout breaks the silence, making me scamper behind Mr Alcazar.

"I didn't do it," the shout echoes through the dark hallway.

"Shut it, Marcus," Mr Alcazar grumbles as we pass his cell. "Tell it to the judge."

We exit the jail cells and traverse a bright white hallway without him uttering a word. With every step, I can't help but feel anger emitting from him. He stalks up another hallway and we reach the end, where it becomes a dull white. An uncomfortable defining silence accompanies us as we pass through a pair of off-white doors. An empty white desk sits in the middle of the room, with some uncomfortable-looking overused chairs on either side. Mr Alcazar walks so quickly around me that I feel the breeze on my face and smell his unusual and pleasant scent.

He pulls out a chair and motions for me to sit. "Before we go in, we need to chat," he states in an unhappy tone. His eyes narrow as he slides on his glasses, magnifying his big green eyes. He sits opposite, and I notice they're a beautiful shade of emerald.

"Yes, Mr Alca—"

"First, please call me Rafael. Here, we are equals. Next is toughen the hell up. I can't have you acting all shy and scared, especially with clients like we have today." He places his glasses onto the table and entwines his hands together.

I nod nervously, trying hard not to look at my feet. I can't tell whether I fear him or fear my first day?

"Now a quick brief. This family lost their twenty-two-year-old daughter, Eliza Thomas, last year. She was found tied up with rope and murdered. Her stomach was ripped open, her small intestine and kidneys missing. Definite foul play, of course, but she had also been sexually assaulted." He spoke with rhythm, barely stopping to breathe.

I listen intently, wanting to get this right the first time.

"Backstory: she had told her parents about a man." He takes a deep breath, and his lips curve downward. "She went on a date with him once and said he was stalking her. Her parents thought she was overreacting. She had also contacted the police two weeks before her death, and the day she died, she was under police protection. She disappeared from her bedroom at two a. m. without trace. We found her three days later in an abandoned house. But nothing was left—no DNA, nothing leading us to the murderer."

My jaw is tight as he finishes his speech, my heart palpitations skyrocketing.

"Sir, this is my first case. I don't think I'm the best to be—"

"Don't be silly. Just get up, use your head, take notes, and for god's sake, don't say anything stupid." He forces a grin, then pats my shoulder as he crosses me towards the door.

I rise swiftly, still wrapping my head around the fact that he's told me not to say anything stupid, and follow to where Rafael is holding the door open for me. I pull my skirt lower down my knees and lead the way, letting my hair fall in front of my face as I pass him.

"By the way, good job. You look very professional, except for the bite on your neck," he says, his voice low and sweet.

My cheeks burn up, and he opens the door across the hallway to reveal another dull white room. The seats, though, are a little comfier, with soft white cushions on the backs.

A woman and a man sit opposite two empty chairs. The woman's cheekbones protrude wildly through her sunken, paled skin. Her hair falls limply at her shoulders, the grey shining through her dark brown hair. The man beside her is emaciated—the remains of someone who once was large and strong, now thin and weak. His shirt hangs off his body.

I greet them confidently, a firm shake. My fingers tremble, and my palms sweat.

"This is my partner, Rosalie Lockwood. She will be working alongside me on your case." Rafael speaks to them with a gentle voice, one which I have not yet heard.

"Is she experienced? She looks a little young," the man says, his voice lifeless.

His wife readjusts herself in the chair. "Have you had any news yet?"

"Mr Thomas, I assure you she is as good as you can get, a brilliant mind. But no, we've found some more DNA samples from her body but still no matches. The cause of death is being redetermined. We have reason to believe she died before she was, well ... cut."

Mrs Thomas shudders, her eyes brimming with tears before they fall on me, as if expecting me to have some answers.

"Did she ever mention what the stalker was threatening her about?" I ask carefully.

"Of course, but we've answered these questions a hundred times." The mother's voice rises as her cheeks flush. "I just want to bury my daughter, not babysit an intern." She sobs into her husband's shoulder.

"I'm so sorry, to you both. We are doing absolutely everything possible. I will not stop until we and the detectives find and punish the killer," I say, hoping to assure them, but it seems to make Mrs Thomas just wail louder.

Rafael rests his hand on my hip and pushes towards the door.

I comply and make to exit.

"I know this is hard for you, but you cannot speak to my partner like that. We are working for you, not against you," I hear Rafael say as I leave the room.

I suppress a shaky grin as I stand against the hallway wall. I'm speechless as Rafael exits the room, his face a deep shade of pink.

He passes me, nodding towards the door ahead.

I follow his lead and enter behind him.

"Sorry," he murmurs.

"For what?"

"They shouldn't speak to you like that." He turns back to the door. "We're going to the office now, but I need to stop at my place, if that's okay," he states more than asks.

I nod and follow him out the door. We exit through the front of the building this time. Rafael nods towards several police officers, of whom multiple take an involuntary step backwards and look the slightest bit nervous. The wind howls through the trees that surround the building. The sun tries to make an entrance, but a large black cloud blocks it. A drop of rain hits my cheek like a tear.

"Let's take your car," he says as he directs me to my car.

"But what about yours?"

He chortles. "I have another I can use."

I stare at him, blinking dumbly. I fumble to find my keys in my bag and unlock the car.

He appears at my side and opens my door to allow me to sit before shutting the door.

I put the keys in the ignition and turn to watch him climb into the car.

He, who is much taller than me, moves his chair all the way back, allowing leg space.

I pull off as he fastens his seatbelt.

"You. Are. A. Lawyer." He puts his arm around me, my heart hammers, and my eyes widen. He slides the seatbelt around me. Oh Shit.

"I ... I forgot."

His green eyes pierce into mine.

My cheeks rise in heat and fill with colour as I follow his directions out the police station. We drive in absolute silence except for his directions every now and again. Twenty minutes pass, and I turn onto a country road. With each passing house, they get bigger. Soon enough, fountains and statues decorate the huge front gardens. I glance at him, realising he is watching me. I'm suddenly fixated out the window as the dark clouds compound.

"Here, turn left here," he mutters, now studying me.

I obey, and two large gates, decorated with silver snakes at least three meters tall, creak open slowly. I follow the road leading to what I would describe as a mansion.

He clears his throat. "You don't say much do you?"

"I guess not, not unless I have something to say. And I'm pretty sure we don't have much in common." I snicker as I stop at the front of his home and stare at the patterned glass windows.

"Don't judge me like that." He faces away from me. "Where I live is not who I am."

I sit still, leaving the engine on, and give him an 'I'm waiting' smile.

He frowns as he walks around to my door and opens it "Please, come in. I have to find the documents first." He laughs, waiting expectedly for me to get out of the car.

I attempt to leave my seat without removing my seatbelt. It pulls on my shoulder, slinging me backwards so I hit my head off the doorframe. I hastily undo my belt and climb out the car, not looking at Rafael. His laughter bursts through me, like a balloon popping. I turn on my heels to see him bent forward with laughter.

"Whatever." I stomp to his front door.

"Wait." He stopped laughing at once. "Did you just say, 'Whatever,' to me?"

"Yes. You are laughing at me like I'm an idiot."

He chuckled. "I'm laughing at you, because you hit your head, not because you're an idiot." He retrieves his keys to unlock the door.

CHAPTER 8

A beautiful long tapestry hangs on the landing of a double staircase that winds up the white stone walls. A chandelier reflects lights across the high ceiling leaving glitter spots across the walls in the entrance. I step through the door, my muscles in my legs hold me back, stopping me from moving any further when I notice how many hallways and doors are contained in this vestibule. I gulp as I make an effort to unstick my legs.

A young lady appears from the door at the end of a hallway to the left. A beautiful black dress with white trimmings fits her thin body. I feel a surge of jealousy at her curves and tight figure. She hurries towards Rafael, her hand outstretched. "Good morning, sir. Your jacket?" Her voice is high and full of admiration.

"Sure." He shrugs off his jacket and hands it to her. "This is my new partner, Rosalie."

The young lady smiles at me. "Your jacket, miss?"

I slide off my jacket, hand it to her, and smile.

She's already facing Rafael, her eyes lock on him again.

"Lucy, please stop staring and fetch me and Rosalie a coffee." He retorts with shocking distaste.

My mouth hangs open, and I stare at Rafael, shocked he speaks to his help in such a bad way.

Lucy's face turns a violent shade of red. Her eyes divert to the floor, and she spins to walk down the hallway, clenching our jackets.

Rafael watches her leave the room, his eyebrows furrowed, seemingly in deep thought.

I can't help but survey his face, trying to understand why he'd react that way. In silence, we stand in the massive entranceway.

He grins as he peers into my eyes, and to my complete confusion, my body jolts with fear. For what reason am I feeling fear, I don't know; nothing about this situation screams wrong or worrisome.

"Sorry, Lucy is ... well, she's a bit obsessive. A long time ago, I was drunk. Shit happened. I have tried to let her leave. I have offered her money and other jobs. But she just won't go." He laughs.

"Oh ... so she's, like, in love with you?"

He chortles. "You could say that."

I sigh. "I was worried you were just an asshole to everyone for a moment."

He raises his eyebrows at me with look of disbelief on his face, then chuckles, and gestures for me to follow.

He approaches the stairs and my heart starts slamming in my chest. His eyes dart to me. Can he hear it?

He stands still, holding the rails of the stairs. "Welcome to mi casa." He gestures again for me to follow.

I almost forgot he has an almost unnoticeable accent. I follow him up the marbled winding staircase and stumble on the last step. His hand flings out to grab me with such force I might have been better off falling. I steady myself, wrapping both of my hands around the stair rail. I nod wearily in thanks, trying to catch my breath after being winded by his sturdy palm.

He refuses to let me go until we're two steps from the top of the staircase. His face is tense and, if I'm not mistaken, angry.

My stiff and motionless legs tremble, not because of my almost accident but because of Rafael.

He eyes the staircase and takes a deep breath. "Please don't get yourself killed on my stairs." His tone is displeased, but his lips lift into a forced smile.

"I'll try not to. Have I annoyed you with my accidental trip?"

Rafael pauses. "No, I'm annoyed I hurt you when I tried to stop you from falling."

"You confuse me."

"I could say the same about you, but here I am, keeping my mouth shut." He turns and saunters down the hallway.

I run to keep pace with his brisk gait, marred by a barely visible limp. If I hadn't been staring at him in awe at how graciously he can almost run down a hallway, I wouldn't have noticed. We pass too many doors—some old, dusty, and untouched, others beautifully bright and white. The handles shine, and I notice the reflection as we pass. Orbital lights, opposite each other, adorn the white walls, casting spotlight-like circles on each door. Inside the spotlight circle is a letter of some sort—a language I'm certain no-one uses in today's age.

"This writing, what is it?" I ask between deep breaths, my ribs hurting with all this speed walking.

"Enochian, the language of the angels. My father was obsessed, so I named my rooms in Enochian in his honour." Rafael chuckles and halts at a bright white door engraved in gold with hundreds of symbols, in shapes of circles and stars.

I reach to touch the etchings. A charge of electricity flows through my arm—excitement.

Rafael knocks my arm out of the way as he shoves open the door, his gaze never leaving my hand. "Don't touch. Please ..." He adds as if trying to be polite.

A cold wind blows through the open door, making my breath hitch. I see shining lights reflect brightly from a crystal chandelier that hangs low over the middle of a large black table. Mesmerising gold engravings adorn the walls. Long gold-lined white curtains cover the windows, letting only a sliver of light through from the outside. I walk to the walls, drawn to the beautiful engravings. Rafael keeps on my heels, inches behind me.

"I don't—" He stops as I reach again and takes my hand in his cool hand, then puts it to my side. "Do not touch, Rosa. It's fragile. Don't make me regret bringing you here."

The stiffness in his voice hits me fast. "Sorry. It's j-just so beautiful. You won't regret this, sir. S-sorry." I step backwards, making space between the tempting walls and myself. I squeal and fall backwards onto a white leather sofa.

"Calm down, Rosalie. Just stay, stay still." He laughs.

My body tenses as he wanders around his office, looking for papers. Staying still is harder now than ever before. I tap my fingers together, my eyes following Rafael rummaging through what seems like hundreds of folders and drawers. A soft knock sounds at the door, and I watch Rafael rush to open it.

I hear Lucy the maid. "Sir, I'm just checking that—"

"Lucy ... everything is fine. You are checking on *me* ... not checking that everything is okay." Rafael says slowly, clearly losing his patience.

"Sorry, s-sir." She peeks around the door.

"That reminds me, Rosa. I've asked, just call me Rafael." He turns to put his hand on the door to close it.

"Sir, can I call you Rafael?" Lucy asks timidly, though she glares at me from behind the door.

"What? No. Where's the coffee?" He closes the door harder than necessary. He turns his back and stands in the middle of the room, looking confused.

His dashing beauty hits me like a snowball to the face. Goosebumps rise up my arms, forcing the hairs on my neck to stand.

He clasps his hands on the back of his head in frustration, staring hard at the mirror opposite him. "Sorry, Rosalie. You must think I'm a terrible person. I don't want to be like this with her, but I also don't want to lead her on. I have none nor have ever had any intentions for her, other than work." He speaks through gritted teeth, trying to control his surfacing, frightening rage.

I laugh, shrugging as I rise. "Any luck with the documents?"

"Yes, I found them moments before Lucy knocked. Let's go."

"What about the coffee?"

"Never mind the coffee," he says with a frown. He holds the door open for me as we leave. His right hand guides me from behind, not touching me, just inches from my waist, as if waiting for me to fall or suddenly drop to the floor.

Silence follows us through the house and down the stairs, but I'm too preoccupied with not tripping or making a fool out of myself and, most of all, not letting him save me.

Lucy stands at the bottom of the stairs, our jackets hanging off her arm, her eyes glued to Rafael. "Sir." She holds his jacket open for him.

He simply pulls it from her hand.

"What about your coffee?"

He ignores her.

"Miss," she says, still eyeing her boss. She pushes my jacket into my arms and turns on her heel.

I follow behind Rafael to the door, and he holds it open for me.

"Lucy, don't cook tonight. I'll get some dinner later with Rosa." Rafael says, his voice harsh.

I raise my eyebrows, a bemused look crossing my face. *What*?

We get to my car, and, as always, Rafael, being a gentleman, holds open my door.

His green eyes pierce mine. "Please, after work, get dinner with me." He must notice my wide eyes because he hurries on. "As partners, I don't mean anything by it. I just want to get to know you more and brief you on some more cases."

"Sure, but I have to be back by seven o'clock."

"Of course, Cinderella. By the way, the trial is over, Rosa. You're easy to work with, mostly. Let's give this partnership a go." A smile spreads across his face.

CHAPTER 9

The rest of the day flies by. We return to the office and process a small stack of paperwork. Rafael hands me several photographs to take home—photo evidence that has been recovered from the crime scene, which is almost as useless as having no evidence at all in this case. My stomach growls in anticipation for this evening.

I stand and put some papers onto Rafael's desk then grin. "Done."

"Me too. You ready to go?"

I take a deep breath. "I think so."

We leave the office together. Several of Rafael's employees greet me with a nod and a smile. I try to smile, but the air feels dry as I think about the upcoming dinner.

"I'll drive us, Rosalie. Leave your car here, then I'll ask my driver to drop your car back. I can take you home so you can change."

I survey his shiny dark grey Lexus in a huff. How many cars does one need? I glance at my timid old Mini Cooper and back at his Lexus. Show Off.

"I can just drive mine back. It's fine. You can meet me at mine," I say, recognising the inconvenience of him driving me back.

His cheeks redden. "Look, it's a new car, and I've not managed to show it off to anyone yet."

"Sure, it's very nice." I laugh. "So, is that the day finished? It's only four o'clock."

"Yes, tomorrow we have a lot to do. You'll get a temporary contract tomorrow until next week so we can figure out the final details."

I climb into his car. My hair flicks wildly in the wind as he shuts the door behind me.

"Seatbelt." Rafael grins at me.

The drive is once again silent. He's peaceful and relaxed. I like that about him. I watch the trees and townhouses pass, thinking of angels. Rafael is as beautiful as an angel. I chuckle to myself.

"So, how long have you and your boyfriend been together?" He asks conversationally, looking neither bothered nor interested.

"I don't have a boyfriend." I laugh. "He's just someone I met, barely even dating."

"Ah, okay. That's good. Is he from around here?"

I don't know how to react or what to take from the words, 'That's good.' I don't answer Rafael as quick as I could, as I try to ascertain the meaning behind this conversation. "Well, from what I can gather, he is. At least, originally, but then he moved away and is back for family reasons. Anyway, what about you? You don't have a wife—"

"And your brother, you've mentioned him. What does he do?"

"Funny story actually, my brother is going to be in a production written by the guy I'm seeing, Dale," I say with a large grin.

"Cartwright?" Rafael flits his eyes from the road to me.

"Yes, how do you know?"

"I've just heard of him before ..." Rafael clears his throat.

The car shoots forward, forcing the back of my head into the headrest. "Hey. Slow down, Mr Lawyer."

We arrive outside my house, and Rafael seems preoccupied, studying a tree.

"How do you recommend I dress?" My cheeks redden.

"Quite formal will be good." He forces his eyes from the tree and onto the steering wheel, a frown etching deep into his olive-coloured skin. "I'll wait here."

I rush up the stairs, only greeting my brother with a quick hello. I rush into my room, pull off my skirt, and hop to my wardrobe. Formal, I contemplate, then grab a black low-cut dress.

Looking in the mirror, straighteners in one hand, hairbrush in the other, I try to tame my blonde frizz. I stare at myself, proud of what I've achieved in ten minutes. The dress is tight, coming to just above the knee. It accentuates my body in the bright light of the bathroom. The neck comes down low and crosses my chest. My hair flows over my shoulders. I have only a couple hours until Dale will expect me at his house.

My heart jumps and flutters. I refocus on the mission at hand. The heels compliment my legs. My dark makeup enhances my blue eyes; they're bluer than ever this evening. I hurry down the stairs and to the front door to find it wide open.

Benjamin's talking to Rafael. *Oh god*.

"Ben!" I say as calmly as possible.

He turns to me, the etchings of laughter all over his face. "Just meeting Rafael. I'll get out of your way." He shakes Rafael's hand and winks at me.

"Sorry, Rafael." I grin at the floor. "My brother likes to know everyone I talk to."

"Rosa, no need to apologise. You're a beautiful woman." He stares at me, as if just realising I'm a woman. "It's for a good reason he worries about you ..." Rafael places his hand on my upper back and escorts me to the car door.

My shoulders tighten, and my head tilts upwards as I spy him. His grin is undeniably handsome—not handsome like you see in the movies, not handsome like Dale, way beyond that. His manly features, imperfect skin, and messy hair radiate a boyishness in his beauty. Even the stubble on his slightly crooked chin is beautiful.

"Watch your head this time." He sighs and rests a hand on the top of my head.

I scowl and don't reply. I can't help but feel annoyed at my idioticness around him. I just wish I wasn't so clumsy. He's in the car by the time I stop cringing at myself. His hands are already clenched around the steering wheel. I stare at my knees, the car's engine growling to life.

He checks the time on the dashboard. "It's five thirty. We've got just over an hour. I will drop you near Dale's house when we finish." His jaw tightens.

"Yes, thanks." I fixate on the road ahead. "You seem like you know him."

A slow minute passes as I watch the trees pass.

The houses have grown scarce when Rafael finally answers. "Not really." He pulls in front of a small restaurant just outside of town. Lights and vines travel up the building, making it a deep shade of green.

The bitter wind hits my shoulders, slithering a gentle shiver down my spine.

The valet opens my door, and Rafael's already outside the car, holding out his hand. "Watch your head, Rosalie," he says monotonously with an unmistakable smirk.

I slide as carefully as possible out the car, my focus on the manoeuvre in these heels and this dress. *The Riviera* is lit in bright white writing across the top of the petit building. The glass doors emit a bright white glow onto the dark floor below.

He gestures for me to enter first as he pulls the door open.

"Table for two?" the waitress asks, her eyes on Rafael.

Several white-clothe tables for two comprise the little Spanish-inspired restaurant. Yellow and red flags, little statues of bulls, and various sunsets on golden beaches hang neatly on the pale grey walls. The sound of a beautifully romantic Spanish guitar tickles my ears as the waitress guides us to a table in the corner alongside a large window looking onto a fast-flowing and deep river. The setting sun is nowhere to be seen through the thunderous clouds forming overhead.

"Red please," I hear Rafael say to the waitress.

Rafael holds a chair out for me. "Sit,"

"I never knew this restaurant existed," I mention, still taking in my surroundings.

"Yes, not many people do. People, they only see what is right in front of them, instead of looking into the distance." His deep, slow voice calls my attention.

He hangs his suit jacket on his chairback. I watch his work-worn hands loosen his black tie and unbutton the top four buttons on his light-purple shirt. My eyes narrow in on a bright white scar stretched across his chest, which is only revealed for seconds as his hand brushes across his collar. I refocus on his face, the high cheekbones, and the bouncy curls.

"I hope you like red wine." His eyes lock onto mine.

"Well, who doesn't?" I giggle and ramble on. "I couldn't imagine a world without wine, or whisky for that matter."

His grin disappears as my phone rings. He gestures for me to take the call.

"Dale?" I answer.

"Rosalie, why are you in a restaurant with another man?" His voice echoes down the phone.

Rafael scans the darkness outside the window.

"It's my boss, Dale. How the hell do you know, anyway?"

I keep my eyes on Rafael. He bends down to mess with his shoelace, but I know he's listening.

"I came to surprise you at your house and watched you get into his Lexus." His voice gets quieter. "Well, I'll see you later, Rosa."

My heart pulsates out of its cavity as the phone goes silent. I drop it on the table. "Sorry." I raise a glass of wine to my lips and drink the lot.

"I thought you weren't that serious with him yet."

"I'm not. I have no idea why he'd follow me here. Maybe he's got the wrong idea of me and him," I say, more to myself than to Rafael.

He refills my glass and slides it to me. My phone beeps, and Rafael turns his face, his eyebrow raised.

"BTW, you look sexy in that dress. Can't wait to rip it off you. Dale."

I read the text, my cheeks filling with heat.

Rafael turns back, his face tense, his hand that was resting on the table now balled into a fist. "Okay, Rosalie, let's just drink. I'll drop you off at Dale's soon."

"I didn't mean for this, Ra—"

"Don't. We can arrange another one, sort this out first." He waves his hand over my phone, then signals for the check.

"I want to stay."

"Right, let's have one more drink."

The waitress rushes over, her face shadowed with confusion.

"Sorry." Rafael smiles. "We'll be staying a little longer."

The waitress nods and does an odd courtesy, before realising what she's done, going bright pink and rushing to behind the bar.

Rafael holds a bemused expression as he watches her for a moment longer, then he refocuses on me. "When did you know you wanted to work in law?"

"When I found out that was what my father does. He's amazing."

"I have a feeling you'll be amazing too."

"I'm quite nervous. When I came in for the interview, I could never have imagined getting to work with you."

"You're nervous to work in law?" Rafael leans in a bit closer.

"Uh, no. Nervous to work with someone like you."

Rafael smiles. "Why? What's wrong with me?"

"Nothing." I blush. "I just mean, you're the big guy—the whole entire boss."

"Ah, naturally." He snickers. "I'm not that scary, though. I think you'll be okay."

"I'm very sure of that." My phone dings loudly, and Dale's name pops up again.

"Is it time for me to deliver you to Dale?"

I glare at Rafael. "I'm not sure I want to go anymore."

"C'mon, you can go give this Dale a piece of your mind." Rafael laughs and raises his hand again, asking for the check.

The waitress rushes over with the bill, and he hands her some money.

He snatches his jacket off the chair and heads for the door. "Come."

I hurry behind him.

The sun has disappeared already, the dark clouds making the setting more dreary than ever. My hands shake with nerves—what a terribly embarrassing dinner.

The valet pulls up beside us, and Rafael opens the passenger door but does not speak.

My skin shines in a sheet of fresh downpouring rain.

He wraps his jacket over my shoulders. "You'll catch a cold. Put it on."

CHAPTER 10

He pulls off quickly, his eyes on the road and one hand turning on the heating. "Will you put on your seatbelt, Rosalie," he snaps.

I realise I had just been sitting there, staring at him with my mouth open, and force myself to look away. I pull my seatbelt around me and notice Rafael looks furious, though his face is still so beautiful, if not more so now he is frowning. I can't understand why he's so annoyed. I rack my brain, considering all the possible reasons, but none make sense. The car slows outside the gates to Dale's house, and his finger taps on the gear stick.

"You're to be in tomorrow at eight thirty. My office." He looks at me for the first time since outside the restaurant.

I take a deep breath, relieved his sudden annoyance hasn't lost me my new job. He lifts the seatbelt over my head, and his hand brushes my cheek. I smell the leather on his hand from the steering wheel. His hand moves to my face. I stop breathing, my heart thumping with all its might, then he tucks a strand of wet hair behind my ear.

"Will you text me please, just to let me know you get home all right?" He forces his gaze off me and back to the window.

"Why wouldn't I get home safe?"

Rafael shrugs. "He seems angry."

I nod and hurry to reach the doorhandle, watching the hallway light to Dale's house flick on and filter through the dark, stormy night.

"Goodnight, Rosalie," I hear as I shut the car door behind me with a weak smile.

I stand motionless, breathing deeply, the cold air rushing into my lungs. I linger a moment, then approach his house. The door opens as soon as I reach the first step, and Dale stands there, as sweet as ever, as he waves to Rafael's car, which pulls off slowly.

"Hello, hun."

"Hey," I say through a tight smile, my jaw tense with annoyance.

He proffers his hand and leads me through the dazzling hallway and into the front room. Several candles are lit on the beautiful fireplace's mantel. The light crackling and the smell of burned wood feels inviting and warm.

I sit on the sofa, and he brings forward two glasses of wine and sits next to me. He's so close to me I can feel the heat of his body on my own.

"You look delicious." He puts his hand on my knee and kisses my cheek. The electricity in his kiss fails to impress me.

"You followed me."

His shoulders tense, but his face looks ashamed. "I was wrong. I'm sorry. I shouldn't have followed you." He puts his hand under my chin, his face full of regret. One hand slides to the back of my neck and pulls my face close to his. "You're different, Rosalie. Every time I think of you, my heart leaps into my chest and pounds away, as if my world is about to cave in." His voice quivers along with his hands.

His sweet warm lips touch mine, the surge of electricity back at full power—a different type of electricity, so strong it almost hurts. He pulls away, leaving my lips feeling cold; my cheeks flush as they burn in his loss. His finger delicately traces the shape of my face. He reaches his other hand behind the sofa and produces a single rose. "Forgive me."

"Of course," I say before I think. I want his lips on mine again; I want to feel the new and strange electrical current he emanates. I take the rose and wrap my arms around his neck, pressing my lips against his. The passion in his lips awakens the pit of my stomach. I recall last night, his body dancing in the moonlight.

He holds my hips and slides his hands around to my back. He lifts me with ease onto himself, his tongue flicking playfully over mine. It's so easy to forget to breathe when life shoots by so fast.

Over his shoulder, I watch our shadows move and become one in the light of the fire-lit room, our breathing erratic, his hands uncontrollable against my inviting body. My eyes close as I give into my desires.

***

"What are you working on?" he asks as he caresses my hair. The firelight shines off his pale body, his arms wrapped around me, our bodies close, and the heat from the open fire burns against my back.

"What do you mean?"

"I mean ... what case are you working on at work?"

"A stalker, a murder." A shiver creeps up my spine at the thought of what happened to the woman.

"Oh, and the stalker ... he's been captured?"

"No, we will be working alongside the police. This ... this bastard who murdered this young woman needs to be caught and handed his judgement."

"And what about Rafael? What's his deal?"

Before I know it, I am standing rigid, holding my dress against my body. "What do you mean?"

"Nothing bad, Rosalie. I just meant, he's a weird character."

"He's fine; he's a good man. He's just doing his job." I pull my dress over my head. An odd sense of unease overwhelms my body as Dale gets to his feet.

He inches towards me, closer—as close as he can possibly get—his face against mine. "You have feelings for this man?" His voice is a deadly whisper.

I feel paralysed. Slow-motion takes over. He puts his hands on my face unnecessarily hard. With his fingers wrapped around my face, squeezing my cheeks so hard I can feel my teeth against my inner cheeks, he lifts my face to look at his own. "Answer me!"

Spit splashes across my face with each word, his hot breath not enticing but fear-inducing. A great knot sticks in my throat, forcing me to choke out my words of denial, with no chance to swallow or even breathe before he pushes my face away. Where his hands have been, a burning sensation remains.

He turns his back to me and thunders from the room, leaving me with nothing but the crackling of the now dying embers in the fire.

My heart pulsates in my empty chest; my eyes well up with unstoppable tears. Each fleeting thought ends ridiculously with calling Rafael. I need to feel safe. I fall to my knees, an unmistakable mess. I want to cry. I want to scream, to run, but my body cowers to the floor as he enters the room and walks in my direction. I glance up, and for a split second, I'm not scared; I'm horrified.

"Rosa," his shaking voice whispers. "I'm so sorry."

I look up again. He's on his knees next to me. I jump back a little, my body pushing against the sofa.

He holds his hands together, prayerlike. "Please, I didn't mean this. I have been cheated on too many times before. I am scared of being hurt again." He pauses, his eyes red and filled with tears. He puts his hand on my shoulder, ignoring my wincing, and lifts me to my feet. "My father left me with some bad traits, but I'm trying."

I keep my eyes focused on my bare feet.

"I saw a part of my father in myself tonight. Listen to me, baby. Believe me when I say this won't happen again. I will not let my father, nor his ways, break what we have." He puts his finger under my chin and lifts my head, then wipes a tear from my cheek with his thumb. "Please."

"I don't know, Dale. Right now, I just want to go home, please." I stutter between sniffs and hiccups. My body quivers.

"Okay, of course. I'll drive you." He proffers his hand and passes me my shoes, then leads me from the house.

I focus on my feet and follow like a puppy. Home is where I need to be, where I long to be, and where I'll feel safe again, away from him.

CHAPTER 11

Rushing through my front door, I give Dale no sign of goodbyes or forgiveness. I notice my car parked on the road outside my house, just like Rafael said, before I slam the door behind me, letting my emotions really kick in. My head pounds relentlessly as I fall to the floor in a heap.

"Rosa," I hear a voice echo from up the stairs. "Rosalie!"

Warm and familiar arms lift me off the floor. I'm safe; I'm home. My brother huffs as he carries me into the front room and sits on the sofa with me still safe in his arms. He rubs my back and tries to sit me upright, but my head falls back then lolls onto his shoulder. "What's going on, Rosalie?"

"Nothing, Ben. Just a stressful day."

"You don't collapse on the floor because of a stressful day, Rosa."

I stare into my brother's wide, diamondlike eyes as they home in on my red cheeks.

He surveys me, then focuses in on my love-bitten neck and shoulders. "Who did that to you?"

"Nothing, Ben. Please ..." I wobble from his arms and stand shakily. I walk to the front room door. "It's just stress. Trust me."

He jumps to his feet and grabs my wrist. "I don't believe you for one second! What happened?"

I yank my arm from his grasp. "He's just a bit rough." My lip quivers before I sob out, "He wasn't happy that I went with Rafael for dinner."

"Did he hurt you?" Benjamin whispers.

I step closer to Benjamin, my skin crawling. "Not purposely," I whisper, barely making a sound.

Benjamin's arms shake as he wraps them around me. "Rose, I don't want you near him again."

I nod in agreement and turn to go upstairs. I drag my feet up the stairs as fast as my stiff muscles allow. I push open my door and scan my bedroom, half expecting to find Dale sprawled across my bed. I sigh in relief, then drop my dress onto the floor, and climb into bed. I squeeze myself into a little ball as mascara taints my tears that stain my white sheets. What could I have possibly done to make Dale do this? Maybe I was rude; maybe I didn't consider his feeling. I question my ability to think. Of course, it must have been my fault to bring the worst out in him.

The ding of my phone jolts me from my trance. "*I'm sorry.*"

I hiccup as I smile sheepishly. "*I'm sorry for making you mad, let's start again.*" I reply.

Another text comes through almost instantly. "*Of course, I'll text you tomorrow. Good night.*"

I ponder what Ben has just said, about not seeing him again. Guilt fills me to the brim. A lump forms in my throat at the thought of Dale coming close to me.

Another loud ding startles me. "*Rosalie, Rafael Alcazar here, just a reminder for 8:30 a.m. tomorrow, my office. Hope all is well. Hope all went well.*"

My heart skyrockets, as if it has a mind of its own. "*All's fine, thanks. See you tomorrow.*" I triple check the message before sending it and lie on my side. With closed eyes, I review Rafael's weird reaction to Dale. Rafael's smile is the last thing I remember.

*****

I wake with a jolt much earlier than usual to an ignored phone call from my mother. I reluctantly listen to the waiting voice message.

"Rosa, see you soon, I love you. Tell Benjamin I love him too." Her voice is quiet and croaky.

As guilty as I feel for never talking to her, it is for good reason. Her constant badgering of me never being good enough for her much-too-high standards, me not trying hard enough, me not meeting the men she'd throw my way. Together, my mother, Eleanor, and Father, Walter, make a good living. Her job as a prestigious estate agent ensures that.

A black skirt and vest with a black cardigan will have to suffice for today. I can't seem to focus on the upcoming work; the unanticipated happenings of last night are still burned freshly into my mind.

*****

I arrive at work with ten minutes to spare after spending twenty trying to find a parking space. Eyeing the illuminated lights, my heart skips a beat, which has been feeling quite normal these days. The dark, gloomy English morning makes walking into the warm and well-kept entrance feel ten times better. I direct myself straight to the lift to not talk to anyone on the way to Rafael's office.

"Morning, Rosalie." A voice startles me as the lift doors slide open. A firm hand holds my shoulder, and I turn.

"Mr Alcazar. Good morning," I say between several deep breaths.

I step in, Rafael by my side. His face is tight, with a smile forcing its way through. Rafael's suit is light grey today, with a bright red shirt and a grey tie. His hair is a bit scruffier than usual.

"We have a day full of research today. I hope you're ready."

"I'm always ready, sir."

"*Rafael.*" He holds his office door open for me.

The room looks the same, except for another smaller dark wood desk next to his own and a black shiny computer. I hold my breath as I stand in the middle of the room like a lost child.

"Rosa," he says with a laugh. "It's for you." He turns the metallic plaque on the front of the shiny new desk. In bold words, it states, MISS LOCKWOOD.

"Really, in your office?" I grin, walking up behind him.

"Our office. I told you we're partners. Now make yourself comfy. This data stick contains what little video evidence we have of who was supposedly stalking poor Eliza." He hands it to me, lingering a moment. "This is the petrol station, but we need to find the time he and she entered. There is twelve hours of footage here that you need to watch." He sits at his own desk. "I've got another twelve hours here, so we're splitting the load."

Five hours pass and neither of us say a word between us, nor do we see anything incriminating on the recordings. Dale sends me a text, explaining he is going away for the night to visit a friend, and with a confusing feeling of happiness, I fill myself with an endless supply of coffee.

"How did last night go, anyway?" Rafael breaks the silence with the worst question imaginable.

"It was fine, just chatted." I remove my cardigan, my body heating up.

He pauses his video and ponders across the desks at me, sliding his glasses from his head to over his eyes.

I stare at my screen, preoccupied with an old man paying for his petrol. I watch from the corner of my eye as Rafael leans forward onto his elbow.

"Really? He wasn't mad?"

"No ... well, a little bit, but I was angrier at him. He doesn't own me." *Or does he?* I run my hand over my cheek, the fear I felt last night rising in my chest once again. I stand, about to rush to the bathroom, before I burst into tears, but Rafael is faster.

"Tell me what happened," he asks, his voice dark.

"Nothing. He just got a little bit mad, as he should. I shouldn't have made him mad." I rush my words. "It's fine; it's just my first argument with him."

Rafael regards me blankly, his eyes emotionless, and he puts a hand awkwardly around my shoulder.

My heartbeat slows almost to the point of stopping, my breath catching up in my throat; a sense of calm engulfs my body from head to toe.

"It's okay. New relationships are hard," he says through gritted teeth. He holds my shoulders and studies my face. He sighs, forces a smile, and leaves the room.

Nothing can stop the incoming panic attack that overwhelms me for the next ten minutes. The thought of Rafael finding out that Dale hurt me makes me feel sick with embarrassment. I collapse to the floor, with my head between my knees, and breathe deeply several times. My heart rate slows. I take one last deep breath. "You'll lose this job," I scold myself, pulling myself off the floor, and sit back at my desk.

Hours pass—too many to keep track of—and he's still not back. My eyes water from watching a screen for so long.

"Miss Lockwood? I have a Mr Lockwood on the phone for you." A male voice startles me from the office door.

"What? Oh, okay." I outstretch my hand, waiting for him to pass me the phone.

"Well, uh, Miss Lockwood, just ... press the number nine on your phone, and you'll ... get connected."

I nod and blush, lifting the black wireless phone off my desk, and press Nine. It rings for a moment, then goes silent.

"Rosa, your mother. She's gone," my father's voice rings down the phone.

"Dad? Dad? What do you mean?" My eyebrows lift.

"She's gone missing, Rosalie. She left for work three days ago and just never came home. I thought maybe she went on one of her drinking escapades. But still no sign of her."

My head spins, and my heart leaps. "She's probably in a hospital somewhere, having her stomach pumped, Dad. Have you contacted them?"

"Darling, I've done that already. I'm with the police now. I'll call you soon. Love you."

The phone goes deadly silent. My jaw hangs wide open. Of course, it's not serious, I try to calm myself. It's happened too many times for me to care. My idiotic mother getting trashed, shacking up with a man, then coming home and begging for forgiveness.

I slam the phone into its charger unnecessarily hard and face the screen, my head in my hands.

"Rosalie ..." Rafael rushes in. "I've just been notified that—" He stops talking abruptly, and I look up. "What's wrong?"

"Nothing. Carry on," I say, my eyes bulging with tears.

"It can wait. What is going on with you today? This isn't how we work, Rose. This is your job, not a joke." He lowers himself to my desk.

I continue to stare at my computer screen, it gets increasingly hard when I notice his hand resting on the table. His fingers are long; another mysterious circular scar is embedded into the centre of his hand. I glance at his face and see his features seem annoyed, his eyebrows at a severe angle. Our eyes connect for a split second, and I frown as I try to bring myself to talk.

"I can't help you if you don't communicate, Rosalie." He turns off my screen and moves it a few inches aside.

"My drunken mother has gone missing. Again. She'll turn up again soon. I'm just so angry she's done it again. The stupid ..."

Rafael's eyes narrow. His scarred hand taps on my desktop. He stays silent, flipping through the pages he has in his other hand. "Here." He puts a piece of paper on my desk—a photo of a white Toyota Prius parked in a petrol station, blurred, and in black and white, the outlines of two people stand out through the dark windscreen.

The feeling of dismay envelops me as I realise one of these figures is dead, the other is her murderer.

"So, we know the killer is here. She filled her tank before disappearing off the maps, until we found her body." Rafael stows the paper into a large file on his desk. "Evidence for her family."

"So, where do we go from here? This leaves us no closer to slamming anyone in prison," I say, my palms wet with sweat.

"Well, I've already sent this to forensics. They should get back to us soon enough. But tonight, there's nothing we can do. It's time for you to focus on your mother."

I clear my throat. "My mother—her name is Eleanor—does this a lot. Gets drunk, runs away, comes back the next day."

"Your father would not call unless he was worried."

"My father will work this out himself. I don't need my boss telling me what to do when it comes to my whack-job mother." My temper rises fast, and I say the words before I can stop myself.

Rafael lets a loud laugh escape his lips and nods, then paces the room a couple times in silence, his hand raised to his chin. A look of deep contemplation embeds on his beautiful face.

My anger has time to evaporate into the cool air. My body succumbs to a great shiver. "I'm sorry, sir. This isn't my usual attitude." My voice trembled along with my body. "I will sort myself out for tomorrow."

"It's fine, Rosalie. If you have not heard any news from your mother, please, tomorrow, let me pull a few strings." He talks low. His eyes are vivid from beneath his glasses.

CHAPTER 12

My life has become a huge search party. I search for my mother and a murderous stalker, and I'll cope with how I know best: a large coffee and a shot of whisky. The sky is a dark blue, empty of clouds and sun, by the time I leave work. Agreeing to let Rafael help me if my mother isn't found is, even if unknown to him, a huge relief that I won't have to do it alone. My drive home is fast through the small town's dark and empty streets.

"Rosalie," Benjamin calls out as I walk down the front path "Rosalie!"

"What?"

"Did Father call you?" he asks slowly, waiting at the front door.

"Mom's missing, I know."

"You told me she called this morning." His voice gets higher with each word, his voice now matched with a blotchy pink face.

My head spins for a moment, faster than the waltzers Benjamin and I used to ride as children till we were green in the face. My hands fly to my phone, understanding nothing other than she spoke to me. I ignored her, but she spoke.

"Rosa, see you soon. I love you. Tell Benjamin I love him too." Her croaky voice seeps quietly from my phone.

Ben's face changes into an angry contorted mess as he steps closer to me.

My throat becomes irritatingly dry, seemingly sending all its moisture into my eyes.

"She's been missing for three days, Rosalie. She contacted you this morning, and you, being the selfish git you are, ignored her." Ben's voice rises hysterically with each word.

"I didn't know she was missing." I stare at the floor, my eyes burning and filling with tears. "You never answer her either!"

He turns, stomps towards the house and slams the door shut. The little line of light coming from the open door disappears, leaving the garden as dark as midnight. The sky is black now, with no stars or moon to shine any light onto my garden.

I slump onto my knees with my head in my hands for what seems like an eternity.

A typical English night, however, tonight feels different. The whispering of the wind seems to be trying to convey a secret message. The hair on my arms stand up as the night slows down. The large, old tree in the centre of my front garden creaks with the strengthening wind, and I find myself glued to the spot. The closest streetlight is at least a hundred feet away, its dull light not reaching anywhere near the garden. The security light has not yet activated, because of my continued stillness. I've completely lost track of time, but the cold is creeping up my legs from the damp grass below me.

My head jerks to the left, instinct perhaps, to the streetlight in the distance. A dark silhouette of a man stands facing me. I stare back, stuck on my knees. Unreasonable fear surges through my body. A quiet crunch of leaves from behind force my legs into action. As I run to the house, the security light finally snaps on. I do not dare to look back as I push the front door open and lock myself in.

I stand silently staring through the misted decorative glass panel on the front door. A dark frame that stands still is only visible because of the security light. My heart pounds, and my palms are sweating. I wait, wanting to scream for my brother, but my lips don't even release a gasp of air. The light goes off. My heartbeat now shoots into my head, and a dangerous throb forces me to the floor. Shaking my head, I crawl up the stairs. I aim straight for Ben's bedroom and shove his door open.

"Ben." A sharp whisper escapes my mouth.

He is sitting at his computer. The only light in the room is from the monitor, but straight away, I feel safe. I feel stupid. He looks down at me, his eyes wide, and jumps out of his seat. "Rosalie, what's going on?" He grabs me under the arms and lifts me to my feet. "What is it?"

"Outside." Is all I manage to say.

He heads downstairs. I hear him unlock the front door, and my ears ring in the deafening silence.

What have I done? What if he gets hurt? It was probably just a neighbour, just a passerby. I talk myself out of being terrified, trying desperately to stop my shaking insides, at least enough to approach the top of the stairs. The seconds feel like hours as I wait for Ben to return. The security light flicks on again, and I hear footsteps approach the house.

"I can't find anything, Rose," he splutters between breaths. "I ran all the way to the end of the street. What's going on?"

He locks the door and switches off the light as he climbs the stairs. This time, he leads me to my room and sits on the end of my bed, his head in his hands, fingers tying up into his straight brown hair, catching his breath.

"I was outside. I lost track of the time. Then I saw someone staring, then I ran into the house, and the security light was on, and I could see a shadow outside." I trip over my words in a rush to get them out.

"I think you're just tired. Get some sleep."

My phone vibrates, startling both of us. I take the chance to check the time—2:30 a.m.

"Why is your boss calling so late?" Ben's voice fades into the background.

"Hello?" I answer with a lump in my throat.

"Rosalie, I'm sorry to be calling so late. I need you and your brother to come to the hospital now," Rafael says his soft-but-urgent voice.

*****

Time passes with unbelievable speed when what you fear most is approaching, only to slow down, almost to a stop, when what you fear arrives. My hands shake violently as I hold her cold, stiff fingers. A horrid scream pierces my ears as I stare at her battered and bloodied features.

I love you. Please, let this not be true, just another taunting nightmare.

The scream gets quieter as I recognise it to be my own when a hand rests on my shoulder, spiralling me back into reality. Each breath I take attacks my heart with a sharp stab, and I turn to bury my face in Rafael's chest.

His tense arm wraps around me.

Shuddering, I take a deep breath and step backwards. I see Benjamin kneeling at the other side of her body, his face buried in his hands, with his body vibrating intensely. His cries torment me, forcing my pain to rise from the inside once again. My knees weaken.

"Rosalie," Rafael whispers and holds my face steadily between his hands. "We will find whoever did this."

I turn back to my mother, her body stiff and bloody. Her mouth droops open, blood staining her lips and nose. My stomach flips, and bile spurts from my mouth onto the floor as I try to focus on her eyes. They are gone.

Blood-crusted voids mark her barely distinguishable face where her large blue eyes used to sit. My legs give way, my trembling knees no longer able to hold my weight.

Benjamin scurries around the hospital bed and wraps his warm arms around me. He lifts me off the floor and cradles me like a baby when he walks me out of the room and into another. He sets me onto a cold leather sofa.

"I'll get her a blanket," I hear Rafael say in the distance as Benjamin sits next to my head.

Benjamin's hands shake as he strokes my hair. He is humming something beautiful, his voice on the verge of breaking. Footsteps approach me, and someone throws a warm blanket over me.

"Is she asleep?" Rafael asks, tucking the blanket around me.

"Asleep? Passed out? Anything's better than being awake right now," Benjamin says, barely breaking his melody for a second to reply.

"The poor girl, just too much for her brain to handle. She needs this bit of rest." Rafael's hand brushes my forehead. "I'm so sorry for your loss, Benjamin. You have the best working on this case, myself included."

Benjamin doesn't answer. His melody falters. He clears his throat and starts again.

I let myself drift into a dark and empty slumber.

*****

My eyes burn as I force them open. It's pitch black in the room. I can see a brightly lit corridor through a small square window on the pale cream door. Benjamin's light breathing above me soothes me enough to think straight for a moment before my heart pounds in my chest once more.

I stand before my scream breaks free and run to the door. I pull it open and fall into the corridor. My face hits the cold tiled floor, tears spilling, my sobs uncontrollable. I hear an exasperated sigh behind me, the feeling of someone staring at me, probably standing there in shock; well, I don't care.

For a long moment, I stay still, pouring my heart onto the icy floor. I gather the energy to look up to see who's watching me have a meltdown. Shakily, I lift my head, pulling myself into a sitting position. No-one. I'm completely alone in a cold and deserted corridor. I snap my head back to look behind. Still, I see no-one. A light flickers near the end of the corridor as a dark shadow rushes towards me. With each step growing louder, I clench my eyes shut, as if it will protect me from whoever is running in my direction.

"Rosa." A concerned familiar voice eases my fears instantly.

"Rafael," I say with a deep exhale.

He takes my hand and stands me up, then throws me straight into an awkward hug. My body is stiff as he walks me through the hallways.

"It's four thirty in the morning, Rosalie. You need sleep." Rafael murmurs after a long silence.

"Don't, Rafael. I couldn't sleep now if my life depended on it," I shout, unable to control what is left of my emotions.

"Nothing you do right now will help," he whispers. He holds my shoulders as we reach the end of the corridor and he pushes open a cream-coloured door, the empty and cold night hitting my face. "Let me get you home."

The drive home is silent. I barely remember how I got out of the hospital or even how I got into my house. Rafael barely spends two minutes with me before he rushes out of the house apologetically.

I sit in the dark, staring numbly at the blank TV screen, just trying to make sense of anything—sense of me living, or her living, of love for a parent, or the pain of death.

"Did it hurt? Did she suffer?" I cry out loud.

CHAPTER 13

I shakily wrap my arms around a mustard-yellow cushion, the grey-fabric sofa beneath me teeming with memories of my mother—a housewarming present from her. I never liked it, although now, I couldn't see why I didn't love it. I stare aimlessly at the reflection of the TV which shows the empty double window behind me. It's dark in the front room, the light from the hallway not making much of an impact on the moonless early morning.

I force myself to rise unsteadily and sleepily off the sofa and drag my feet across the carpet and into the brighter hallway. My head pounds as the light burns my eyes. Squinting, I crunch my hand against the light switch and turn the hallway pitch black. I feel my way to the staircase and climb slowly. With each step, my vision adjusts.

I look at the top of the staircase, so used to seeing the empty window which shines onto my back garden. I don't even use the energy to focus.

Seven steps from the top of the staircase, I count.

Six steps from the top of the staircase, my peripheral vision alerts me of movement by the window. My heart jumps, but it soon regains its natural rhythm.

Five steps from the top, I try to force myself to stop, to run down the stairs, but my body is already on the fourth step.

Three steps from the top, I speed up, my heart thudding against my chest. With a drop in my stomach, I remember the events of earlier that night.

Two steps from the top, a shadow jumps out from around the corner.

I let go of everything around me, the force of hands whacking against my chest pushes me down the stairs. A rush of adrenalin pulsates through my head, forcing me to keep my eyes open.

I see nothing but blackness and am unable to figure out where I am when I finally stop falling. My eyes, which are still wide open, fill with a warm liquid that I can feel dripping into my hair.

***

Finally, a peaceful and dreamless sleep. I don't feel cold, but somehow, I'm shivering. I hear a jingle of what could be bells, though I don't really care; I'm in my own world here.

"Rosa!"

I stay silent. If I don't answer, maybe he'll leave me alone. Why can't he just leave me to sleep anyway?

"Rosa."

The owner of the voice shakes me violently. He lifts my head and tries to pry open my left eye. It feels quite stuck. My eyelashes tug on each other. My head pounds to the thump of my heart and quickens as my memory returns. It hits me like a tonne of bricks; my mother is dead.

I open my mouth to shout, but nothing comes out. I flail my arms about, searching for the body to the voice. Cold water falls onto my closed eyes, making me jump, my eyes finally unsticking.

The pale face of a shocked Dale looks down on my fluttering, blurry eyes. Concern fills his dark brown eyes as he lifts me into a sitting position. His hand traces my face and stops just above my hairline. "Rosa, darling. You're lucky it's not deep. Can I help you up?" His voice sings almost happily in my ear.

I stiffen nervously as he puts his head under my arms and slowly lifts me to stand. We walk together to the sofa, his hand wrapped tight around me.

I sit silently for a moment, slowly straightening out my head. My eyebrows rise, and a sharp pain jabs through me. "How are you in here, Dale?"

"Surprisingly, your brother called me. He couldn't get hold of you and, for good reason, got worried. What the hell has happened?"

A moment of silence passes as I ponder the idea of Ben calling Dale after what Ben said the other night.

"My mother has been murdered." I say, finally.

"Darling, I know. I'm so sorry." His lips brush my forehead. "But I meant, what happened to you?"

"Someone pushed—" My body shakes uncontrollably as this morning's events catch up to me. I grip Dale's arm and pull his body across mine, as if to shelter myself.

"What? What do you mean, Rosa?" Dale doesn't wait for my explanation; he is gone before I can inhale deeply enough to stop shaking. His heavy footsteps thunder around the house, checking every corner, every room, every window and door for a sign that someone was in here. "It couldn't be. No-one could have been in here. The doors and windows are all still locked.

I unlocked the front myself." His hands lock onto my face. Looking into my eyes, he kisses my lips.

My body still trembles under his large, pale hands. "I know what happened to me, Dale." I pull my face from his.

"What if you were just tired, darling? Seeing things. Stress and anxiety can do horrible things." His hand caresses my cheek, and I turn into it and rest my lips against his thumb. His explanation makes so much sense that I close my eyes in relief.

My eyes fill with tears, and again, Dale rubs my back as the tears flow from my eyes onto his chest. He doesn't say a word. I listen to Dale's uneven breathing as he rests his chin on my head.

"What do I do now, Dale?" I ask, my voice trembling.

"We wait, doll. We wait."

I watch Dale through the TV's blank reflective screen as he regards me with what I swear is a grin. I turn my head and look up. His lips are the opposite of a grin, turned down at both sides. Through clouded eyes I look at him again, unsure as to why I feel so disturbed, why his upside down smile seems like a charade.

Silently, we sit. He cleans the cut on my hairline and reassures me that no-one can see it through my hair. He flicks through the teleshopping programs and stops every now and again to look at a product—a blue diamond necklace, a back massager, and a hunting set equipped with fishing knives.

"Maybe, one day, I can take you on a hunting trip with me," Dale whispers and inhales deeply into my hair.

"I don't think I'd be any good at that." I peek at him through a sheet of my hair.

"You, in a tent with me all night, completely alone in the wilderness, needing to keep warm on a cold English night? I think you'd be great." He chuckles.

"I didn't picture you as a hunter," I say, watching his face.

Dale's lip twitches before he laughs loudly. "You'd be surprised at what I like to do."

The room grows lighter with every kiss from Dale, and with every touch, I'm left craving something else, something comforting. And for some reason, Dale is not helping with that on this hellish morning. Maybe he plans to distract me, but instead, each time I take a deep breath, a powerful nesting fear fills the pit of my stomach. I'm surprised at the lack of comfort I'm feeling. Nothing can hold back the growing monster I feel the second I close my eyes. It's tearing me up inside. I feel almost reliant on his firm grip around me, to keep me from falling apart, even when I don't particularly feel any safer with him now than I did before.

"I best get dressed," I whisper, tugging my hand free.

He rises quickly, wrapping an arm around my waist, and walks me into my room. The last time we were in this bedroom was when all I wanted was him. Things change so quick. It seems like a lifetime away since I felt safe within his arms. An embarrassing tear builds in the corner of my eye.

Dale's lips touch my eye before it falls, wiping it away with his plump lips. "It's okay, baby." His hand slips to my lower back. He sits me on the end of my bed and heads for my wardrobe. He retrieves some blue skinny jeans and a grey button-up shirt. He stands in front of me, taking my hands, and eases me into a standing position. He looks at me, his eyes desperate. Maybe he's waiting for consent or searching for any emotion at all. He seems pacified with my weak smile, and he lifts my shirt over my head. His eyes linger on my chest before putting the shirt on me.

I can see the hunger in his eyes, but he makes no attempt or even mention of what is inevitably on his mind.

He doesn't fasten the buttons on my shirt; I reach for them myself. He pushes my hands away and barely looks at me when he drops to his knees. He silently unzips the side of my skirt, and his hands tremble on my thigh. "Rosa ..." he says with a deep breath and bites hard onto his bottom lip. His hands clench my thighs, forcing my heart to thump in my chest. He jumps up and locks his lips onto mine.

I grasp his hair to pull his face back, not ready for this type of intimacy.

He gasps for breath and steps backwards, his frame as hard as stone. "Sorry," he says in a groan, his eyes shining mischievously.

I nod, unsure of how to feel, now desperate to be alone.

"You're crying." He comes closer, slower this time, and looks me up and down. His eyebrows angled so high they might have merged with his pale hair. "Here." He almost throws my jeans at me. "Get dressed." He sits on the end of my bed.

An unexpected expression of rage flickers across his face when my phone which is on my bed, rings. His face changes—not a single trace of annoyance left in his expression—as he answers the phone and stands to hand it to me. "One moment," he says sharply into it. He smiles at me as he gives me the phone, his eyes curiously lingering on the screen: *Rafael*.

I glance at the time—6:15. "Sir."

"Rafael," he corrects me with a sigh. "How are you?"

"Well, as fine as I can be after—" I have to stop the words coming from my mouth as my chest rips at its seams.

Dale comes closer to me, definitely able to hear the voice on the other end of the phone. His hands clench into fists as he puts a possessive arm around my waist.

"I want you here, at the office with me. You will feel much better helping out here. We will find out what happened, Rosa." His tone is thoughtful and powerful. It eases the never-ending throb in my head. The phone goes silent. "Come now. I'm already at the office."

Dale turns and paces to the other side of my room and back. "Are you going?" he spits, his sharp voice piercing my heart.

"Well, of course. I want to help in any way possible, Dale. Surely you understand." I grab his arm and pull him to face me as I speak.

He violently shakes his arm from my grasp, then grips my shoulders. He lowers his face to mine, his brown eyes darken as he closes in on me, leaving not an inch between our faces. "He doesn't need you, Rosalie. He wants you, and you like that," he whispers fiercely, his hot, sweet breath washing over my face.

"Oh 'Sir'," he mimics. "I'll come and sit with you..."

I push away from him and rush to button my shirt, but his lips force themselves upon mine.

He removes his shirt, then tugs at mine. He opens it further and pulls my body against his own. His hands tighten painfully around my arms so hard that his nails dig in.

I deserve this. My arms grow numb against his tight grip, and he bites hard on my lips, my neck ... "Stop!" I struggle to get away.

Dale's grip only tightens as his teeth sink sharply into the skin of my collarbone, and finally, they break through my skin.

I struggle against his groan of pleasure, my hands pushing against his forehead.

He releases me and jumps backwards, his eyes wide with excitement, my blood smeared across his face. "Rosalie, my darling." His soft voice does not match his violent expression.

I stumble backwards and fall onto my bed. My body trembles as I push myself farther back against the wall. My mind can't seem to figure out how to complete a coherent sentence to shout at him.

He follows me and leans across my bed, his face inching closer to mine. "I got carried away, Rosalie," he mumbles breathlessly. His hot breath brushes my cheek, making me recoil, my back pushing hard against the cold wall. He reaches for me again and licks his lips dangerously. His fingers trail over my body, caressing and pinching, until his hand wraps around the back of my neck. His sinisterly vacant eyes stare into mine; I can feel a large tear building in the corner.

A jolt of pity shoots through my body, and I push his hands away.

His pale chest and shoulders tense, stretching his skin over the muscles. I don't look at his face but at the veins in his arms, which slowly shrink in size as the seconds pass. His breathing slows, his hands collapse around his face, and he falls face down onto my bed.

To my horror, I hear a sound erupt, one that causes pain a thousand times worse than a bite. He's crying. "Dale?" I whisper timidly. "I'm sorry."

"Sorry for what? You haven't done anything. It's me. It's always me." He can barely finish the sentence before his sobs return.

My stomach grumbles painfully with anticipation as I move around him and stretch my arm around his body. "Dale, please. It's okay. Look, things are tense. I think we need a few days apart." I slowly move backwards, as if the words will cause less ache the farther away I get.

He leans onto his elbows, tears streaking down his utterly perfect face.

My muscles ache with loss, desperate to forget what is happening.

"I'm damaged," he whispers between pained sobs.

"As am I, Dale. This whole fucking world is damaged." I shake my head. "I've got to go." I turn my back on him and hurry out the door before he can respond.

It pains me more than it should. I don't understand my absurd reaction to this man. My hands are still shaking on the steering wheel, and I stare absentmindedly out the window as I drive towards Rafael's office. I don't focus on the early morning traffic, instead, my thoughts are back in my house, where Dale could still be. My pain for him, for who he really is, is barely a tiny fragment of the pain I feel for losing my mother, but still, it burns deep into my heart. My physical pain from Dale's bite is fizzing out fast, and now that I am finally away from his allure, any sympathy turns into cold anger.

How can he be like this, after what has happened? I struggle to think straight as my body trembles with rage. I slam my car across two spaces in the car park of the office.

"Rosalie." I hear a sigh of relief from behind me as I step from the car. Rafael's hand rests on my shoulder before I get the chance to turn around.

"Mr—" I clear my throat. "I mean, Rafael." I turn to face him.

His anxiety-riddled eyes scan my face. "What's happened? And don't give me no crap."

I stare at him for a moment, my eyebrows furrowing with bewilderment. "What?"

"I know he did that to you." His voice trembles angrily with every word, a scarred hand brushing across my collarbone.

The tears of pain and anger flow at an unstoppable force, my cheeks reddening with every self-conscious whimper I let escape from my tired lips.

He directs me into his building through the back door, his hand resting lightly on my quivering shoulder.

I focus on the colours that flash beneath my closed eyes as he sits me on the comfy leather sofa I know well.

"Why?" His voice is as soft as velvet, but his breath is shaky. He's unable to completely hide the anger threatening to overflow.

I stare at him again, my eyes hurting, prickling every time I blink. "It's not his fault," I lie, my voice steadier than it has been since yesterday.

I drop my gaze not wanting to see his disappointed eyes. He watches me and turns around to bang his fists against the wall in frustration. He puts his hands on the wall and leans into it with his head bowed, his previous attempt to hide his anger evaporates. His large, rugged shape moves shockingly fast and he stands staring out the large office window into the dark morning. His husky appearance is more vibrant as his emotions strengthen—rugged but safe. I sit there, surveying Rafael from afar, I don't fear his anger; I can't fear this man who seems to be trying so hard to protect me. His light-green shirt is unusually messy and untucked from his suit trousers.

"Rafael," I croak. My endless crying has tortured my throat.

He turns, pushing his brown curls off his face, and approaches me. His shirt has several buttons undone; brown and red colouring circle his eyes. "Miss Lockwood... Rosalie, please." He sits opposite from me and takes a drink from a cup on the table then leans his elbows on his knees. "I feel like we're missing something huge."

My eyes linger much too obviously on the glinting white scar on his exposed chest.

"We've had the top men working your mother's case. No fingerprints, not one bloody clue as to who has done this," he says, his voice getting louder.

I shuffle nervously, wrapping my arms around myself, holding together what little I have left. "I just don't understand who could ..." My voice breaks as my mother's eyeless, tortured face flashes through my mind.

"Does your family have any enemies?"

"My father was a lawyer. Of course, he has enemies," I whisper.

"Listen, Rosa. She was found very close to your house. No more than two hundred feet from your front door." He rushes towards me, and his arms wrap around me as I break into terrified sobs.

My hairs stand on end as I remember the shadow, the outline of a man watching me the night my mother died. My skin prickles painfully, and my throat fills with blood from the inside of my cheek, which I continue to bite to stifle my cries.

"Your mother passed. She died at about ten o'clock that evening. Your brother has told me you saw someone ..." Rafael's voice becomes unsteady. "Benjamin said you were terrified that someone was there."

"I saw a man by the streetlamp at the end of the street. Then someone was very close. I heard them walk. I saw the shadow. I ran. I locked the door. I was too scared to look back."

"Your brother told me this was at, like, two a.m., correct?"

"Yes, minutes before you called." I shudder violently against his solid arms.

"I wonder if whoever was outside so late at night has anything to do with it?" Rafael asks himself out loud.

I raise my eyebrows. "That makes no sense."

"It makes sense if it isn't just your mother they are after. Because your mother, from what can be gathered, was coming to see you."

CHAPTER 14

I lie on the cold, wet grass, unable to move an inch, as the outline of a man, tall and broad, bludgeons my mother to death under the eerie white streetlamp across from my house. Her screams turn into muffled gargles as she chokes on her own blood.

*****

"Rosa!"

My hands fly to protect my face from the monster who killed my mother. I can still hear her screams as my eyes open, and Rafael holds my face close to his own. He breathes a shaky sigh of relief as I stare into his vivid green eyes.

He makes me drink a cup of sugary tea before he agrees to talk to me again. It's not until he offers me a biscuit that I realise how hungry I am. I eat as he talks again; my other hand is wrapped in his insanely chilly hands. I let him hold my hand tight, as if that will protect me from his words.

"The detective, he's asking whether you or your brother have any enemies. This is a small town; they feel this is personal, someone trying to get to you or your brother." He watches me swallow the cookie, my throat suddenly dry.

I shrug slowly, concentrating, recounting the years, but nothing comes to mind. "No-one. We are friendly people."

"I want to take you home with me, Rosa. I'm concerned."

I laugh. It sounds strange in my humourless mind. "No. No, I have Ben."

"Will Dale be with you?"

My hand raises to my collarbone. It stings as my fingers run over the blood-red teeth marks which have coloured purple and blue after all these hours.

"No," I whisper. My hand trembles in his.

"He's hurting you."

"Not intentionally," I lie to myself again.

"Rosalie, you can't unintentionally bite someone so hard they bleed. He's a goddamn creep." He stands, his hands raised behind his head in complete and utter disgust, as if I meant enough to him for my pain to be his own.

"It was just the heat of the moment."

"I don't want to leave you alone. I can't even sit still, never mind sleep, knowing what you're going through right now," he whispers, dropping to his knees in front of me. "I don't want you hurt, Rosalie, and you know you'd feel safer with me there."

His sincere words puncture my already crippled heart. He stands again and wanders out of his office. Within seconds, he's returned, back on his knees in front of me, wiping the black smudges from under my eyes with a soft cloth. "Just think about it." He stands again. "I have to meet with the detectives about the Eliza Thomas case. Stay here please." His tired, red eyes look sad. He slips his glasses over his eyes and smiles weakly then tucks his shirt into his trousers as he leaves our office.

I stand and shuffle towards the window. The silence hurts my ears as I suppress the tears forming in my eyes. The low and mid-rise buildings look grey and empty in the gloomy light of day. I watch the few cars pass, people going on with their day-to-day activities, tiny problems causing petty headaches, whilst my life is imploding. I can't stop wondering about Rafael, about his need to protect me, even if he is doing it for a clear conscience.

My phone screeches—at least, that's how it sounds to me in the silence of the office. Dale is calling. My blood rushes to my face, and a bead of sweat builds on my forehead. I'm unusually apprehensive as I answer the call. "Dale."

"Rosalie, will you forgive me?"

"I just want some space right now, Dale."

"I want to see you."

"Not now. I need to be alone for a while. Please, just let me be."

"I'm coming to see you, now!"

"*No.*" My voice switches between two octaves. I end the call and slam the phone onto Rafael's desk. My cheeks flush as I stomp to my desk and sit with my head in my hands.

I hear his voice before I see him. "Rosa!" He bursts into the room, his hands stacked with paperwork. "They called me at the front desk, said you're shouting." He drops the papers onto his desk, next to my phone.

"Sorry," I say, my voice feeble. "Dale called. He wants to see me. I said no, and he just wouldn't listen."

My phone vibrates on the desk and dings.

Rafael spies my phone. His eyes narrow, and his mouth opens and closes twice, as if he might say something. "He's outside." Rafael slowly approaches the window.

I rush to Rafael's side. My heart trembles as I focus on a bright white Jaguar parked next to my car. I can barely decipher the shape of Dale in the front seat from all the way up here.

"I'll sort it." Rafael grabs my phone and calls Dale's number.

The phone hardly rings once before Dale answers. "Get down here, now. Rosa, we need to talk."

"Ah, Mr Cartwright." Rafael says, his voice deepening.

"Put Rosa on."

"We're busy right now." He grins and nods towards the window.

"I just want to see her!"

I watch him exit the car and head towards the front.

"My security will not let you in, Dale."

Dale spins and strolls towards his car, then punches the bonnet as he leans against it. I can't discern Dale's expression, but he's definitely angry.

As bored as Rafael sounds, his smile begs to differ.

"I'll wait."

The phone goes dead before Rafael has the chance to reply, and Dale gets in his car. Rafael puts the phone on my desk and furrows his eyebrows at me. He allows the corner of his pale pink lips to turn up into a grin. "It's okay."

"Come home with me," I whisper, and he nods.

I check the time; my mother's death brings my father to Woodbury town. He's due to arrive today after not visiting here for many years. Benjamin will collect him and review the necessary steps. I can't bring myself to help; seeing him will be painful enough.

Rafael rushes around his office, finishing what he can and organising his early leave. Rafael suggests we go to his house first, because he's sure Dale will follow.

I stand, surveying the Jaguar parked so close to the driver's side of my car it would be impossible to get in from that side.

Dale steps out a few times and smokes a cigarette whilst staring directly at the office window, then gets back in his car.

"Rosa ..." Rafael's hand grasps my shoulder. "Ben has your father. They're with the police. We are going to leave here now."

I face him, startled. "Already?" I whisper and grab my phone off his desk, my hands shaking.

"Don't worry. I won't let him hurt you," Rafael whispers, pulling me into a gentle and short embrace. His hand which strokes my hair shakes too, so sightly I barely notice it. He smiles reassuringly as he rests a hand on my back and leads me from the office.

I feel safe as he takes me out the front door, then we almost jog to his car parked only several cars from Dale. My leg muscles tense up so bad I struggle to take the next step, when a car door slamming startles me.

"Rosa!"

I keep my focus on the car I'm about to get into.

Rafael tightens his grip on my upper arm and pulls me forward. We reach the car, and he swings the door open leading me inside so fast I don't even have the time to look at Dale. Dale storms up to Rafael, his hands balled into giant, bony fists. The door slams shut at the same time the tiny beep indicates the car is locked.

Rafael and Dale stand face to face, Dale is taller, but Rafael makes up for it in sheer ruggedness. Dale glares down at Rafael, who simply squares his shoulders and smiles. Rafael, my boss, who has no reason to protect me, stands in front of the car ready to fight, ready to protect me. Rafael steps backwards from the car, his eyes smouldering with excitement for the oncoming confrontation.

"Dale," Rafael says bluntly.

"Rosalie, what are you doing?" Dale asks, ignoring Rafael.

"Dale, you've been harassing this poor woman all day. Don't you think she's going through enough?" Rafael's eyes narrow.

"I just want to talk to her. Why are you preventing me from doing that?" Dale steps towards Rafael.

My hands tremble against the locked door handle as I watch helplessly from the sidelines. I fear for Rafael, his head barely reaching Dale's jaw. I only just realise how tall Dale really is, or how small my five foot seven is. *Rafael, please walk away.* My hand closes on the door handle, ready to get out to protect Rafael.

It happens too fast for my jaw to drop. Dale's fist crashes into Rafael's jaw with immense power, which knocks Rafael into the side of the car. I struggle at the door handle, trying to force it open, but it remains firmly locked as Dale grabs Rafael's shoulders and stands him upright.

"Open the *damn door*!" Dale shouts.

"Make me." Rafael grins, shrugging away from Dale's grasp, and steps backwards. He wipes the blood from his lip, smearing it across the sleeve of his light-green shirt, as he opens his arms, seemingly ready to embrace the beating.

Dale straightens his shirt and looks at me through the window. His eyes fill with tears, no trace of anger left. "I told you, Rosalie.

I knew he wanted you." Dale moves closer to the window and bends to look at me.

My eyes fill with angry tears.

"What? Want her?" Rafael says in a barely audible but disgusted growl.

"Don't bullshit me." Dale straightens up and bangs his huge hand on the car's roof. He turns to face Rafael. "I'll talk to her soon enough." A lopsided grin spreads across his face as he turns to me and blows a kiss.

A shiver runs down my spine, chilling me from inside out.

Rafael watches Dale stroll to his car, as if nothing happened.

Dale's car revs loudly before speeding off. Once Dale's car is out of sight, Rafael clicks the car key, finally letting me out.

I stumble from the car, rush to Rafael, and warily wrap my arms around him. "Thank you," I cry on his shoulder.

Rafael's hand pushes on my shoulder as he shrugs out of my embrace.

With a burning pink face, I look up at him, embarrassed by his rejection.

"Sorry, I don't want you covered in blood." Rafael laughs.

"Raf—"

He turns and walks towards the car. Blood still seeps steadily from his lip, down his face, and onto his shirt. His face could easily pass as being made from stone as he holds his car door open for me and waits for me to get back in.

I reluctantly get in and watch him cross the car. The wind gusts as rain spits onto the windscreen.

Rafael unbuttons his shirt and opens the driver side door. "Can you pass me my jacket, please?"

I avoid looking directly at him, my cheeks growing an even brighter red. I hand him his jacket, which is draped over the back of my seat, without making eye contact.

He turns his back on me and removes his shirt.

I glance at him again, surprised to see layer upon layer of muscle.

His muscular shoulders flex as he flicks his shirt onto the driver's seat and slips on his suit jacket, covering his light-olive skin. "I'm sorry you had to see that, Rosalie, but we need him to know you'll not be alone." He sits beside me and starts the engine.

"Why do you protect me?" The words slipped out before I could stop them.

"Come to mine. It will be safer at mine for now."

I nod, unable to think of a reason not to, unable to even imagine a scenario where I'd feel safe tonight.

He turns to study me, his thumb rubbing his lower lip, which is now raw and sporting a large lump. He's clearly assessing my face as we speed down the winding roads towards his home. His eyes narrow on the road as we take a sharp right. The sun's efforts to shine through the dark grey clouds cease, and we take the last left and stop at the large gates that protect Rafael's home. They open, creaking loudly as they did the first time I was here. He pulls up outside his house, and I clamber from the car. Rafael hurries to my side as we walk to his towering front door.

The door swings open, and Lucy stands waiting expectantly. Her face is seemingly much paler than the last time I saw her.

Rafael leads, almost pulling me into his house. He hurries my jacket down my arms and holds it as we walk through the first door on the right.

Lucy rushes behind and flicks on the light.

A large circular room lights up before my eyes. Its white walls stretch high, revealing several beautiful diamond-shaped lights dotted across a black ceiling, like stars. An empty log fire sits in the far side of the room. A desk with a computer, a small circular coffee table and a curved white leather sofa is the only other furnishing in the room. A large window faces the wooded area just beside his home.

"Anything I can get you?" Lucy mutters to Rafael as she stands awkwardly at the door, her gaze falling on me.

"Some drinks please. Some wine will do. And some snacks," he says, not looking at her. "Take a seat, Rosalie. You're safe here."

"Why is she here?" Lucy regards me with distaste.

"Because of a personal issue. You will tend to her as you tend to me." He sits on the sofa next to me.

Lucy leaves the room, and Rafael watches me silently, his chest still bare under his suit jacket.

I can't help my eyes flittering towards his obviously chiselled physique.

His finger absentmindedly traces along the large silver scar. He looks down at his chest and up at me, then jumps up. "I'll go grab a clean shirt. Sorry." He opens the door and rushes out.

"It's okay," I mutter.

My shaking hands are easing. I feel safe here. Somehow, this house feels comfortable. The sofa, though cold, is invitingly soft. I watch the outline of trees sway in wind through the window, almost certain that if I stare hard enough, I will find Dale, staring back.

Lucy pushes a silver trolly that carries a bottle of red wine, two glasses and a platter of sandwiches into the room. "Here." She pours two glasses of wine. She strolls straight back out, brushing past Rafael as he reenters.

He's wearing a tight black t-shirt, dark blue jeans, and is carrying what seems like another shirt. He glances at me with a smirk, grabs the two glasses of wine, and sits at the end of the sofa, his body turned to me. "Sorry about that. I forgot I took off—"

"No, it's fine. You stood and protected me today, Rafael. Thank you."

He moves his wine glass to his lips, and I follow. Together, we finish our first glass within seconds. Its fruity burn flows roughly down my dry throat.

"Well, I wasn't going to let him touch you. Will you be wanting to press charges?" He fills the glasses with more wine.

"I'd rather not. I have enough going on."

I drain the next glass as fast as I did the first.

Rafael grins, drinking back his glass too, and refills them. We drain the rest of the bottle before he speaks. "Would you like to stay here tonight, Rosalie? I'd feel better if you did, and in the Morning, I can drive you home."

I swallow my wine, only stopping because the room spins around me. I nod as I think through my options. My heart thuds at the thought of Dale sitting outside my house now, waiting for me to get home, my father's raw pain and crying with Ben. If I stay here, I'll at least feel safer. "My father can have my room for tonight."

My head feels lighter than it has for ages. My body can loosen up after being so tight for the last couple days.

Rafael laughs as I shake my head in a daze. "Good, because I couldn't drive you home anyway."

His smile shines like a beacon of light in this time I desperately need it, and his green eyes glitter like emeralds in the white spotlights. My head feels even lighter as the alcohol has time to travel through my body, reaching my hands and feet at a wonderful pace.

"Lucy, wine please," he says to his phone. He must have called her. He raises his eyebrows at me. "I know it's hard, but try just relax tonight. You're safe. I'm here." He puts the other shirt between us, a cheeky smile spreading across his face. "I'm sorry. I don't keep women's bedclothes here, but you're welcome to use this." His cheeks redden with every word.

I smile and nod in thanks, unsure of what to say.

Lucy throws open the door, holding a bottle of wine. She looks at Rafael, curiosity filling her childlike eyes. She places the wine on a tray and waits patiently.

"Rosa will be staying here tonight."

"Oh ... I'll prepare your bed, sir."

My heart thuds as I contemplate what she's saying. I stare at Rafael, and my mouth drops wide open.

Rafael's laugh echoes around the tall, circular room.

Lucy's eyebrows rise in surprise, and she steps backwards, almost scared.

Rafael looks at me, then again at Lucy. His head drops into his hands and says towards the floor, "Lucy, prepare my bed, yes. But can you also prepare the guestroom opposite my own?" He looks at me sideways, head still in his hands. "Am I really that undesirable, Rosa?" He straightens up, smiling, and pours more wine.

"I didn't mean that. Of course, you're not."

"So, I am desirable to you?"

I grab my wine and sip slowly this time. "Does it matter?"

Lucy coughs, as if to alert us of her presence.

Rafael dismisses her without even glancing in her direction as he moves farther from me. He looks me up and down, his smile hesitant. "No, not really." He stretches his arms, leans back, and rests his arms on the back of the sofa. His stature relaxes around me, and suddenly, he's no longer my boss. He's settled quickly into the position of a friend.

We finish the bottle, chatting about life—my life, mainly. The sandwiches I start to eat nearing my last drink are perfect on my empty stomach.

We're still laughing as he leads me upstairs, walking almost as wobbly as me. He requests with a chortle that I hold the stair rails extra tight. The staircase moves in a blur with every step I take. Rafael's warming hand wraps around my upper arm, comforting on the otherwise strange marble staircase.

"My room. Your room." He points out, then opens my door. "Good night, Rosa. I'm straight across if you need me."

I survey the swirling bedroom; it's simple but elegant. A large double bed, two bedside tables, and a wardrobe occupy the white, open room. I flop onto the bed and unbutton my shirt. The room spins in synchronisation with my thudding heart. I force myself into a sitting position and slip off my shirt and jeans. I pull on Rafael's blue shirt; it doesn't cover much of my legs, but it'll do. I unsteadily fasten the buttons and lie back on the bed, staring out the double glass door that leads onto a balcony that looks across the driveway.

My body shakes irrationally as I picture a tall, blonde man staring back at me from the dark balcony. My breath heaves. An unnatural fear for a man who has barely even threatened me spills out, and I rush from the bedroom. Not looking back, I slam the door shut and burst into Rafael's room.

CHAPTER 15

This room is massive; his bed is easily the size of two double beds and covered with a dark red blanket. A desk sits in the corner of the room, and a computer and a large bookshelf is on the other side. Two large glass doors are directly opposite his bed, with a view of the forest that sways in the wind.

Rafael runs towards me, and his body feels like a block of ice as he pulls me into his arms.

My cries morph into embarrassingly loud sobs as he awkwardly pats my back.

"I've been waiting for this," he whispers, pushing my hair from my face.

I struggle to understand what he means as my sobs soak his bare chest.

"I noticed you hadn't cried much," he says softly, his body angled from me. "It's about time you let out some emotion."

Minutes pass whilst he rubs my back. He whispers that I'm safe now and that it'll all be okay as he wipes my tears with his thumb. It feels as if my tears will never end. His cold skin feels soft beneath my trembling fingers, but his body is hard. Each time I suck in a breath, I smell an earthy smell, maybe sandalwood, emitting from his neck. His chest slowly warms the longer I stay attached to him. After what could easily have been hours, I finally control myself again.

Rafael's patience is endless; he smiles gently as he slides himself from my grasp and makes a large space between us.

"Sorry," I say, finally able to talk coherently.

He laughs again. His cheeks rise spectacularly. His face is angelical in the shadowy lamp-lit bedroom. We sit on the edge of his huge bed, and the mattress shakes in unison with my body.

"Don't worry about it, but you need sleep," he says with a deep breath. He stands and holds my hands to pull me upright.

"No ... I can't be alone." His eyebrows furrow at me, and he turns to lift the covers off his bed. "Hop in."

"Huh?"

Rafael rolls his eyes. "If you won't sleep in your own bed, at least get in mine and let me get some rest."

"Oh, right. Sorry," I murmur, sliding under the covers.

The warmth of his bed embraces me instantly.

Rafael walks to the other side of the bed and lies on top of the blankets. His olive-coloured skin shimmers in the light emitting from the lamp next to him. His stomach is defined in his stillness. His hands rest behind his head, and his arms and shoulders seem to be carved perfectly from marble. Each band of muscle stretches his skin. His whole body seems to be toned. His stubble lines perfectly accentuate his chin and jaw. He stares at the balcony doors ahead, too preoccupied to notice my constant admiration.

The thick glistening scar stretches across his stomach and thickens on his hip where it finally ends. I try to imagine what could have caused it, but I cannot conjure anything but horror-worthy nightmares of murderers and psychos. My eyes relinquish to the night, and I fall into a restless sleep.

The shadow stands tall at the foot of the bed. The only thing visible in the dark night is the white-blond hair and the twinkle of the raised knife.

I wake up shivering, my arm wrapped around an unusually cool and solid body. My eyes snap open, and I stare, horror struck, at Rafael.

He's squashed uncomfortably at the very end of the bed. His arms are still behind his head, the way I saw him before I fell asleep.

I shove myself off him. *Oh my God, how embarrassing,* I cringe to myself. My cheeks burn as I make as much space between us as possible.

Rafael's long eyelashes flutter open as he awakes. A huge grin spreads across his bright face, and his eyes glint in the early morning sun. "Sleep well?" His grin only gets bigger.

"Umm, yeah. Better than I could have hoped." I shrugged, my hopes that he didn't notice me cuddling him rising.

"Comfy?"

"Cold." I look down to let my hair filter across my face.

"Well, I dislike blankets. And it was you who chose to sleep on me." His cheekbones rise in an effort not to laugh.

My heart flutters at the sight of his elated mood. *At least he didn't mind.*

"You did kiss my chest once or twice and dribble on me. But I'll forgive you." He chuckles and sits upright.

I reach for my lips and focus anywhere but on Rafael. My face burns as if it's on fire.

He emerges from his bed, and I sit upright, staring at my hands.

I risk a peek at him and see his hands resting on his hips, he's silhouetted in the morning sun, which glares ever more powerfully through the glass. I dart my gaze to my hands again as he faces me.

"What's up?"

I don't even need to look at him to know he's smiling.

"S-sorry." I entwine my fingers together. "I don't know,. I don't even remember doing that." I glance up at him again.

He takes a deep breath and sighs, his chest rising. "It's fine, Rose. You were asleep. You were safe."

My eyes fill to the brim with tears. I put my hand on my head and let my hair fall over my eyes again. My head feels full with so many emotions that must be impossible for any single human to handle. An icy hand brushes my cheek, then moves my hair over my ear. Rafael's face is barely an inch from mine, and I freeze; everything from last night hits me with all its might.

"It's okay," he says with a breath into my ear.

A warm shiver rolls through my body as I inhale his skin's earthy scent. I almost fall out of his bed to get out quickly. I jump and shrink away from a full-length mirror stretched across the left wall. "Why?" I nod towards the mirror, allowing myself to survey the mess which is me.

Rafael stares at me and coughs up a laugh. "For a better view."

"What?" My eyebrow raises, confusion spreading across my face.

"It just gives me a full view of my bed, Rosalie." He flops onto his bed, now wearing a sapphire-blue shirt. He leans on his elbow and surveys my face as I pan from the mirror to the bed several times.

My lips tighten in a straight line and slowly curve up at the edges.

His laughter shakes the bed, and he stands again.

I turn back to the mirror and straighten the borrowed shirt I'm wearing.

Rafael stands next to me, now wearing a pair of tight black trousers. "That colour suits you." He taps the shirt collar. "I had Lucy wash your clothes. They're here." He points towards a table at the end of the bed.

I collect the clothes into my arms and stand, staring expectedly at Rafael for him to leave the room.

He watches me for a moment, then jumps and mumbles something as he wanders out the bedroom. "Let me know when you're ready." He closes the door.

I dress fast, not enjoying the feeling of being alone too long. My gaze darts to the balcony every few seconds, as if Dale will just appear. I open the door to let Rafael back in.

With him, he brings a hairbrush and some mascara. "Lucy bought them up. She said you might need it." He barely acknowledges what he hands me.

For a moment, I feel a wave of affection for Lucy. I stand in the mirror, hyperaware of him watching me, caution in his eyes, probably waiting for my next breakdown. My stomach tightens uneasily when I think of my mother. A lump rises dryly in my throat when I imagine what I'll say when I see my father.

Rafael approaches me, holding out my phone. "You left it on the bed in the other room."

"Thanks." I nod, taking the phone, and see I've received several missed calls and even more texts from Dale last night but only one from my brother, which simply says that father is asleep in my room. I shove my phone into my pocket, ready to go home.

Rafael is ready to leave a few minutes after I am. It's only 8:30 a.m. when we leave his house. The morning air is cold and sharp against my cheeks.

Rafael wraps his black suit jacket over my arms and mutters something about me needing a decent coat. He starts the engine and turns on the heat. "Let's get you home," he says, his tone businesslike again.

The journey home is quiet; my stomachs in tight knots. The closer I get to home, the dryer my throat feels. I try to focus on the passing trees and the blue sky over my head like a halo in the white fluffy clouds.

Rafael pulls the car outside my house, which appears strangely small compared to Rafael's unnecessarily huge house, and glances at me. "I've got to pop to the office. "

"What?" I rush my words. "You're not staying?"

As the words slip carelessly from my mouth, I realise, in the last couple of days, I've come to rely on Rafael, as if he's my protector. The only problem is he's nowhere near my protector. He's my boss. My cheeks burn like fire, and I look sharply to the window.

Rafael's laugh eases my fearful and trembling body. "I'll be back. I'm not going to leave you alone. Unless that's what you want? I just feel like you need some extra support, after what happened yesterday."

"Please come back," I say quietly.

He creases his eyebrows at me, the lines on his head visible for the first time. His plump lips pull together to force a smile before he waves me off.

I take that as my time to exit his vehicle. I placed his jacket onto the seat before I walk towards my house. The door is open before I get there. My father's ashen face awaits there; his shoulders are slumped, his greying brown hair messy and unkempt. I turn to take one last glimpse at Rafael, but he's already gone.

I refocus on my father, my hands shaking and throat aching. So many emotions bubble to the surface. First, love, to just see my father's warm face. Next, shock, as his usual tidy appearance is worn and tired. And finally, the almighty rib-crumbling pain. My tears turn into a smudge of mascara on his shoulder. I regret not seeing him enough. I regret not seeing her enough. Her—

My father squeezes me hard, then pulls me into the house. "Darling," he says with a cry. "Are you all right?"

"I'm okay, Father. How are you holding up?"

"I'm still breathing. Your mother had been threatening to leave for so long I just thought she had finally found someone and left." He chuckles through his tears.

"I love you," I cry out, losing myself in tears.

He enters the kitchen, and I click on the kettle and sit at the table. His fingers tap noisily as he sits opposite me. I stare at the kettle, the loud hum of the slowly boiling water helping me focus.

"Ben told me you have a tall, blonde hunk of a boyfriend."

I snuff out a laugh with a cough, my eyes wide with astonishment. I forgot Benjamin doesn't know, and has absolutely no idea of the hurt Dale was causing me, that he punched my boss in the face yesterday, or that Dale won't leave me alone and that's why I slept at Rafael's.

"No, Father. I'm not. I just saw him a couple times." I stand and busying myself with making tea before my poker face cracks.

"From what Ben said, you and this blonde bloke are getting on very well." My father's cheeks blush a crimson red.

"What has Benjamin told you?" I stomp around the kitchen, getting sugar from the cupboard and slamming the door.

"Not much, just that you are an unstoppable force when it came to 'getting some.' And that he doesn't approve much." My father makes a huge effort to sound casual and humorous as he inquires about my life.

"It wasn't like that." I turn from his view, my face burning hot as memories of Dale collapse on me. "It was just a fling."

"Just be careful," he mumbles, his voice a pitch higher than usual. "Your mother was just like you, you know. Knew what she wanted and got it, too."

The lump in my throat blocks my airways. I can't talk. Hearing about how my mother 'was' and not 'is' somehow makes it more real.

I hand my father his tea, and we sit opposite each other in silence. I hear movement from upstairs; Benjamin must be coming down soon. I ready my argument with Ben for telling father about my love life. I'm ready to spurt out that the perfect Angel Benjamin has several different girls over each week. But then again, my father will probably be proud.

"Rosa, how was your sleepover with your boss?" Benjamin asks loudly on his way down the stairs.

"Sleepover with your boss?" my father repeats curiously.

"I had to work late, and then I remembered you were coming, so I thought you'd rather sleep in a comfy bed," I say defensively to my father.

My father grins as he sips from his cup.

Benjamin rubs our father's shoulder. He moves around and sits on the chair next to our father. "You okay, Dad?"

"I'm okay, son. I'm just grateful I have you both."

My father and brother have always had a much closer and more fun relationship. Benjamin is both my parent's pride and joy. Firstborn, of course, he's absolutely perfect in their eyes.

I watch with a frown as Ben hugs my father, then heads towards the kettle as he asks me, "Will you be working today?"

"I'm not sure. Rafael will call me." I check my phone and see it is 10:30 a.m. already. I get up in a hurry, desperate to jump in the hot shower and cry where no one can see me.

I hop up the stairs, taking two steps at a time, and rush into my bathroom, undress fast, and only turn on the hot water. The bathroom slowly steams up. I stare into the mirror, my fingers tracing the light brown circles around my eyes. My face is much paler than it was three days ago. My hair is a curly mess. I drag my brush through it, letting the pain on my scalp ease the agony in my heart.

I step into the burning heat of my shower and sigh as the water stings and runs down my back. I lean against the wall, watching the water induce a red glow on my chest. The running water disguises the tears streaming down my face. My shoulders shudder with each ragged breath I try to take, and I fall to my knees, unable to hold myself together anymore. My arms wrap around my legs, holding myself in a ball and letting my pain run free.

My phone rings and snaps me from my bubble of internal misery. I step out of the shower and wrap my towel around me.

I grab my phone from my jean pocket on the floor. I hear my brother and father laugh from downstairs as I answer the phone.

Rafael speaks fast. "Dale is at your house, Rosa."

My heart thuds faster than ever as the sound of light footsteps move on the stairs. I close the bathroom door and hold myself against it. "Raf, he's here," I say in a barely audible whisper.

"I'm on my way right now. Don't worry."

The phone cuts out.

With all my might, I push my body hard against the door, bracing myself for Dale.

"Rosalie," I hear his whisper against the door, and the handle twists.

I push my body against the door harder now, my knees cracking violently on one another. I count the seconds in my head, praying for Rafael's arrival. I try to shout, to scream for help, but my words are trapped inside the prison I like to call my brain. My wet bare feet slip across the white tile floor as he applies pressure. "Please ...!"

"I just want to talk, sweetheart." He nudges the door once, easily able to overpower me.

I move backwards, clenching the towel around me. My heart's battering rhythm that's booming in my ears deafens me, and I scramble to the corner and sink to my knees.

He smiles when he sees me—a gentle smile, the type of smile one has when talking to a child, a sickeningly sweet smile. He's in a black suit. His tie is loose around his neck. "Why are you acting crazy?" He steps closer.

"Just stay away, and we can talk." My voice breaks near the end. My stomach flips angrily. A wave of nausea causes my forehead to sweat.

He charges towards me and proffers a hand. "Stand up, love."

My body tenses harder, my leg muscles cramping. I ignore his hand and stand.

He grabs my arms and pulls them apart.

I swing my arms outward, knocking his hands out of the way, and throw my palm against his chest.

Dale grunts as my hand hits him and smiles again; this time, his teeth are bared.

I stare at his face, fear forcing its way up my chest. I squash myself farther up the wall. With a small gasp, I reach to my back to secure the loosening towel around me and hold it as close to me as possible. "Go away," I growl through gritted teeth.

His grin distorts and turns into an angry frown. His eyes become snakelike slits as he tightens his grip on my upper arm, his nails digging into my soaking wet skin. He holds my arm at a dangerous angle, my shoulder smarting with pain. "What are you trying to hide from me?" He releases my arms but grabs my wrists and pins them against the wall above my head. His tongue flickers playfully over his own lips as the back of his hand moves over my neck and slowly reaches my chest. His fingers push roughly against my towel, forcing space between it and my skin, and with his breath held, his fingers reach farther.

I squeeze my eyes shut and swallow a cry that's building in my desert-dry mouth. I'm sure my heart has stopped, its usual thunder frozen alongside my muscles. An unusual silence fills my ears.

"Dale." Rafael's deep voice breaks the eternal silence.

Dale's one hand moves from my body to his side. His other hand keeps my hands pinned above my head. I hear a string of swear words as my brother's face appears at Dale's shoulder, and one of Benjamin's hands clench Dale's white-blond hair.

"Get out of my house," Benjamin whispers almost seductively.

Dale chortles—a wrong move, as not a second passes when Benjamin's fist collides with Dale's perfectly structured cheekbone. He releases my wrists, leaving me to collapse in a wet, shaking heap on the floor.

"Ben," Rafael says and reaches for Benjamin in a lazy attempt to stop him from hitting Dale in the gut.

I shake my head. "*Stop!*"

The room freezes with confusion as Ben and Rafael stare at me.

"Just go, Dale," Rafael murmurs.

Benjamin's chest heaves. His clenched fists tremble.

Dale regards me with watering eyes and a ripe bruise forming on his cheek. "You have me wrong. I mean her no harm. What have I done but love her?" He leaves the bathroom.

We listen to Dale stomp down the stairs.

My father's head pokes around the bathroom door, his eyes wide and face pale. "What the bloody hell just happened, Rosalie?"

"Let her get dressed, then we can talk about it," Ben mutters to our father. Benjamin's face is purple with anger, and he straightens his shirt. He squints inquiringly at Rafael.

Rafael nods and watches them through the door as they leave my room. "Can I help you, Rosa?" Rafael's gaze falls to his feet.

I grip my towel uncertainly as I rise off the floor. Rafael still doesn't look my way as I cross the bathroom and stand opposite him. My legs are trembling, my stomach somersaulting again and again as I reach for his face.

CHAPTER 16

"Rosa," he says with an unsteady and hot breath against my wrist. His cheeks burn where my hands rest on either side.

I tilt up his head enough to look at me. His green eyes lock with mine for a small moment. A curly lock of his dark brown hair drops in front of his eye, and I brush it back, my fingers trembling. I watch his Adam's apple jolt with a hard swallow as he collects his thoughts, and he exhales an exasperated sigh.

"It's all right." He strokes my head like a dog. "Get dressed. I'll wait in your bedroom." He turns his head, not looking at me, his gaze still on his feet, takes my hands off his face, and holds them. "It'll be okay," he whispers, turns to the bedroom, and gently closes the door behind him.

I hide my head in my hands as I try to calm my erratic breathing. I bang my hands on the wall, horrified I'd made a mindless move on Rafael. As terrified as I am, Rafael makes me feel safe, like I mean something to the world, like he truly cares. I long to feel the fire in the pit of my stomach which only his presence can seemingly ignite. I shake my head again, staring at the door.

"I'm being irrational," I whisper to myself and get dressed as fast as possible. The black skinny jeans and green buttoned shirt will have to do. I apply only eyeliner and mascara and flatten my hair with a brush before I open the bathroom door.

I stand in the doorway and stare at Rafael, who's lying on my bed, hands behind his head.

He flashes a smirk at me before sitting upright, his lips forming a straight line. "How do you feel?"

I sit next to him at the end of my bed. My breathing shakes loudly, and he rests a hand on my shoulder. "I don't feel safe."

"Would …" He clears his throat, surveying my face. "Would you like to stay with me for a few nights? I've taken the week off work. We can't do much until the police get back to us anyway."

I nod silently; my tears are all he needs to see.

He stands, proffering me a hand, and together we go downstairs to explain the problem with Dale to my family. I'm pretty sure Rafael has rehearsed the story; he tells it perfectly. He graciously skips over anything too intimate, maybe to protect my feelings. He tells them about how he noticed Dale's attitude and offered to help, that I want to be away from Dale.

Benjamin stands in frustration as Rafael recounts the confrontation in the car park. He reiterates how I was safely locked in the car. He tells my father how his priority is my safety right now, because not only is he worried someone had targeted my mother, he's worried Dale will try again.

"Targeted?" my father stutters.

"The police mentioned this morning that one of Eleanor's coworkers told them that Eleanor had received a call before she went missing, telling her to come to Woodbury. They don't have much information yet, but, of course, I'll tell you when I know."

"And you believe Rosalie—"

"I believe Dale will be back, and I'd like to offer her the protection of my home so you can both focus on coming to terms with what has happened to your wife."

"You're Rosalie's boss?" My father stands.

Rafael steps forward, his hand extended. "Forgive me, sir. I'm Rafael Alcazar. I am her boss. She works with me in my law firm."

My father grasps Rafael's hand and firmly shakes it. His eyes lock onto Rafael's. "I'm Walter Lockwood." My father smiles. "Rosalie, I'm pretty sure you chose the wrong man."

No one notices Rafael's rapidly reddening cheeks; my father is too interested in chuckling at his own joke. He slaps Rafael's shoulder in a friendly manner, and the chatter soon begins. Rafael reveals information he's heard concerning my mother's murder.

I ignore their talk and sit, silently letting my tears sting my eyes and topple unsteadily down my cheek. "I'm going to get some bits together."

"I'll come up soon and help." Rafael glances at me, too immersed in conversation to fully stop.

I drag my feet up the stairs. My body still hasn't completely stopped shaking as I reach my bedroom and grab my phone off the side. I see several texts from Dale and lie back on my bed to start with the first.

"Rosa, I have my father's funeral this morning. Please accompany me."

"Rosa, can I see you? I'm going through so much, and I know you are too."

"I beg of you to forgive me, Rosa. I told you I wasn't good. My father influenced me too much."

My hands shake and tears splat messily on my phone's screen. I sit upright, breathing deeply.

"I'm going to come to see you after the funeral. Please, let's just talk."

"Is it wrong of me to love you? To see the threat of Rafael and want to keep you mine?"

"Nothing will change how I feel about you. I'd rather die than part with you hating me."

I throw my phone onto my bed and thrust my head into my hands. "Why?" I cry out to myself as silently as possible. With silence being my worst companion, I wish Rafael had come upstairs with me.

I shove my clothes, makeup, some perfume, and my toiletries into a backpack—I can always pop back here if I need anything—and sit on my bed. I close my eyes for a moment. *"If wanting you is a crime, then send me to Hell."* Dale's words echo in my mind, tugging dangerously at my already torn heart. I wrap my arms around myself, pulling myself together.

A finger brushes my forehead, then moves my hair from over my face. "Come," Rafael whispers.

I open my eyes slightly.

He takes my hands to pull me up. "Let's get you settled at mine." He grabs my backpack and puts his hand on my back to lead me from my room.

I exchange a hug with my father, and he whispers for me to be good, before kissing my head.

Benjamin smiles and stage whispers for me to not do anything he wouldn't do.

Rafael's lips press into a hard smile, and he turns to leave my house.

My father's and Benjamin's laughter fills the house as we approach the front door.

Rafael keeps his hand on my back as we head for his car. He drives slower now, glancing at me every few seconds.

I stare ahead, watching the clouds disappear. The sun shines through the window, warming the car. I lower the window a little. The fresh, cold wind blows invitingly on my warm face.

"Are you hungry?" he asks, his eyes back on the road.

"Umm, sort of."

He nods. I see his cheek rise with what seems to be a smile, and he presses his foot to accelerate the car along the winding country road.

Fifteen minutes pass, and we say nothing. We pull in front of a small coffeehouse and park next to a Range Rover, with large, darkly tinted side windows. Two large blossom trees sit sturdily in front of the building, the branches hanging loosely to the ground.

"Come." He turns off the engine and gets out.

I clamber from the car and stand by his side. We walk together to the door. THE HIDDEN COFFEE, the small sign reads above the door.

I raise my eyebrows at Rafael. "How do you know this place?"

"I bring clients here. It's a quiet and private place." He smiles and opens the door, chiming a little bell.

Bright lights illuminate the coffeeshop's black walls and white tables. Small spotlights guide us down a pathway between the candlelit tables.

A waitress wearing a small black dress rushes up to us, smiling. "Mr Alcazar." She greets him with a small curtsey and motions to us to sit.

He smiles at her and pulls out a chair for me. "Two cappuccinos to start with, please."

She nods and pirouettes. Her dress doesn't conceal much of her body, and she sashays behind a small bar in the corner of the room.

Rafael watches her go, his eyes move over her body, once, then sits opposite me and hands me a menu. "How are you feeling?"

"Confused. Maybe a bit scared." I answer stiffly, watching him as he glances back over to the waitress.

He opens his own menu. "Why?"

I peruse my menu. "I think it's obvious why, Rafael."

He sighs and looks up at me. "Why are you confused?"

The waitress appears and sets down two mugs. "Any food I can get you, Mr Alcazar?"

"I'll have the roasted vegetable and goats cheese sandwich, please. What about you, Rosa?"

I stare at the menu that I hadn't even read, then make eye contact with Rafael. "Same …"

The waitress disappears into a door next to the bar.

I watch her while I add a lump of sugar to my coffee, and Rafael's still waiting for my answer. "I'm confused, because you're protecting me," I say, sighing.

His hand runs through his curls, and he lowers his glasses to rest over his eyes. "Because I care about you, Rosalie. I know we haven't worked together long, but it's been long enough for me to care—it's long enough for anyone to care. It's human nature. Any decent human would."

"Then you're very selfless."

"Maybe." He chuckles and loosens his shirt cuffs. He rolls up the sleeves and leans his sturdy forearms on the table. A long prominent vein runs from under his shirt and down the side of his arm. He tilts his head, searching my face.

I pull my eyebrows together and grin. "What?"

"Are you sure you're okay?"

I shuffle in my seat. *Of course, I'm not! I'm absolutely not okay!* I smile instead and whisper, "I'm fine," worried if I speak too loudly, my voice will break and out me.

The waitress brings our food, and it looks nothing like the sandwich I am used to. The brown bread is slightly toasted, the smell of roasted peppers seeping from the steaming insides. A yellow vinaigrette dresses the sides of thick cut chips and the salad.

"Thank you." Rafael smiles beautifully to the waitress, who returns the gesture. He beams at his sandwich before he takes a bite. Obviously, he's eaten here many times.

I start on my chips, chewing more times than I usually would, and I notice a faint tattoo on Rafael's arm. "What's it say?" I point to his arm.

He runs his hand over the grey tattoo, barely visible unless under the bright light. "For he will command his angels concerning you to guard you in all your ways," Rafael says quietly, smiling. "Psalms 91:11."

I stare open mouthed at Rafael, who chuckles to himself and takes another bite of his sandwich. Just like an angel, Rafael has guarded me, though he hasn't seemed to make the connection yet.

"Why don't you get it redone?" I sip my coffee.

"Because I like it like this. Only those who really want to know me will notice it." He resumes focusing on his sandwich.

"Are you religious?"

"No, not in the church sense. I believe in God, if that's what you're asking."

"I just don't see how a wonderful and loving God can allow so much travesty." I look down at the table.

"I ask myself that question all the time, blaming the fallen for the problems of the universe." He takes a deep breath. "God abandons his creations and his children but blames the world for that. Says it's our fault because we sin."

I think for a moment. "So, you believe in God but don't think he's a good guy?"

He nods in agreement, his face blushing.

We finish with just a little bit of small talk. Rafael pops up to the bar to pay the bill, and we head for the car. It's cooling down outside as the clouds roll in.

We drive to his home, and he mentions the case of Eliza Thomas with irritation in his grumble. "The police are still no closer to finding her murderer."

Chapter 17

We arrive at his home, and I get out of the car. It feels more familiar when I approach the large doors.

Rafael walks behind me, carrying my backpack. He takes me upstairs to the room opposite his own. "Yeah, we'll just leave your bag here. I must do a little bit of work. You're welcome to join me or just relax. I have an entertainment room downstairs where you can—"

"I'll come with you." Yes, I feel safer in this giant house; however, Rafael is the real reason I feel safe. Without his presence, I'm sure to just crumble.

Rafael's cheeks lift into a grin, and he throws my bag onto the bed. "Then let us go." He smiles and turns for the door. He stops, sighing loudly, and steps backwards.

Lucy stands at the door, hands on her hips. "Sir." Her eyes flitter in my direction.

"Yes?" Rafael moves backwards a few steps to stand next to me.

"Your brother called. I've left a note in your office," she mumbles. Her eyes widen as Rafael's arm wraps around my waist.

My body stiffens at his unexpected touch.

"Miss Lockwood will be a houseguest here." Rafael grins at Lucy. "We'll need towels and soaps for her."

Lucy's eyebrows rise, her cheeks reddening. "For how long?"

"As long as she'd like, Lucy."

Lucy nods, and her gaze lands on the floor when she turns for the door.

Rafael watches her as she leaves, the pale flush of guilt flooding his face.

"What the hell was that about?" I remove his hand from my waist.

His answering smile stuns me. "I'm sorry. I just want her to move on. And since she already thinks we're a thing, maybe it'll help her."

"What *thing*?" I say before I can stop myself.

Rafael frowns at me. "She thinks we've been sleeping together, Rosalie." His slight Spanish accent somehow makes him more attractive.

I laugh loudly, then choke on the words as I repeat them.

Rafael's lips spread into another dazzling smile, and he shakes his head.

We leave the room and walk down the long hallways and into his office. I sit on the white leather sofa, staring at the beautiful gold print on the walls opposite me.

Rafael sits as stiff as a board opposite me, his eyebrows knitted together, reading some paperwork. He glances up at me from time to time as I check through some paperwork of another case—house theft, very boring compared to our current case. I watch a curl drop over his eye several times. He removes his glasses only to push them onto his head to hold back his hair. I watch as he unbuttons his first three buttons on his sapphire-blue shirt. He unravels his tie so it hangs on either side of his shirt.

He stands, then strolls around his office. "Rosa," he starts after a couple hours of silence, then shrugs off his jacket and flops onto the sofa next to me. His arm drapes lazily over my shoulder, his friendly manner completely back.

"Raf."

"Can I tempt you with some wine?" He smiles as Lucy walks through the door, holding a tray.

"Absolutely." I slap Rafael's upper thigh.

Lucy's eyes snap in my direction, and Rafael stares at me before jumping up and swiftly taking the tray.

"Some tapas, *por favor*, Lucy," Rafael says.

Lucy mumbles something I can't hear as she leaves the room.

Rafael chuckles knowingly and pours our wine. "What was that?"

"Well, I thought I'd play along." A smile stretches across my reddening cheeks.

We both drink deeply from our first glass and finish it in seconds.

He pours me another and stands, proffering a hand. "Let's go relax, Rosalie."

I always forget how very elegant and gentlemanly he is, even when he sometimes seems reckless and impulsive. I take his hand and stand much too quickly, knocking into his other hand holding his wine. The deep red wine splashes across his shirt, soaking the breast pocket.

He steadies what's left of his wine and places it on his desk. "Rosalie." He laughs.

I put down my glass. My cheeks burn uncomfortably at my moronic moves.

He unbuttons his shirt a bit more, then pulls it over his head, his arms stretching high. I stare at his toned abdomen; the scar glistens across his stomach. My mouth is still hanging open when his shirt lands on my head.

"Eyes up here, Rosa." Rafael laughs.

His shirt smells strong of wine and sandalwood. I pull it off my face. I'm unable to suppress a laugh as I throw the shirt back at him. "Hey, that's my line." I giggle and steal another glance at his abdomen.

"Well, apparently, I need it more."

"What happened?" I stretch my fingers to touch the scar.

Rafael takes my hand before I reach his skin. I shiver at his touch. My stomach buzzes lively with butterflies.

"My brother was in trouble. I was protecting him." He pauses to inspect it himself. "It's very sensitive to touch though, a decent amount of nerve damage. But let's not dwell on that right now." He guides my hand along the upper part of the scar.

The scar feels jagged and warm under my fingers, where they touch the unscarred part of the abdomen, its colder, like the rest of his skin. He studies me while I suck in a sudden breath at the heat coming from the scar as it stretches around and down to his hip.

He releases my hand, analysing me, as I hesitantly step closer. He peers down at me through his thick eyelashes and laughs again, breaking the silence between us. "Rosa." He sighs. "You're mad."

"What?" I glare at him.

The door opens, and Lucy stands with a tray of snacks.

I startle and pull my hand from his side.

"Take it to the entertainment room, please," Rafael says to Lucy, not even looking up. He watches me as I grab my glass off the table.

I smile at him as I walk to the door. "Let's go, then."

"May I put on a shirt, or would you rather I just get naked?" Rafael points to his chest.

"Oh ..." I stare at him, my cheeks burning again. "Sorry. Yes."

He chuckles and walks down the hallway and into his room. I ponder my strange attitude towards Rafael, its like he's the flame and I'm the moth. He comes out seconds later while buttoning a dark purple shirt and stops halfway. "Come on, then." He smiles and leads the way.

The bright gold writing on almost every door pulls on my curiosity. The shapes that all mean something to Rafael remain a complete mystery to me. Questions brew inside me faster than I can ask, faster than I can even comprehend myself. "Raf," I say, calling his attention.

He slows down on the stairs. "Yes?"

"What does the Enochian on the doors say?"

Rafael stops midway down the stairs and focuses on the stair rail. "It just describes what's in each room. The one on my room literally says Rafael's room."

"Oh," I mumble, my curiosity dissipating as quickly as it started.

He leads me to the left of his house, past a large kitchen, and into a large, dark, and square high-ceiling room. A huge grey stereo system is central to the back wall, alongside a glass bar. Bottles of alcohol on a mirrored back wall stretch at least two metres high. A piano is set on a small stage opposite the bar, with a pool table nearby, and tables dotted around. I try to stop my jaw from dropping at the sight of Rafael's little bar, but I don't succeed.

He chuckles as I stand in the doorway and flicks a switch that partially illuminates the room, and some music plays faintly in the background. "Surprised?" he asks, obviously smug.

"Well, I didn't expect you to have a bar." I approached a table.

"There's a lot you wouldn't expect from me." He sits opposite me.

"Then, tell me ..." I sip from my wine glass.

Rafael looks behind him.

Lucy pours us more wine, then leaves the bottle on the table.

"You can go now," he says to her, and she leaves the room. Rafael walks to the bar and returns with another bottle and two glasses. "Scotch?" he asks, pouring it anyway. He drinks his back, and I follow. He pours another, then sets down the bottle. "What do you want me to tell you?"

"Well, what is it that I wouldn't expect from you?"

He sighs, and a smile creeps across his lips. "There's a lot, Rosalie, ranging from my childhood to why a man like me works in a small town like this, and even my family. The reason I've not married and settled down is usually one of the first questions I'm asked."

"Then why? Why haven't you married?" I fiddle with my hair, waiting for his reply.

His lips turn upward. "Since living here, I've filled my alone time with women and fun. Settling down doesn't attract me." He frowns at his hands.

I shuffle in my seat with a tinge of jealousy towards these women, then I drink back my drink. "You're single. Why not."

"I feel like a bad person," he murmurs. "I should do better. I'm meant to do better."

"I think we've all done it."

"Done what, exactly?"

"Slept with people just because we want to feel something."

"Really? You too?"

"Uh, yeah, a couple times. It never really helped anyway."

He looks away, his jaw is tight. "You're right; it doesn't. When was the last time you did that?" He still doesn't look at me.

I think for a second. "Maybe with Dale. The more I think about us, the more it doesn't make sense. I've just been so alone recently, and I just thought he'd make me feel less lonely."

"You'll never be alone again, Rose," he mutters. "But my reasoning is maybe a bit more selfish, and I think I'll always feel bad for that." His deep purple shirt hangs loosely off his chest, and he's leaning forward, his elbow on the table and his hand cradling his chin. His beautiful eyes stare at my hands. The most angelic man I've met truly believes he is bad.

"You're not at all bad." I take hold of his other hand.

"I feel like I've failed," he whispers and squeezes my hand.

"Failed whom?"

"Never mind." He brushes his hand across his cheek to wipe away an invisible tear.

"Can you dance?" I ask, trying to distract him.

He grins and stands, pulling me up. "Naughty or nice?"

I splutter awkwardly as he wraps his arms around me and holds me close. I take a deep breath, my forehead against his shoulder.

"We'll start with nice." He laughs, his breath hot against my ear.

I shiver against his body as the music grows louder.

He spins me around the dancefloor, his lead easy to follow. His hands rest delicately on my waist as the song echoes to an end. He looks at me.

Each breath I take trembles when I look into his fiery eyes.

"Are you okay?" he whispers breathlessly. He drops his hands from around my waist and steps backwards.

"I am, with you," I murmur and step closer to him. I study his face and close the space between us.

His gaze travels between my lips and eyes as I trace his set jawline with my thumb. His eyebrows knit in concentration, an unknown internal struggle raging in his head. It lasts only seconds before an upbeat song plays, and his lips stretch into a grin. His hands dance across his chest, and he moves to the beat.

I turn into a statue, my eyes wide as he unbuttons his shirt in a striptease fashion and throws it to the floor. His scar glints, almost translucent in the flashing lights. "Now it's time for naughty," he shouts over the music. He moves expertly to the beat, closing in on me again. His hips swing to the beat, with his arms in the air.

I stare in disbelief, unable to move.

His hands move to his waist where he turns, shaking his bum in my direction. He spins to face me. He dons a massive playful smile when he stops, breathing heavily not even an inch from my face. The heat radiates from his slightly flushed skin. He carefully lifts my chin and gazes into my eyes.

My heart drums loudly. I feel it in my throat, excitement raiding my system.

His eyebrows rise comically as he howls in laughter and falls onto his chair.

I stumble to the table. The room is spinning, because I've had a lot to drink—the fact I forgot to breathe for his whole dance might be a contributing factor too. "Well, I ..." I giggle. "I didn't expect that."

"Why are you blushing?" He leans forward and brushes my flaming cheek with his hand.

I stare at my hands. "Well, I think I'm entitled to blush after that performance."

He laughs again, his mood light and contagious, his chest shimmering with sweat.

I affectionately slap his shoulder.

The laughter carries on through the night. Memories of the last few days seem distant, for now. My head spins dangerously when I allow Rafael to help me up the stairs. He opens the door to my room, and I reluctantly enter.

He leaves the door open and heads for his room without a word.

I fiddle awkwardly with my backpack, and retrieve a pair of jogging bottoms to sleep in. I'm halfway through removing my shirt, my back to the door, when someone coughs quietly behind me.

"Are you joining me?" he asks.

I pull my shirt back around me.

He hands my vest to me from behind and leaves.

I put it over my head and stride from my room into his.

Rafael is looking out the glass balcony door, wearing a pair of shorts and a vest.

I come up alongside him. "You're not shy, are you?"

He chuckles and approaches his bed, offering me the side of the bed closest to the door and, I note, farthest from the mirror.

"I feel comfortable around you, that's all. Keep you smiling and all."

I slide under the covers.

He walks around, gets in on the very edge of the bed, and faces me. "Sleep, Rosalie. Have sweet dreams."

My eyes are heavy as I mumble my goodnights.

***

My eyes snap open to see Rafael already on his feet, the room is dark, and a cold draft blows through my hair, making my skin prickle.

"Stay still!" He pulls the blankets off me and onto the floor at the foot of the bed.

I sit upright, gasping for air, as my heart bangs so violently I'm sure it will explode. The muffled crunch of glass and sudden breeze sends me into hysterics as I realise something has smashed the balcony door. I lean forward, watching Rafael push the door open, his breathing as quiet as the now empty night.

His bulky back moves into the blackness of the balcony.

Fear rips through me like a knife. "Raf," I whisper. I shake as I move onto my knees and lean over the edge of the bed.

Rafael turns, and his face is pale, completely devoid of colour. He scoots around to me. "Come." He approaches the bedroom door and opens it.

I climb out of bed and rush to his side.

He wraps his arm around my waist and directs me down the never-ending hallway to the beautiful white door.

My head spins disturbingly fast, the alcohol still at work deep inside my body.

Rafael pushes his office door open and pulls me in beside him.

I stand disorientated in the centre of his office. I bend forward, trying to catch my breath. The bright lights sting my watering, weary eyes.

Rafael paces his office several times before standing against the wall, leaning his elbows against it, and bowing his head. "Someone threw a large rock through the balcony door."

I stumble towards him, my legs jellylike.

His hard arms catch me as I fall.

I wrap myself around his body. My face against his chest cools my burning cheeks.

His arms unexpectedly wrap around me. For the first time, he truly embraces me. His hand trembles as it climbs my back, pulling me into an even tighter embrace. "Rosa ..." he mutters, his lips brushing against my hair.

"How?"

"Whoever it was must have been standing on the balcony. It's too big of a rock to throw that high" His murmur sends a shiver down my spine. Rafael's hot breath blows against my ear as he breathes deeply. Of course, he must have come to the same conclusion as me. It's Dale.

A loud ring snaps me from my thoughts, and Rafael lets me go to rush towards his phone. "Hello?" Rafael smiles reassuringly at me before his other hand rises to the phone. He spins on the spot and walks to the corner of the room. "When?" he asks with a sense of urgency. He faces me, and his eyebrows furrow in a way that makes my stomach tie itself into knots. "What about her father?" he snaps.

The knots in my stomach pull dangerously. Bile rises into my throat.

"Stay with them." He puts down the phone and rushes around his office, pulling open a wardrobe. His hands move fast through the rack of light-green and purple shirts. "Your home has been broken into about thirty minutes ago." He puts on a shirt and buttons it up.

"By whom?" My heart throbs so ferociously I feel it pulsating in waves in my fingertips.

Chapter 18

I pull on my black leather skinny jeans and a white vest, barely thinking. By the time I get downstairs, Lucy is already standing there, looking wide-eyed. She hands us two coffees in takeaway cups, and within seconds, we're in the car. We speed down the winding country roads.

"I'm sorry I can't say much to comfort you, Rosa," Rafael says, his eyes on the road.

"You've not said a thing since we were in your office, Raf."

"Because I don't know either!" Rafael bangs his hands off the steering wheel.

My eyes fill with unnecessary tears at his unprovoked anger.

Rafael glances at me, and the car halts on a small dirt-hard shoulder.

The very early morning is still dark. Dirty grey clouds cover a sky empty of stars. I stare ahead of me at the only space the headlights are illuminating.

"Rosa." Rafael takes my hand in his own. "I'm sorry."

"Right," I say, still looking ahead.

"Look, someone has just smashed my window in the room where you were staying." His voice rises again. "Though, at almost the same time that happened, your home got broken into."

His voice shakes, and I put my other hand on his face. The quiet of the night is more prominent now I've only got his steady breathing to listen to, the smell of whiskey still lingers on Rafael.

"This can't have been a coincidence. It doesn't feel like your mother's murder was random. It feels like your family is a target." His jaw tenses beneath my hand, and my breathing stops. Pain floods his face, and my heart aches to see him like this. "Forgive me." He holds my hand against his cheek. The raw reminder of my mother sinks deeply into the scars on my heart.

"Already forgiven."

His lips graze my hand before he lets me go.

My heart pounds, and electricity shoots into my elbow from where his plump lips touched my hand. The car moves again whilst I sit in my own little dazed bubble. Targets, that's what Rafael thinks. But maybe Dale went to my house and Rafael's attack was purely coincidental. Guilt evades me like a dark cloud, and before I know it, Rafael is standing at my door with an outstretched hand.

"Do you mind?" he asks, as he unusually entwines our hands after helping me from the car.

I stare at him speechlessly and nod.

He tries to smile, but it becomes a painful grimace, and he leads me up the path to my house.

Two large police officers stand outside the front door. "Rafael." The largest of the two nods knowingly, then eyes me. "Rosalie, I guess?"

"Yes, is everyone okay? Was anything taken?" Rafael questions.

The officer's eyes bulge at our laced hands, then his large forehead creases when he focuses on Rafael. "The ladies' room, her wardrobes were all opened. The father was left unharmed though." He moves out the way for us to enter.

Rafael releases my hand once we're in the house, and I rush into the kitchen where I can hear my father's voice.

Benjamin's sitting on the countertop with a bag of frozen peas on his hand, and my father is sitting at the table.

"Father. Ben." I rush in and wrap my arms first around my father.

Ben hops down and stands next to Rafael. "Thank you so much for having Rosa with you."

Rafael nods with a grimace. "What happened to your hand?"

"He punched whoever broke into the house," my father says proudly and stands.

"Yeah, he wore a mask. He wasn't as tall as me; that's all I could see. I fell asleep downstairs and woke to someone trying to get out the back door. I threw a punch, but they got away," Ben says angrily and puts an arm around me.

My father shakes Rafael's hand, saying something about him being happy I could be safe with Rafael.

"Rosa, do you want to check your room? See if anything is missing?" Rafael asks.

"Yeah, but not alone," I whisper to him, my hand tightening on his jacket.

My brother and father leave with a police officer to go to the hospital after the officer notices Ben's hand has swollen to double its usual size.

Rafael shrugs off his jacket. His thick forearms contract as he pulls up his sleeves and leads the way up the stairs.

My room looks much the same as always, except for my bed covers are on the floor and my wardrobe doors are open, as well as two of the drawers. Nothing else has changed, but I feel lost in my own room. A claim made that wasn't me, I survey the now strange room. I peek inside the drawers and see the underwear stuffed messily back in. My cheeks burn as Rafael stands by my shoulder. I check the other drawer containing jewellery boxes, all of which they left untouched.

Rafael sits on the end of my bed as I finish checking my room. He leans back, deep in thought. His eyes are closed when I finally finish, and I stare at him in awe. How anyone can look so still and calm. His handsome features are easier to appreciate when he's not staring at me.

"I don't think anything has been taken," I say, pulling him from his reverie.

He sits upright. "I don't understand."

"Maybe it was Dale looking for me." I sit next to him.

Rafael shakes his head. "No, it can't be. He'd have no reason to look through your drawers."

"Dale has never seen the inside of your house. He wouldn't know where you or I were sleeping." I stand again and pace the floor.

Rafael grabs my hand and pulls me down to sit next to him. His eyes fill with curious excitement. "What if someone is working with him?" Rafael wraps his arm naturally around my shoulder.

I shrug, unsure. "It seems a bit much. We weren't together long. He wasn't even staying here long, just sorting out his father's funeral."

Rafael stares at me. "But Dale's lived here for years. His father died years ago."

I can feel my anger bubbling to the surface. The betrayal and deceit, the lies he's told me. "W-what?" My legs tremble as I leap to my feet.

Rafael rushes to my side and grabs my shoulders. "Tell me everything."

"He lied."

Rafael hugs me stiffly with a reassuring smile, my body shaking in his embrace.

I close my eyes; Dale's brown eyes stare lovingly back at me through my watery lids. How could he do this? Why would he do this to me? I stare at my bed where we lay together only days ago, a shiver rolling up my spine as I think of his lips on mine.

After some silence, Rafael coaxes me from my room and down the stairs.

I follow mindlessly—another realm of pain to add to my ever-growing list. I hug myself tight, afraid if I shed a tear, the rest of my heartbreak will be evident. I haven't allowed myself to feel the full extent of the pain of my mothers murder nor the agro Dale has been causing me. Rafael's presence, like glue, holds me together.

A cool, reassuring hand wraps around my mine as we rush through the dull front path and to his car. He doesn't say much on the journey, just an angry murmur about Dale being a weirdo. He requests that I tell him everything when we're safe in his house.

I ignore him mainly; just a squeeze of his hand is enough to show I'm sort of listening. My lower lip trembles threateningly every time I try to talk.

We enter his house together, and Lucy's holding the door open, her arms open to take Rafael's jacket. "The police have been here, sir," she says as he heads upstairs.

"Okay, great. Have you called someone to fix the glass?"

"Yes, they're coming in an hour." I swear she smiles at me as I follow Rafael up the stairs.

Without replying, he walks to his room.

I follow, having to run to keep up. I reach his door to see him sitting on the end of his bed. The glass is now cleared from the floor, and the room is very cold. I suppress a shiver when I sit next to him and stare at the glassless door ahead. "I wonder who did it," I whisper, letting my hand rest on Rafael's shoulder.

"I might know," Rafael says with a scowl, his voice deep.

Rafael leans back on the bed, I shuffle all the way back, until I'm sitting against the headboard. We sit in silence, my brain erupting and aching. Questions and pain filling every thought I have. Who broke the window? Who broke into my house? I close my eyes trying to block out external noise. The cold wind tickles my cheeks and envelopes my arms. I lose myself in so many thoughts and theories, I can't keep count.

My eyes flutter open to Rafael's soft voice, he stands and proffers a hand to pull me up.

I'm move slowly, a few steps behind Rafael. We head for the circular room. He collects two glasses and a bottle of whiskey before sitting beside me. I fidget awkwardly as I watch Rafael get comfortable, bringing the table between us for our drinks and pouring us both a glass.

He gets a notepad and pen from under the table and spins the pen between his fingers. "I know it's a bit early for alcohol, but it might make it a teeny bit easier." He takes a deep breath. His face is serious and his eyes troubled. "Tell me, then, Rosa. From the start."

My breath shakes as I exhale, preparing myself. I finish my glass of whiskey, letting the burn travel down my throat and into my empty stomach. I help myself to more before I finally bring myself to talk. "We met at the library. I was reading a quote out loud, and he spoke. I thought I was alone. That's why I was reading out loud."

Rafael notates as I speak, only looking up to encourage me to carry on.

"He guessed my age, told me he'd been able to guess it, because I had mentioned I just finished university for law. He tells me to call him, to meet him for coffee soon. I agreed." I shuffle in my seat again and sip from my glass. "I met him not even an hour after my interview with you. We were in a coffeeshop when the waitress spilled coffee on me. Dale insisted we went to his place to clean up and told me his father was a doctor, that he had recently passed away, and Dale was hanging around to sort his family's affairs. We met a few more times. I felt infatuated with him, desperate for his touch—for him. He was perfect." I stop, allowing a single tear to burn down my face.

Rafael hands me my glass and drinks his own. His usual bright green eyes seem dull and filled with malice and hate. His expression surprises me, a savage grimace ripping through his angelic charade.

"I told him we should spend some time away from each other, that we were moving too quickly. As much as I wanted him,

I didn't want to spoil things. That night, he ended up at my house. My brother said Dale had written the play he was rehearsing. Then he followed me to the bathroom." I stop and hold my breath. I rub my hands together, my palms wet with sweat. I drink again. This time, the room wobbles. My emotions fog over, making it easier for me to speak.

Rafael's fists are clenched, his bones and tendons too visible on his bulky hands. "Did you …?"

"Not exactly. My brother heard. He wasn't happy, so I went upstairs. Dale followed again, and yeah." I cross my arms and look away from Rafael, not wanting to see the judgment in his eyes.

"I'm not thinking bad of you, Rosa." He leans forward and untangles my arms to hold my unstable hands. The rage that shows on his face, I know is only the tip of what he really feels. "Keep going," he whispers, his eyes on mine.

"The night you and I had dinner, when I went to his, it was late in the evening, and he asked what your deal was, asking whether I had feelings for you, though he didn't even give me chance to deny it before getting threatening. He got in my face and squeezed my cheeks. I went home that night." My back gets hotter.

Rafael encouragingly squeezes my hand, sending vibrations into my elbow, and shuffles a bit closer to me. This time, his hand rests on my knee. "Rosa, do you want to take a break?"

I stifle a loud sob, nod, and clasp onto Rafael. The dust mote that glitters in the bright sunlight appears to move with my emotions, twisting and twirling in a never-ending spiral.

He brushes my hair back, gazing softly into my eyes.

My heart flutters as I move closer to him, my lips not even an inch from his. I watch his face, confused and conflicted.

"Why are you doing this?" Rafael whispers.

My insistent lips touch his, parting them. I feel his trembling minty breath. I taste the whiskey on his sturdy mouth, my insides bubbling passionately as his lips relinquish and mould against my own.

Barely a second later, not anywhere near long enough for me to feel satisfied, Rafael releases me. He stands swiftly, his hands on the back of his head, and paces the room. His phone rings. "My brother." Rafael sighs and glances at me. His face is flustered, and he grabs his glass off the table, drinks it all, and answers the phone. "Adriel. You're always welcome here. I do have company though." He eyes me. "Rosalie, my brother is arriving in town tonight. Do you mind if I have him here?"

"Raf, this is your house. Of course, I don't mind." I can't help my heart sinking at the thought of no longer being alone with him.

Rafael laughs for a moment and ends the call, grinning, and sits at the other end of the sofa. He looks at me, his face suddenly serious again and reddening with every passing second.

"Did I ... Did I do something wrong?" I mutter, staring at my hands.

Rafael laughs, shaking his head, his beautiful, troubled face, his lucid green eyes staring at me. "It's not about what you've done. It's about what I've done. You're in a sensitive place. I shouldn't have allowed you to kiss me."

I slide across the leather to get closer to him. "Can you at least sit by me?" I scowl.

"How have I made you mad?" His eyebrows rise.

"You aren't allowing me to have feelings," I say, looking down. "Unless you're rejecting me, gently." I turn away again. If I were embarrassed before, it's nothing to how I feel now.

"Rosalie." He moves next to me. "Don't." He brushes my hair back from my face.

"Don't what?"

He frowns. "Just let me protect you for now, and when this is over, you can see how you feel." He puts his arm around my shoulder. His body, for the first time, feels unnaturally hot against mine. He's more rigid than usual. His body angles away, and his hand barely touches my shoulder.

I behold his face, my eyes still teary from rejection.

He takes a deep breath and kisses my forehead, then rolls his eyes when I give him a little grin. "You're something else, Rosa." He chuckles and hands me my drink.

CHAPTER 19

R afael calls Lucy to bring some snacks.

She arrives soon after with continental meats and cheese.

I munch on them in silence, not wanting to disturb Rafael, who sits as still as a statue, deep in thought.

The day moves swiftly in silence, the cloudy day barely brighter than this morning. Rafael comes in and out of the front room with different paperwork each time, and at one point, he sits with his iPad in silence for what felt like hours. I occupy myself with double checking Rafael's paperwork, and I must have fallen asleep, because when my eyes flicker open, the room is dark, and the sky outside is almost pitch black.

Rafael smiles wearily at me from the other side of the sofa. "You ready for some more questions?"

215

"How long did I sleep for?" I ignore his question and rub my eyes.

"About three hours," he says with a chuckle.

My mood shifts when Rafael moves around again, ready to throw questions at me—questions that tear at my already broken heart. My heart throbs painfully every time I think of Dale. A simple sweet smell causes a tsunami of emotions to overwhelm my body to a point that it aches.

Rafael smiles cautiously when he brings in a stool and sits opposite me. "Tell me."

"The night we found out my mother was missing, you know, I was outside, and I saw the shadow. Then you called to tell us you found her, and you took me home. I fell down the stairs, and Dale let himself into the house. He found me lying on the floor and told me Ben called him and asked him to check on me." I can feel the confusion on my face as I try to remember through the haze.

Rafael leans forward, his elbows on his knees. "Then?"

"Then he stayed with me through the morning. I went upstairs to get dressed. He was with me when you called and asked me to come in." My eyes brim with tears again, and I peek at the bloody scabs on my collarbone.

Rafael leans forward, his fingers stretching towards my collar-bone. He stops just before he makes contact. He retracts his hand and focuses on his knees.

"That's when he got physical. He pulled open my shirt and bit me. He touched me," I whisper, unable to say it out loud. "I told him we need to be apart for a while, and I left. You know the rest."

"So, he told you he was sorting his father's funeral?" Rafael asks, after a moment of stunned silence.

"Yes. Actually, he messaged me yesterday and said the funeral was yesterday morning. He asked me to go. I ignored him."

"Rosalie, his father died about three years ago. My firm dealt with his will." Rafael scribbles something on his notepad.

"W-what? When he came in yesterday, he wore a suit, as if he had been."

Rafael stares at me. For a moment, he looks as if he might just crack, until his lips turn into a stone-carved smile. "Then maybe he's lying about more than just his father," Rafael whispers to me and places his hand on my back pulling me a bit closer. He allows himself a small reassuring smile and whispers, "It'll all be okay." He rubs my back in circular motions. I move into his shoulder, resting my head and wrapping my trembling arms around him. His body is close, closer than I had ever felt it before. His muscles contract teasingly as he loosens his grip. "I

won't ever let anything happen to you like that again, Rosalie."
He lets me go, but I take his hands in mine, not ready to let go.

Our hands are still entwined when a man enters the room.

His dark brown curls are what I notice first as he stands still just
inside the doorway, his gaze on me. He pans wearily between
Rafael and me before deciding it's okay to come in farther.
He has bright blue vivid eyes that stand out against his dark
olive-coloured skin. He smiles greatly as he stands in front of us.

Rafael drops my hand like it's a time bomb and jumps up,
"Brother," Rafael says, his hands on his brother's shoulders.

"Rafael," his brother replies, his voice smart, dignified, and a bit
higher than Rafael's.

They stare at each other for a second, as if they are having a silent
conversation, then the brother raises his eyebrows at me, waiting
for an introduction.

"Rosalie, this is Adriel, my older brother," Rafael says, still staring ahead at Adriel.

Adriel takes my hand and kisses it delicately. His cool lips linger
on my hand for a moment before he moves back, smiling. "It's
wonderful to meet you, Rosalie."

I stand awkwardly at Rafael's side, staring open-mouthed at
Adriel.

Adriel grins at Rafael, his smile contagious.

"Yes, and you," I say and look to the floor.

"Come drink with us, brother." Rafael points towards the sofa.

I go to the sofa first and sit near the end.

Adriel follows Rafael to the little bar. His thin hand wraps around Rafael's wrist and raises it, staring at the faint tattoo on Rafael's exposed arm. Their chatter looks heated as Rafael shakes his brother off his arm and turns to walk back, holding another bottle and glass.

Adriel smiles as he comes to sit next to me. He leans back comfortably, his legs wide open so his knee touches mine.

Rafael pulls the stool in front of us and sits.

I stare at Rafael, wishing he at least sat by me. I swallow hard when I accept that Rafael must sit opposite to make good conversation.

"So, Rosalie. How did you meet my darling little brother?" Adriel asks.

I shift awkwardly. "I work with him."

"A coworker, Rafael? You shouldn't shit where you eat." Adriel laughs and pats Rafael's leg.

"Number one, it doesn't matter where I chose to shit, Adriel," Rafael says with a scowl. "Number two, we aren't together." Rafael's eyes flitter to mine so fast I can't tell if he really looked at me.

Adriel's grin becomes seductive as he drapes his arm over my shoulder. "Then, you won't have a problem with me getting to know her better?"

"Adriel," Rafael says with a sigh, frowning. "I'm glad you're here. I actually need your help."

"Baby brother needs my help?" Adriel coos but sits rigid in a businesslike position, his heavy arm still draped around my shoulder.

"Well, I would appreciate it if you'd listen," Rafael snaps, the authority in his voice sounding harsh. He shifts in his seat, his eyes darting from Adriel's hand on my shoulder to my face.

"Rosa, do you mind if I mention some details to my brother?" he asks, studying my reaction.

"I don't mind."

Adriel's eyes widen at me.

"I know you can pull strings, Adriel. I need you to ask for details, and as many as possible, about a man named Dale Cartwright." Rafael leans forward towards his brother. "This man has been harassing Rosalie. Her mother was murdered a few nights ago, and Dale doesn't seem right to me."

Adriel lifts his arm from my shoulder and takes a long drink from his cup. "Raf ..." He leans in. "You must not mess. Let the police deal with it."

Rafael's eyes are piercing, glinting dangerously in the bright room. "Please."

"I'll look. But that's it. I won't involve myself." Adriel spies me again.

"Bottoms up?" Rafael smiles and swallows his whiskey.

A gentle knock comes from the door, and Lucy enters, squinting at me. "Adriel, can I show you to your room before you settle in down here?" Lucy flashes him cheeky smirk on her pretty face.

Adriel chuckles before standing and following her out the door.

Rafael stares at Adriel's back as he leaves the room. He looks at me, his facial features relaxing, and flashes that smile that lights up the room. "Sorry, Rosalie." He grins. "My brother thinks a lot of himself."

"I can see that. You look alike." I smile at Rafael's raising eyebrows. "You though are more muscular," I say in hopes of making him feel better.

The difference, now that I think of it, is staggering. Maybe they have similar features, like their olive-coloured skin and slight accents. The curly hair matches, but the major differences are in eye colour, the darker tones to Adriel's skin, and his slim and tall build against Rafael's lighter skin and bulkier body. I stare at him for a while before I realise he is watching me.

"Rosa, sweet. Are you okay?"

My heart thuds foolishly when he calls me sweet. Something about the sincerity in his eyes holds me together as I face the truth of my words. "I'm scared."

Rafael leans forward and tenderly wraps his arms around me. His shaking breath blows across my face, and I notice I, too, am shaking.

"Don't be scared. You're with me. Nothing will happen to you," he whispers and gently lifts my chin, his rough fingers cold against my rapidly heating face.

I try to stop myself, I know I shouldn't. I know I need to give myself space. My body struggles against my mind. With closed eyes, I take a deep breath and before I can move back, my lips press against his for the second time this evening. This time, it feels different. His lips mould to mine without hesitation and in perfect harmony. My fingers move around his back and onto his neck, and I lean deeper into our kiss. His fingers tickle nervously down my spine and stop on my lower back.

A cough shocks us apart. I stare for a second, dizzy from excitement, and notice Adriel grinning.

"I thought you said you weren't shitting and eating." Adriel faces Rafael, who is sitting stiffly on the stool, his skin reddening.

"And what I said was true. We're not *together*." Rafael wipes the corner of his lip with his thumb.

"Lucy mentioned you've been sleeping together for the last couple nights." Adriel takes a large gulp from his glass. He sits back, comfortable again, and puts his arm around me.

Rafael hands out refilled glasses of whiskey, and our glasses meet awkwardly in the middle. Yes, Adriel, she sleeps with me. Not like that though. You should know Lucy can be a bit dramatic when it comes to my life."

"Why does she care so much if we're in the same room?" I ask.

Adriel's laugh booms around the echoey circular room.

Rafael's lips press into a very straight line, his eyes narrowing at Adriel. "I told you, I slept with her once." His eyes dart to Adriel and back to me.

"What about the fact that you slept with her mother too?" Adriel laughs harder.

I chuckle while staring at Rafael, waiting for an explanation.

"I know it sounds bad, but I didn't know. Lucy got a bit obsessed." Rafael's lips turn upward. "I was expecting a new client, and apparently, Lucy had set it up with her mother so we could meet and that it would make her closer to me."

Adriel remains silent, as if waiting for a punchline.

"We were on my office desk when Lucy walked in with some coffee."

Adriel's wave of laughter hides Rafael's guilty sigh. *"Mother, I didn't expect you to be here,"* Adriel mimics a girly voice.

"She still believes she has some weird claim over me, and, well, she likes to check I'm not sleeping with everyone who walks through the door." He chuckles awkwardly before turning to look me in the eyes to assess the damage.

I laugh slowly, my giggle turns loud, and before I know it, I have a tear streaking my face. I feel so free, to laugh again.

Both Rafael and Adriel stare at me, their mouths open, before joining the contagious laughter.

"Sir," a timid voice comes from behind Rafael. "It's one a.m. Is it okay if I get some sleep?"

"Of course. I'll be going up now too," Rafael says to her with a smile.

She giggles annoyingly and turns to go upstairs.

I stand, automatically ready to go up and have the alone time with Rafael that I crave.

"I'll hang down here a little longer, request that information you need," Adriel says, glancing in my direction.

Rafael stands, nodding in thanks, and leads the way upstairs.

The walk to the bedroom is charged with a different energy than I remember. I feel excited as I rush into my room and change into my shorts and vest. I trip over my jeans and giggle dizzily. My heart beats so fast it feels like a constant vibration in my heated chest. I go to Rafael's room and knock on the door.

He calls for me to "Come in."

The glass is firmly back in place, so the room is warm and cosy. The lamps at the end of each bed light the room just enough, projecting a drowsy atmosphere. I hear water trickling in his bathroom, the shower running. My heart seems to skip a beat when I lean back on his large bed, pulling the covers halfway up my body.

The room's warmth feels amazing on my face and arms. I heat up much too quickly, and suddenly, I'm wishing for the cold wind to be blowing through the balcony door to cool me down. The calming sound of the running water in the bathroom stops, and silence inhabits the room. For reasons, I shy from admitting to myself my stomach flips in somersaults.

Only seconds pass before Rafael opens the bathroom door and walks through, a light grey towel wrapped around his waist. He glances at me. "Sorry." He grabs something off the top of his table.

"No, I don't mind," I say, surprised at my confidence. "I definitely don't mind."

Rafael chuckles, studying me. He steps forward, a grin spreading across his wet face. "You sure you don't mind?" He climbs on the bed and leans over me. He holds himself in a prone position, his bare chest hovering only inches above me, his lips closing in on mine.

My heart pounds as if I've run a marathon, and I stop breathing.

"Rosalie." Rafael laughs, lifting off me, and heads to the bathroom.

My face flushes. I'm sure I must look like a cherry. I take several deep breaths and move the blankets farther up my body.

Rafael returns, wearing only a pair of baggy shorts. "You like?" He twirls on the spot.

I laugh loudly. "Beautiful."

He winks at me before lifting the blankets and getting in at the other end of his bed. His eyes linger on my legs, then he pulls the blankets over me, leaving his side of the blankets only covering his lower legs.

I lie there, watching him from my end of the bed. I struggle to focus as the room spins around me. I feel miles from him, even though if I am to just reach out, I could touch him.

He regards me for a long time. He seems perplexed, his eyebrows furrowed unevenly. "Rosalie," he whispers, watching my lips in the dull light.

I nod in acknowledgement.

He props himself on his elbow, turning his whole body to face me. "You're so brave." Awe and amazement fill his eyes.

I can't stop my eyebrow from rising so high in confusion.

"Just ... Everything you're going through and you're still so strong."

"This isn't easy for me."

"I know."

"You know, I don't think I'd cope with this half as well if I didn't have you here."

A look of grief crosses his face as a silent tear builds in the corner of my eye. He slides closer to me in the bed, and his cool arm slithers under my back and heats up within seconds. "I like it when you cry," he murmurs.

The tears stream faster down my cheeks, and I turn my face against Rafael's chest.

"It reminds me that you're only human," he whispers, and his lips brush my hair, "like the rest of us."

I cry silently on his chest for a few minutes more, his hand carefully rubbing my back. "Sorry ..."

Rafael's thumb runs across my face to wipe away what's left of my tears, and he kisses my head once more. "Sleep, Rosalie. Tomorrow is a new day," he says gently, almost as if he is singing a soft lullaby.

"Wait," I whisper, my eyes barely open.

"Yes?"

His chest still nestles my face, and I kiss his warming body once and let my dizzy eyes close.

CHAPTER 20

I open my eyes, the room a blur. I hear the quiet singing of the early birds and feel a cool breeze coming from the balcony. I snap my eyes shut again, pretending to sleep, when I hear a voice chattering quietly on the balcony.

"Yes, it's not right. The police still won't do much about what Rosalie is saying," I hear Adriel say.

"Dale has done more than enough to warrant arrest," Rafael replies in a strained voice.

"Dale is a well-respected man and rich. Money talks, Rafael."

"I'm worried he will come for her again," Rafael says quieter.

"Then, be ready. I agree with the possibility of Dale being involved in Eliza's case. Now the police will call him in for questioning today, although I really can't imagine them having enough evidence to keep him past questioning," Adriel says a bit louder now. "Does she know about ...?"

"Don't be daft. I can't ..." Rafael's voice turns into a whisper.

My heart throbs uncomfortably, and I jump up fast, focusing on the balcony door. I tumble dizzily to the floor. The world spins as my head bounces on the hardwood. I get up again, and the room spins worse now than it was last night. I ignore it as much as possible and stumble to a very shocked Rafael.

Adriel stares at me, his eyebrows raised comically high.

"What did you say?" I point at Adriel.

"W-what?" He turns to Rafael.

"What did you hear?" Rafael answers instead of Adriel.

I stomp up and down the balcony a couple times. "Enough."

Rafael coughs to buy himself some time.

Adriel steps forward. "I had some friends investigate Dale. It was noted that the late Eliza Thomas, the one who was murdered, had mentioned being in a relationship with Dale not long before her death." Adriel takes another step forward.

"We don't know the specifics yet, Rosa." Rafael interjects, watching Adriel step forwards to close to the gap between us.

Adriel reaches an arm around my shoulder and walks me to a small table, adorned with a tray of tea and some toast, and chairs at one end of the balcony. "Eat."

I sit rigid and stare at the cup in front of me, my hands shaking. My stomach feels knotted and so does my throat as I try to swallow. My back heats fast, my whole body burning. "Dale was with Eliza?"

"We don't know for sure," Rafael answers, "but she mentioned it to her friend."

Adriel pats my head. "They're looking into it, Rosa."

"How? What are you?"

Adriel stares at Rafael, as if I'd figured out a top secret.

"He works in London," Rafael hurries.

Adriel composes his face. "I work in London." Adriel side eyes Rafael, "I can't really specify where, but it enables me to be able to help. If you would allow, I'd like to stay a little longer here." Adriel smiles tentatively.

I look at him, confusion flitting across my face. "It's not my house."

Rafael laughs loudly. "Yes, Adriel. You can stay."

My world tries to catch up with me in the brief few seconds I have to gather my thoughts before Rafael sits next to me.

"Good morning," he says, watching Adriel leave the balcony.

"Hey," I mumble into my cup of tea.

"You look like shit." He laughs. He brushes my hair back and laughs as I stare at myself in the back of a spoon.

The remains of my mascara are spread across my face like an abstract piece of artwork. "Oh, God." I laugh and stand.

"Yes, God ..."

I leave for the bathroom and scrub my face in the mirror. The mascara is stubborn under my eyes. I brush my hair back, letting it cascade over my shoulders. I stare at myself, then relinquish the idea of trying to look even half decent on a morning where nothing is going right. I take one last attempt at cleaning the dark circles around my eyes before concluding it's not makeup and giving up. I return to the balcony and sit opposite Rafael.

He smiles, a silent compliment.

It's cooler on the balcony now the initial adrenalin rush is subsiding, and I sink into the nightmarish news. My knees crack against each other, and I hold the hot tea in my hands.

Rafael stands silently and leaves for his room for a moment before returning with a warm-looking grey cardigan. "Rosalie, it's freezing out here. You're shivering." He holds it open for me to insert my arms.

An amazingly warm smell comes from his cardigan as it wraps easily around me. I take a deep breath and let a shudder run down my back. "Yeah, I didn't feel it until I had time to come back down to earth."

Rafael refills my cup with hot tea.

I watch the steam spiral from my cup, and I add a bit of milk.

"Try not to think about this too much, it just questions. He probably has nothing to do with any of this, and he might even help us." Rafael frowns darkly at the thought.

I blink furiously at Rafael, at the thought of having to be around Dale again.

Rafael stares at me, understanding washing over him like a slap in the face. "Rosa." He stands quickly. "You won't talk to him, and neither will I for that matter. I don't think I can after what he's done. I just mean he could talk to the officers working the case."

My thudding heart falters at Rafael's apologetic smile, and it finally slows down, giving me time to take a deep breath. "I really—"

Rafael leans across the table, his hands cup my face, and his lips graze mine.

My lips fix to his, and my hands hold the back of his head, pulling him closer. I allow a second to break from his slowly stiffening lips and notice his muddled face. I press my lips against his once more.

This time, he doesn't respond. "Sorry," he says, smiling shyly. "I hated seeing you look so scared. I don't know why I kissed you."

My shoulders slump at his repeated rejection, his confusing and reasonless rejection. "You like me, though?"

He nods and stands to turn to the door. "I'm going down to Adriel. I'll probably be in the kitchen. Get dressed." He gives me one more smile and leaves.

I stare through the glass barrier between me and the ledge, watching this morning's fog filtering down, a billion tiny drops clouding the sky. I think back to those times abroad when a foggy sky meant unbearable heat, and compare it to England, where it's sure to mean the cold is only getting thicker. The birds still sing through the empty courtyards below me, which lead to a wooded area. I search for them through the trees which surround the beautiful house, and the flowerbeds which spread across the grass. I try to focus on one spot but my eyebrow starts twitching annoyingly as it does sometimes when I'm scared. The feeling of fingers moving slowly along my back, as if the smoky fog has hands of its own, has me momentarily rooted to the spot. I stand hurriedly when I finally gain movement in my legs, and the hairs on my arms prickle as I pull the glass door shut and yank the curtains across, leaving myself in Rafael's dark bedroom.

Ding. My phone illuminates from the bedside table. I manoeuvre around the bed and slide along the edge, then move my fingers up the wall to search for the switch. My phone's ringtone sounds noisy, startling me. I abandon the light switch and hurry to answer it. I realise it's a number I've not seen before. "Hello ...?"

"Rosa," a soft male voice replies.

I know at once who it is, and my fingers tighten around the phone. "Dale." I ready myself to put down the phone. I scan the bedroom's darkness and stride towards the bedroom door.

"You enjoying staying with your boss? I've seen you throwing yourself at him," he mutters, breathing heavily down the phone.

"What?" I say, trying to prolong the conversation. I tiptoe from Rafael's room and down the hallway.

"He's rushed to your side fast enough in the last few days. I see things, Rosa. You are so desperate for him, it's embarrassing." he spits dangerously.

"No, you're wrong, but what's it to you if I were?" I rush down the stairs and run into the kitchen.

Rafael stares at me as I bounce around with the phone and press the loudspeaker.

"Well, you never gave me a real chance, Rosalie. What can he give you that I can't? Surely his lips make you think of mine."

Rafael's jaw drops, and he approaches the phone. He doesn't breathe when I scramble to reply.

"What kisses, Dale? You're being crazy." My voice squeaks at the end.

"I'm thinking about us, about you. I miss you. I can't not see you," he says as if out of breath.

"There is no us."

"Hey, Raf." Dale's voice changes tauntingly.

"What the hell do you want?" Rafael growls in a low voice.

"Nothing. Just checking that you weren't doing anything regrettable. She'll be with me soon enough." Dale snickers.

Rafael snatches the phone from my hand. "Understand this, Dale. You have no choice in the matter. You make me sick, Dale, SICK. You're a desperate piece of—"

The phone cuts off, and Rafael's cheeks are as pink as I imagine mine to be. He puts his arm around me, my shivering body unable to move.

A cold sweat has formed uncomfortably on my back. I should have removed the cardigan. Rafael lets me go and Adriel squeezes between us.

"Rose, honey." Adriel lightly squashes my cheeks between two hands.

I jump, only realising he is in the kitchen when his freezing hands are on my face.

He looks at me, his ocean blue eyes shining, his eyebrows creased with concern.

"Breathe," Rafael says from behind Adriel.

I feel a hand on my back, guiding me to the floor, and it cushions my head on the hard tiles. Something wet replaces the cool hands on my hot cheeks.

"Rosalie," a low, gruff voice echoes through my mind.

I focus on the unintelligible words coming from above me and watch the swirl of colours move around.

"She's just stressed. Give her a minute," one voice says

"Should we take her to a hospital?" the other voice, the lower one, asks—the voice I remember, the one that makes me feel safe even when I feel like I can no longer move, or the one who makes my heart thump so heavily that it may just give up.

"She'll be okay. Relax, Rafael."

I feel something cool touch my head, his hand. The fog in my brain is clearing. I can hear better.

Adriel swears several times in the background and moves noisily around the kitchen.

Rafael's hand rests on my head, his breathing audible.

I feel nauseated as I contemplate moving and letting them know I am fine.

Adriel's voice comes closer. "You really like this girl, don't you?"

"Yes," Rafael mutters.

I can see his shadow shift through my closed lids.

"I've never seen you actually care before," Adriel says quieter.

"My whole world has stopped since the day she walked into my office. Everything since then has revolved around her. No matter how much I try to change that, I just can't," Rafael whispers.

Adriel grunts in understanding, and Rafael clears his throat, his hand moving off my head.

I flutter my eyes a bit more dramatically than I would have if I hadn't been aware already.

Adriel stares at me, and Rafael leans over me and slowly lifts my head. "You okay?" he asks as I sit upright.

"Sorry," I say and look around groggily.

"Don't apologise. It's not your fault that asshole won't leave you alone." Adriel hands me a glass of water.

Rafael sits next to me and makes me stay still for another couple minutes before he offers me a hand and helps me stand. He looks away when I regard him and helps me out of his cardigan. We walk up the stairs, and he holds my arm, ready to catch me if I need it. We go to my room, where my bag lies on the bed. All the while I think about Dale's words, 'I see things'. A wave of sickness builds and crashes like a wave. Rafael looks ahead, thinking hard. His eyes are dark and his face looks tired and weary. What he said to his brother moments ago seems unreal, for surely, if he felt that way, he'd look at me for more than a few seconds at a time. Surely, he'd have softened up by now.

"I'll wait outside." He walks to the window and pulls the curtains shut. "Just in case." He smiles humourlessly.

I slip into a pair of black skinny jeans and a green woollen vest. I stare at myself in the mirror and hastily apply some eyeliner. I'll never look good enough when I feel like this, so I just grab my leather jacket and head for the bedroom door, brushing my hair back with my fingers. I don't dare give myself time to think, to remember why he closed the curtains when I dressed. I open the door to see Rafael waiting.

He glances at my face. He bites on his own lip, and we head down the hallway.

"Raf." I grab his arm before we reach the stairs.

He spins on the spot and looks down, fixating on my shoes. "Rosa."

"Look at me," I whisper.

He slowly raises his head. His green eyes hesitantly meet mine, somehow getting more vulnerable the longer he stares. His lips open, but no words come out.

"Are you ... okay?" My trembling hand remains on his arm.

He puts a hand on mine. "I'm just worried about you."

I swallow against an uncomfortable lump in my throat.

Rafael's softening gaze watches emotions flit across my face.

"Then hold me." I step forward and wrap my arms around his tense body.

His arms wrap reluctantly around me. His cheek rests on my head, and slowly, his arms tighten warmly. "I'm sorry ..."

It's barely 10:00 a.m., and the sun shines brightly on the lawn outside his back window. He takes me outside, and we sit in the decking area. Though the air is cold, the sun's rays are warm on my back.

"Lucy and my cook have a day off today, so we'll have to sort our own lunch." Rafael carries two coffee mugs and places one in front of me.

I chortle at how he seems to think that's an issue. "I'd rather her not be here." I wink. "I don't have to keep fondling you when she's not around."

Rafael's laugh surprises me. "Yes, let's pretend you do that just for her." He leans closer to me, his eyes glowing behind his glasses.

My gaze darts around the garden.

"He's not here," Rafael mutters.

My body jolts at the sound of his voice, my racing heart speeding. "W-what if he is? He mentioned us k-kissing. He said he's ... seen things."

"He's taking guesses. He's trying to manipulate you, scare you." Rafael leans closer.

I shake my head and lean into my hands. "But, what if?"

"Then I'll protect you."

The cold breeze blows at just the right moment. My hair flutters around my face, covering my reddening cheeks.

His cold fingers grab my hands.

We sit for a long moment, across from each other, hand in hand.

"Tell me," Rafael says, "if Dale wasn't an absolute nut job, would you still think I'm this adorable?"

Rafael's efforts at trying to lighten the mood work, and I smile freely and squeeze his hands. "I've always thought you were adorable." I roll my eyes.

The door creaks quietly, and Rafael drops my hand when Adriel opens it and sits next to me. His arm automatically rests around my shoulder again, and he grins. "They've got Dale in for questioning."

CHAPTER 21

The minutes pass like hours. We stay in the slowly warming sunlit garden. I watch the grass dance in the wind and listen to Rafael and Adriel chatting about what they think will happen. Rafael smiles several times at me. Adriel's presence clearly no longer hinders Rafael's affection for me.

Rafael stands behind me, his hand on the nape of my neck, his thumb moving in a soft circular motion, relaxingly tingling my skin. "So, do you think he'll guess it's my fault he's getting questioned?" Rafael says and his thumb becomes still on my neck.

Adriel stops pacing. "Probably." He resumes pacing.

"He'll be mad," I squeak, my eyes widening. "What if he tries to hurt you?"

Rafael chuckles darkly. "Keyword being 'try.' But I think he isn't stupid enough to come crawling around too soon."

I shudder at the thought of Dale hurting Rafael again.

He feels me shake under his hand and squeezes my neck, reassuring me.

"My father is heartbroken that we can't lay my mother to rest yet, that her killer is still around," I say lower than usual. I rarely mention my mother's case; the pain is so raw it rips me open each time. Instead, I try to bury it. It works well except for when I do eventually mention it, and my chest gapes horridly.

"The police are doing what they can, Rosalie. And when they find someone, I'll be there to make sure they're put away for as long as possible," Rafael says.

Of course, I've heard a thousand times that the police are doing what they can. Patience isn't a strong quality of mine. I clench my fist until my nails bite into my skin, forcing any feelings back. I can feel them later, when I'm alone. My stomach growls, rudely interrupting my train of thought. "Yeah. How long does questioning usually take?"

Even from this angle, Rafael looks delightful, his handsome jawline enhanced from down here.

"It can take hours, depending on what he has to say, if anything," Adriel answers me.

Rafael smiles apologetically at me. "Hungry?" He heads towards the kitchen.

Where his hands were on my neck burns against the sudden cold. I stare at the door, desperate to follow. I catch Adriel watching from the corner of my eye and grin at him. "So, what's up with Rafael and his aversion to emotions?"

Adriel smiles back encouragingly. "He's just playing hard to get. Though, he's not as shy this morning."

I nod knowingly. "I noticed that too."

"Mhmm." Adriel sits opposite me. His eyes probe my own, as if he wants to coax a confession from me. He looks me up and down once. "You were with Dale, then Dale gets rough, and you run to my open-armed brother. I mean, I can see Raf's concerns about just letting you in."

I shift awkwardly and redden. "That's not exactly how it happened. Plus, I was never really with Dale. We just saw each other a few times."

Adriel leans a bit closer, as if to not let Rafael hear. "So, maybe he doesn't want to be just another fling."

I raise an eyebrow at him. He's right. Of course, Rafael won't want to be with me, his partner at work. Someone who's problems are never-ending. Rafael will end up with a woman who's as smart and as great as he is. I shy away at my idiocy to ever think I can match up to him.

Adriel's phone vibrates on the table.

I startle at the sudden buzz.

Rafael is outside seconds later.

"Hi. Yeah ..." Adriel paces the patio again. "Okay, so they allowed him to leave?"

"Brother ...?" Rafael says through gritted teeth.

Adriel holds up his hand to silence Rafael and walks away.

A couple minutes pass, and Rafael stands silently behind me, I can hear his slow and deep breaths.

I can't stop my leg from bouncing with unease. I stand and face Rafael, his eyes narrowing as he watches his brother's facial reactions from a distance. "Raf."

"Yeah."

"Adriel's taking a while."

"Well, it means there's news."

Adriel approaches us, his face shows no clues. "Dale admits to meeting her at a bar, and they went to her house and slept together. That happened about two to three weeks before her disappearance. He couldn't be sure, because, and quote, 'I slept with several women in that space of time. I don't take notes.'" Adriel's voice trails off, and he looks at me sympathetically.

I nod, hoping he understands he can carry on. I just can't talk yet.

Rafael places a hand on my shoulder and pulls me closer to him. His arms cross over my chest.

"He was happy to cooperate, agreed to stay in town, and that if they have any more questions, to just give him a call." Adriel sighs. "So, they've let him go. The officer said he seemed pleasant and genuinely shocked to hear a woman he slept with was murdered."

Rafael's hands ball into tense fists. "He'll be investigated further though?"

Adriel sits. "Yes, he is on a person-of-interest list. The police seem to think he's innocent. They're checking his alibi now."

"So, it sounds like she was just another one of his one-night stands," I mutter disgustedly.

A ringing comes from Rafael's pocket. He releases me to walk away, just out of earshot of Adriel and me. He stands very still whilst on the phone, careful to keep his back to us

"What do you think?" I ask Adriel.

Adriel's eyes are sympathetic. "I think you should take extra care, just to be on the safe side."

His words ring in my ears. The simple fact he thinks I need to be careful sends a convulsion down my spine. I pull my phone from my pocket, and text my father and brother, asking how they are.

I receive a text almost instantly from my father. "*All's fine, Rosa. You take care of yourself there. Let's get through this together. Love you.*"

His text warms my heart. I miss him. I always miss him; I never had a bond with my mother as I do with my father. My father is warm and loving, and my mother, well, she was warm and loving, just not to me.

I am in my own world, staring at my phone, when a cool hand brushes my hair off my face and startles me back to reality.

"That was the detective working on your mother's case. There's nothing. They're currently searching through CCTV. I told them I wanted an update today. I'm sorry."

Adriel walks towards the kitchen, saying something about food.

I'm much too preoccupied to hear much of anything.

Rafael's fingers trace my frown lines, leaving a trail of cold behind. "It's okay." He wipes a tear from the corner of my eye.

My eyes blur with the tears I hold back. "Do you think Dale will keep bothering me? It's just too much."

"I spoke to your father. He doesn't think it was Dale who was in the house. He says whoever it was wasn't tall enough." His finger trails down my cheek and onto my neck.

I lift my hand and hold his hand on my neck. If he'd only make a move, pull me closer. Until then, I'll be good.

He steps forward, closing what little gap remain between us, as if he heard my thoughts.

"Here," Adriel says from behind me.

Rafael frowns and turns his face towards his brother. Through his serious expression, I can see the slightest smirk. He looks back down at me through his unhappy green eyes, then turns, fixing a big fake smile on his face.

We sit around the table in the garden, snacking on a variety of sandwiches and cakes. The mood lightens as Adriel tells stories from their childhood. The laughter grows as the minutes pass and sounds throughout the garden. "He turned up to school in a mini skirt and a bikini top," Adriel says, chuckling hard.

Rafael is sitting next to me, his face bright red, as he holds his breath.

I hold my ribs and wipe a tear of laughter from my cheek.

"He walks straight up to Brian in the middle of an awards assembly and kisses him," Adriel says as calmly as possible.

Rafael's lips turn up to a smirk. "It wasn't half bad either. I'm sure he slipped his tongue in there."

"That's what you get for trying to steal Rafael's girl." Adriel snickers.

I take a deep breath and try to imagine a young and hot Rafael walking past his whole school to kiss the captain of the football team. "Well," I say, finally able to breathe, "you two were crazy."

Adriel laughs. "We still are, when we aren't caught up in life."

A red-faced Rafael slaps Adriel's arm.

"I definitely want to be there to witness it next time." I grin at Rafael.

He beams at me with warm eyes, and under the table, he gently squeezes my knee.

My heart jumps into my throat at his casual touch.

Adriel watches carefully as my face heats up, obviously reddening. "You okay?" Adriel asks, his voice coloured with concern.

Rafael chuckles. "I've arranged for us to meet your father and brother in an hour. We better get ready."

I follow Rafael into the house, sure I saw Adriel wink at Rafael as we left. I brim with uncertainty with Rafael's constantly changing warmth to me.

"Come," he says.

I follow him up the staircase. I hurry down the hallway and into his office, my heart thrumming like a hummingbird's pulse.

He is rummaging in one of his draws when I enter his office a few seconds behind him.

"What are you looking for?" I ask, staring at the low chandelier.

"Some paperwork. It's something I'd like to check." Rafael's head is hidden in a drawer.

I wander around and stand facing the wall covered in engravings, my fingers mere centimetres away. The same electricity I felt the first time charges through my fingers.

"Rosa ..." He pulls me delicately from the wall and sighs.

I pout and walk to the sofa and sit.

"I have the paper now." He rolls his eyes at me.

I can feel my childish pout on my lips. I cross my arms and look away.

He proffers a hand and pulls me up. "You're relentless." He laughs and pokes my rib.

"What's the paper?" I say as I leave the room/

"Nothing of importance." Rafael answers and follows me out of the house, shouting a loud goodbye to Adriel as we leave.

We get in the car, the clouds are moving fast through the sky. The wind busters as we traverse the empty country road. The dark clouds are full to the brim with thunder as we arrive outside my home.

Rafael opens my door for me and takes my hand as we approach the front door.

I fumble nervously with the keys, my heart thudding for no apparent reason.

"It's okay. I'm here," Rafael says, probably feeling the tremor in my hand. He scans with narrow eyes, his shoulders tensed at my unusual reaction.

My skin prickles as a sense of foreboding hits me. I feel the urge to look behind me, my brain screaming someone's there. The wind whips my hair around my face, and I open the door, almost falling over the threshold.

Rafael's arm wraps around my waist to steady me. He closes the door behind him, takes my key, and locks it.

"Father! Dad?"

Rafael pulls out his phone. "Oh, your father messaged me. He and Ben will be thirty minutes. They're just getting some food. What was wrong with you out there?" His frown lines are deeper than ever.

I shudder and head to the kitchen. I reach for the radio; the background noise always helps. It's the one thing I rely on when I'm home alone, the endless chatter from the radio station in town. I lean against a countertop. "I felt like someone was there, Rafael," I say in almost a whisper, "watching us, like how I felt that night."

"Why didn't you say?"

I gulp nervously.

Rafael's face is uncharacteristically dangerous. He charges through the house and out the front door, slamming it shut as he leaves.

I watch him through the peephole, my throat burning with bile that fills my mouth. The gathering clouds cause the day to be as dark as the night. I can barely see Rafael as he passes the huge tree in my front garden, which is swaying in the strengthening wind.

Rafael turns to face the side of the house.

I can't see well through the peephole.

His body shifts fast, his stance dangerous as he starts running. The rain, which was barely a flutter before, now downpours.

I narrow my gaze but can't see a thing anymore. Surely Rafael can't have seen anything. If he has, he wouldn't chase it. I agree with myself as I run up the stairs and into my room to see out my window, the treacherous rain creating an obscured view. I squint into the distance and see nothing but darkness. I grab a towel off the radiator on the landing; I'm sure he'll be wet. My legs feel stiff when I descend the stairs to the front door, ready to open it for Rafael. I stare at the coloured glass pane as I wait for Rafael's shadow to appear. My heart hammers when I look through the peephole again.

Rafael is standing at the tree again. His clothes are drenched as he walks down the path and knocks on the door, panting. "Rose!"

I open the door, pull him in, and slam it shut.

He stands there, his hair wild. He brushes it back and shakes off his soaking jacket. His eyes almost burn into mine when he drops his jacket. A water droplet drips off his long eyelashes.

A tinge of jealousy fills my stomach; how can he still look so good? I try to swallow, but my throat refuses.

"I thought I saw someone. I ran around to the back of the house but couldn't find anything," Rafael huffs.

Before I know it, I've wrapped my arms around him. My face is squashed against his wet chest. His heart thuds as erratically as mine on the side of my face.

His freezing body shudders under his white and see-through shirt. He pushes on my shoulders for me to release him.

I thrust a towel at him. "Here. Come to my room." I run up the stairs and into my room.

Rafael hands me the now dripping wet towel and peels the soaking shirt off his body.

I try not to stare at him walking into the bathroom. I move to the shower and turn it on. The steam starts to fill the bathroom. "I'm sorry I have no jeans for you, but I can get you a shirt from my brother's room." I reach for his wet shirt off the floor.

"Don't wander the house alone." He grabs my hand. "Just lie them over the radiator in here for now."

I nod and move to the radiator. I hear movement behind me. I take a deep breath at the thought that Rafael might possibly be absolutely starkers behind me. I linger purposely until I hear the shower door open, then close. "I'll just wait."

"I feel even colder now." Rafael voice quivers in the steaming shower.

"I'm so sorry." I automatically look up, then force my gaze to my feet and face the wall. My heart is battering my chest. I try to think, or not to think of what I just saw—Rafael's muscled back, his soaking curls, and ... I dare not even think it myself.

"Don't apologise." The shower turns off. "Can you pass me the towel?"

I grab it and close my eyes, holding it at arm's length.

He laughs as he takes the towel. "I feel frozen." Rafael's teeth chatter as he talks and takes my hand.

He's right. The second his hand touches mine, goosebumps form up my arms. I shiver with him this time, though a feeling entirely different from cold or nerves engulfs my unsuspecting body. I throw my arms around him, his cold and wet chest burning my hot face.

Rafael holds me close to his body, and, for a moment, I stay still, feeling his warm breath on my hair. "Good idea," Rafael whispers and lifts me off the floor. "Your body is warming mine."

I let him squeeze me. I tighten my arms around him too.

Another shudder rolls through his body, less violent than the others. He releases me too soon; the only thing left is his cold hands in mine again. "Okay." He coughs and smiles. "Jeans?"

I jump and rush to the radiator. "They're not completely dry."

"That's all right. I'll definitely need to borrow a shirt though."

I turn and approach the door, then turn back to look at him. "What type of—" My eyes widen. "Sorry!"

Rafael stands in my bathroom, his towel already on the floor. He hides his privates awkwardly with two hands. "Rose." Rafael gasps through a smirk.

My stomach burns as I turn away and run into my brother's room, hyperventilating. I open the wardrobe and breathe deeply several times. I force my eyes shut and listen to the silence of my house. I giggle silently through my embarrassment, my lip curling into a smile. A laugh escapes me as flustered tears bulge in the corner of my eye.

To my surprise, I hear Rafael's deep chuckle.

I exhale, glad he's seen the funny side too, and grab a white long-sleeved shirt. It will be a bit tight; after all, all my brother's clothes are tight. I stand in the hallway, readying a serious face for when I enter my room. I ponder about why Rafael makes everything feel all right. His smile can restrain even the darkest of my demons. "Raf," I call out before entering my room.

He's standing in front of my mirror. His jeans sit just below his hips, his finger tracing his scar down. He doesn't acknowledge me as he usually would, with a smile. His eyes are dark, haunted by something I dare not ask about. He turns to me and smiles weakly. "I'm not cold anymore... After my show."

I ignore his attempt at humour. "You okay?"

"This scar is just a constant reminder of who I am."

"And who's that?" I inch towards him.

He smiles at me, this time with feeling. "A fearsome and ugly beast." He laughs.

I laugh with him. "Really, I don't think you're fearsome."

"But you do think I'm ugly." He winks.

"On the contrary, I think you're gorgeous." I smile and step forward, my finger outlining his cold, jagged scar. "Even the scar."

His answering smile is enough to send anyone to Heaven. I gasp in awe, my chest threatening to explode from the thundering of my heart.

"You didn't see anything before, though. Right?" His gaze is now on his feet as he hitches up his jeans.

I hand him his shirt. "No, just your hands. Not that my focus was there."

He holds it out and looks at me bemused. "Your brother can't be this small."

I laugh and shift awkwardly. "He likes his shirts tight."

Watching Rafael squeeze his muscular body into my brother's tight white shirt has me in hysterics, I bend over, clutching a stitch that smarts painfully in my side. Rafael huffs and puffs, completely red in the face, his hair is all scruffy and standing on end when he finally finishes fighting with the shirt and manages to pull it down his stomach. I bite down hard onto my lip as my eyes travel over each dent and muscle which are clearly visible in the extremely stretched fabric.

My father calls to announce his arrival just on time, Rafael's face is still quite a bright shade of pink when we get down into the kitchen to wait.

CHAPTER 22

My father and Ben rush through the open door, the cold wind blustering through the house.

Rafael's hands, which were on my shoulders, drop to his sides.

Bens notices Rafael's wet hair and borrowed shirt and smirks at me. "Nice shirt, bit too tight for my liking," Ben chortles.

Rafael snorts. "It's still not as tight as your jeans." He smacks Ben's bum.

"Rosalie, sweetheart," my father says, pushing past Ben and Rafael to hug me. He drops his bags, and Rafael grabs them and walks them to the kitchen with Ben.

"How have you been?" I ask, still held in his embrace.

"Fine. Your brother and I were just working out things with the police and talking about what we'll do when this is all over." The wrinkles that outline his face have never been more visible.

"Right, of course." I nod, swallowing hard.

My dad coughs lightly, his arms tightening around me. "I saw Dale," he whispers, his face suddenly colourless.

My stomach flips fast, and my mouth becomes dry. "And ...?"

My father eyes dart around the room before landing upon me. "He says Rafael's bad news. And that you don't know what you're doing."

My face heats fast, my blood boiling beneath the skin on my cheeks. A strange fog fills my vision, and I shrug my father's hands off me. "He hurt me."

"He is trying to protect you. He's told me all about Rafael."

"What about Rafael?" My voice shakes.

He glances at the kitchen door, then refocuses on me. "He's a bad man, Rose. Using you—"

I can no longer control the rage filling my lungs, almost choking me. "Rafael!" I open the front door. The wind slaps my face, the cold rain drenching my hair. I stomp through the wet grass, squinting to see Rafael's car.

I reach the car and can see the light of my house barely through the sheets of rain. I can't hear much through the billowing wind. Some muffled shouting and shadowy movements by the house hopefully indicates Rafael is coming to me. I stand still, unable to breathe through the angry huffs. The lights of Rafael's car blink, and I pull the handle and climb inside. My body shivers from the freezing rain that has soaked me.

Rafael's borrowed white shirt glows in the headlights. "Rosa." He slides into the car. His shirt is wet again but not soaking. He starts the engine, and the heating blows cool at first, making me tremble intensely.

I shrug off my jacket, leaving my arms bare. The woollen vest seemed like a good idea this morning in the sun. Now it just clings onto my body, worsening my annoyance as I try to unstick it from my skin.

"Rose." He turns my face to look at him. His calming fingers squish my cheeks.

The rain thrashes against the car, banging loud enough to drown out my heavy breathing. I look frantically around the car, out the windows, then back at Rafael. "Can you drive? Please." My rage threatens to bubble to the surface again.

Rafael starts driving, the wipers' efforts at swiping the rain away are useless. The headlights give us visibility of barely two metres ahead. Rafael ignores the annoying beep of the seatbelt alarm as he leans forward over the dashboard, his glasses over his eyes. "I can't see," he whispers, the wind shaking the car.

For five minutes, he drives in silence, slowing to 10 mph often. The rain shows no sign of surrender when Rafael turns unexpectedly down a very tight lane and pulls up next to what looks like an abandoned barn. "Rosa, I can't see enough to drive any farther."

I focus on my hands, unable to speak, to explain the anger I have at my father, my outrage at Dale for his lies and manipulation. I glance at Rafael's concerned eyes—Rafael, the man who's done nothing but good; Rafael, who's uprooted his own life to protect me. My heart aches from the betrayal of my father. "I've had enough! I'm breaking! I'm broken!"

Rafael's lips turn down. "Rosalie, please. What's going on?" He says impatiently.

"Dale, he's ... he's told my father it's you who is bad."

"I don't understand."

"Dale told my father he's been trying to protect me from you!"

Rafael's calm response shocks me. He blinks dumbly a couple times and smiles.

"Why are you smiling?" I almost scream again, my rage cracking my voice.

"Well, it's just you should have expected Dale to try to manipulate your family. Your father just wants you safe. He will see sense." Behind his smile is a dangerous shadow. I watch his poker face showing no sign of surrender.

"But—"

"No, Rosa. We mustn't show him any weakness." He takes my wrists and kisses each palm.

Sucking in a deep, shaky breath, I force a grin.

"United," he leans in and whispers. His lips move against my ear and along my jaw. He releases my wrists, and his fingers brush down my neck and across my collarbone. His frozen fingers leave a burning trail across my already cold skin. He brushes my vest strap down my arm and kisses my shoulder with his icy but plump lips.

The pit of my stomach ignites, burning through my skin. I throw back my head.

Rafael's lips move across my neck as the rain pelts the window. The barn across the road looks like it's about to topple in the wind, and long shadows sway in the wind.

My arms prickle painfully as I scan the fields for any sign of Dale. The feeling of not being alone has followed us from my house.

Rafael's lips touch my jaw, and I lose my train of thought.

I try to suppress the next shudder and bite my lip.

He regards me through his long eyelashes.

"United," I murmur.

Rafael straightens up. "This rain won't give up anytime soon. Let's get back to my house."

His chest rises and falls heavier than usual. His wide eyes glance at the side mirror, and he reverses the car. An excitement fills Rafael like I've never seen before. His knees bounce rapidly and his hand on the gear stick taps vigorously.

The rain is a rhythmic pitter-patter on the windows now. I cross my arms and watch the ever-darkening sky illuminate in a flash. The lightning carries its way across a field ahead, the thunder mere seconds behind it. We turn onto his road and wait outside the gates for them to open. I replay his lips on my shoulder, his fingers push my hair off my neck and rubs my tense neck muscles as we creep onto his driveway and stop outside his house.

He rushes around to my door and grabs my hand to lift me from the car. We run to the front door, hand in hand, the tension between us as electrifying as the sky above, which flashes and grumbles. He throws open the door and stops to look at me, his playful grin enticing me completely. I let myself imagine him, imagine what is next and what it'll be like.

"Rafael," Adriel shouts from down the hallway.

Rafael eyes him, then flashes me an impressive smile. "Come on," he stage whispers.

We run up the stairs and down the glittering hallway. He lifts off his shirt before we even arrive at his bedroom. His strong arms wrap tight around my body. I grasp at his bare back, and he opens the door.

"Sir," a small voice shouts from the other side of the room.

"Sonofa—" he huffs angrily. "Why are you here?"

"Sir," she repeats, frowning. "I came back early, and Adriel told me to clear the tray from your balcony." Her bulging eyes and flushed cheeks make her look younger than ever. She ignores me and fixates on a shirtless Rafael.

"Right, you can leave. I'm busy." Rafael scowls as he watches Lucy leave.

My fingers tickle playfully down Rafael's back as Lucy closes the door with one last glance at Rafael.

"Wait," Adriel shouts down the hallway.

Rafael clenches his fists and falls back on his bed, the fire in my stomach burning painfully. Lying back on his bed, Rafael looks more like a Greek god than a man. His muscles stand out, pushing against his beautiful skin. His wild curls stick up and

267

fall messily over his forehead. The disciplined and pampered lawyer look is all but gone.

"The real Rafael," I say, beholding him.

"Huh?"

"Nothing," I say, smiling to myself.

Adriel coughs loudly from the doorway.

"If I were doing something wrong, Adriel, do you think I'd be lying here in a pair of uncomfortably tight jeans with the door open?"

"Uh, sorry ..." He notices my damp hair and clothes, then regards Rafael, who's lying half-naked across his bed, looking perfectly at ease. "I thought you two weren't—"

"We're not." Rafael winks dramatically. "What's up?"

I perch on the end of Rafael's bed and smile up at Adriel's serious face, which has no trace of humour.

He hurries to the bedroom door and peeks around to survey the hallway, closes it, then sits on the end of the bed next to me. "Somethings not right with Lucy," he whispers urgently.

Rafael snickers. "Well, she is obsessed with me."

"No. Actually, yes." Adriel's face is stonelike. "She didn't know I was in. I was in the front room and heard someone enter."

Adriel looks awkwardly, not making eye contact with anyone. "So, I followed her upstairs and into your room." He nodes in Rafael's direction. "I watched her put a candle on the chest of drawers, then open your drawers and remove your belongings and look at them carefully, then fold them back up. I made her aware of my presence. She jumped and claimed to be straightening your stuff. Then about half an hour later, I notice her whispering on the phone."

Rafael walks to the drawers.

"What the hell?" I say, standing up.

Adriel pulls me back down. "Now, this doesn't mean she's done anything wrong. It just seemed weird."

"I wonder what she could be doing in my drawers." Rafael's nose crinkles in disgust.

"I wondered the same. Maybe she was innocently looking at your underwear." Adriel chuckles humourlessly. "I do think we need to keep an eye on her though."

I nod in agreement. "She always ignores me anyway."

"Jealousy," Rafael says and stands. "She thinks we're screwing."

Adriel stands too. "And you're not?" He chuckles, for real this time, "I'll ask her to do some jobs around the house, keep her occupied," he mumbles and leaves.

Rafael's smile fades, and he walks to his bathroom, gesturing me to follow.

I shiver unwillingly when I stand, feeling the cold from my damp vest and jeans.

"Shower, get warm. I'll grab your bag." He reaches behind the glass wall, turns on the shower, and leaves.

I stand alone, looking around. My is heart in my throat when I lift my vest over my head. It's obvious he's no longer interested, and I feel self-conscious. I hurry to the bathroom door and pull it, leaving space for only my head to poke out. I call for Rafael.

"Here." He eyes me funnily and drops my bag by the door. "What are you doing?"

"Well, I didn't want another situation like we had at mine. I sadly don't have enough hands to cover mine," I say as politely as possible.

He laughs and nods. "I won't come in, I promise. I'll wait here." He grabs my bag from the door and throws it on the bed. "You'll have to come to get your bag off me though." He lies back on the bed, resting his head on my bag, then closes his eyes.

I close the door. My stomach growls painfully when I contemplate what's ahead. My jeans are stuck to my legs. I struggle for a moment to slide out of them and almost trip in my rush but catch myself on the sink. The steaming water burns down my cold, bare back. The ice inside recedes from inside out. When my hands finally feel warm, I search through numerous bottles for shampoo. I rush through shampooing and conditioning and close my eyes for a long moment. The events of the day unfold through my relaxed and suddenly tired mind. My body jolts back to reality at a knock on the bathroom door.

"Rose," Rafael calls out. "Use the towel that is folded by the sink."

I unwillingly turn off the water, enter the clouded bathroom, and grab the towel from next to the sink. I wrap it around my body, breathing shakily. I open the door to peek through.

Rafael props himself onto his elbows at the sound of the door.

"Bag, please." I grin and push the door open.

Rafael beholds me and bites his lip, smiling. "Hey ..." He leans forward, his elbows on his knees. "You look fresh."

"I feel fresh." My thumping heart feels almost audible.

"Come here," he whispers, his eyes bright.

Each breath I take increases my pulse. The blood rushes around my head. The water from my wet hair drips down my back, and I carefully step forward, unusually aware of my feet. I stand in front of him. My fingers shake when I run them through his curls.

He exhales loudly, reaching around my back to loosen my towel.

My heartbeat turns into a constant hum.

He mouths, *Wow*, then his eyes flitter between my lips and my shoulders, and he pulls me closer.

I lean forward, letting my lips reach for his.

He kisses me once, then moves to my jaw, now breathing heavily against my neck. "You're amazing."

Our lips entangle; every fibre of my being connects to his. My body tingles as his fingertips leave a blazing trail down my neck. Any worries seem far away from this cloud of passion we create.

"I'm going to let go of the towel," he says between kisses.

My hands tighten on his back, pulling him closer.

He chuckles in my ear. "I want to see this." He guides me a step backwards and releases the towel.

The towel falls graciously to my ankles. I can feel the cool air in the room, but my body burns on the inside. Goosebumps rise all over my body, when Rafael's bright green eyes widen hungrily, awakening every inch of my skin.

The door knocks, making us both startle.

"Busy," Rafael shouts, not taking his eyes off me. His chest flexes as he stands and steps closer.

I reach for the buttons on his jeans, my eyes lingering on his scar, then to his lower abdomen. I let my fingers tickle along the hard muscle.

"Sir, it's important," Lucy's small and irritating voice comes from behind the door.

A surge of annoyance rushes through me at the sound of her squeaky voice—annoyance that didn't exist this morning, when she wasn't the one thing keeping me from Rafael.

Rafael forces his gaze from me, his face pink and chest heaving with each breath. He turns reluctantly to the door and glances at me, biting his lip. "What?" He yanks open the door just enough for her to see his face.

"Can you come here?"

"Not really." Rafael shifts uncomfortably.

I lean over Rafael's bed and grab my bag.

He helplessly peers over his shoulder at me.

I go to the bathroom and dress fast, then leave the bathroom whilst still buttoning my shirt.

Rafael is lying on his bed, his face still flushed. "Sorry."

I shrug. "Just wasn't a good time, I guess." I grin, keeping control of my frustration. "C'mon." I gesture to him and nod towards the door. "I'm hungry."

He grabs a shirt from the wardrobe and moves behind me, his hand on the small of my back. "What do you want to eat." He slides into a shirt and leads me from the room.

"Well, now you're off the menu." I laugh.

He regards me, as if wounded, a hand raised to his mouth, as if damming his words. "Don't," he groans.

I giggle. "Fine. Want to order pizza?"

"Sure. Meet me in the front room. I'll let Adriel know."

"But what did Lucy want to show you?"

Rafael shrugs. "Nothing of importance, just a letter."

We part at the bottom of the stairs. He disappears down the hallway, and I turn into the circular front room.

CHAPTER 23

I sit on the sofa and retrieve my phone. I should take it off silent mode more often. I have several missed calls from Benjamin and, shock, not even one from my father.

"*What is wrong, Rosalie?*" a single text from Ben asks.

I stare at the wall, my anger flaring in my ears. My father's ridiculous warnings, telling me the man who's hurts me more than once, is only trying to protect me. If I were a cartoon, I'd be sure to have steam coming from my ears.

"Umm, where's Rafael?" an annoyingly squeaky voice breaks my focus.

"What?" I snap, not caring to be polite anymore.

She enters the front room after looking behind her. "I said, where the hell is Rafael?"

My mouth opens and closes a couple of times, her insolence shocking me into silence.

"Uhh, looking for Adriel." I manage to say.

"Where though?" she says slowly, as if talking to someone who speaks no English.

I stand angrily at her sour attempt to be rude. "*Look, Loo. I. Do. Not. Know.* I do not have some deranged problem where I must sneak around after him all day long, like a bad smell." I say the words before I think them through and automatically regret my insult. My anger at my father, at the day, hell, after the week, is brimming. I take a deep breath and concentrate on my phone.

She stares discourteously at me for a long moment before retreating.

I sit in silence, listening to her heels click across the hard floor. I try to focus on the wall; it doesn't help. Before I know it, I've dialed Dale's number. I swallow uncomfortably, my throat drying as the seconds tick by.

"Rose." Rafael enters, eyeing my phone, which rings loudly on speaker, and my obvious nervous leg bounce. "Adriel's coming now."

My jaw drops as the realisation of whom I have just called hits. The blood rushing to my ears makes a loud whoosh, and I stand.

Rafael approaches me as Dale's voice escapes from the phone. "Rosa, my love. I knew you'd call."

Rafael's eyes widen. He frowns, unsure as to why I've called this man.

My throat is closed. No words escape, not the screaming fit I was planning to do; not even a breath escapes my lips.

Rafael's finger comes to his lips, telling me to be quiet.

"My love, can you hear me?" Dale draws a sharp breath.

I stand there dumbfounded, and Rafael gestures to me expectantly, his eyebrows raised. "Would you like a cup of tea?" I sigh quietly with my eyebrows creased, feeling like an absolute idiot.

"Rosalie, what?" His voice is venomous.

Rafael grabs the phone. "Uh, no. Rose, you're sitting on your phone!" He puts down the phone before I can reply. Rafael stares at me. "What the hell? Are you mad?"

I shrug, pout, and look at the floor. "I meant to shout at him for contacting my father. Sorry."

"Rose, you've just started a huge problem."

"I know. I'm a moron." I flop onto the sofa with my head in my hands

Rafael sighs loudly and remains still before moving closer to me and resting his hand on my head. "No, I understand you're angry. But we must go about this carefully." He sits next to me and kisses my head. "Lucy found me, said you were mad?"

I blink several times before answering. "She was asking for you. I told her you were with Adriel. She got rude. I told her to stop hanging around like a bad smell." I cross my arms.

Rafael chuckles and takes my hand. "She's super jealous of you. It's weird. I'm continuing my efforts to find a way for her to leave." Rafael's hands hover over my shirt buttons, then unfastens them.

I gasp when his cold fingers graze the skin of my chest.

He smiles and buttons them back up.

"Bad time, again?" Adriel appears behind Rafael.

Rafael chortles. "No. I was fixing her buttons."

Adriel sits, and Rafael's phone rings from his pocket.

I see the capital letters across the screen. WITHHELD NUMBER.

He eyes me uncomfortably.

My neck thuds along with my racing pulse.

Adriel leans forward.

"Hello …?" Rafael answers the phone on speaker.

"You piece of shit."

"Oh, it's you."

"Rosalie, why would you do this?" Dale's voice pleads down the phone.

Rafael's finger flies to his lips, silencing me for a second time this evening.

"She's not here, Dale."

"*Lies.*" A heavy wind blows down the phone.

"Where are you?"

"Rosalie, my beautiful princess. Why would you let him touch you?"

I hold my breath and stare at the window in front of us.

"That's right, baby. I'm here."

Adriel and Rafael run to the window.

My head spins; a tidal wave of nausea hits me.

"Prove it," Rafael taunts.

"Rosalie, let us just talk. Let me have you." His voice cracks, and with one last gust of wind, the call drops.

Adriel pulls across the white curtains. He puts his hand in his pockets. His blue jeans aren't tight like his brothers, and his white deep-neck t-shirt doesn't cling to his skin.

I shake my head. "Is he playing some sort of sick game?"

Rafael stomps around the room, circling the sofa I'm sat on several times, then sits next to me. "Adriel, what do you think about taking a little walk with me? Just around the house, make sure he's not actually here." Rafael smiles mischievously, but I can see the concern behind his smile.

"I've seen that smile before," Adriel says with a grin. "Let's do it."

I sit still, my head tilting to the left. "What?"

"Go to my room, lock the door, and wait in there," Rafael says, not looking at me and heading towards the door.

"Go, Rosalie," Adriel says gently, grabbing my hand, and pulling me towards the stairs. "I really don't think he's here, Rose. It's just precautionary," Adriel adds, trying to reassure me, though his voice is quieter than usual.

I watch Rafael, waiting for him to acknowledge me, to say a simple goodbye or even give a weak smile.

He doesn't. His fists clench when he walks out the door into the darkening night.

I waste no time downstairs. The hairs on my arms prickle endlessly. I run up the stairs, tears brimming in my eyes. If they find Dale, will they hurt him? I laugh at my own idiocy. Of course, they'll hurt him. My lip trembles when I burst through the bedroom door and lock it.

I lean my head against the cold wood, and as much as I try not to, I feel responsible for Dale. A tear rolls down my cheek, and I wipe it off hastily before my panic for Rafael's safety starts.

His passionate green eyes stare into my own through my closed eyes. The simple thought of anyone hurting him forces me onto my knees.

I turn around in the dark room and stare at his bed. A cold breeze swirls in the darkness. My eyes burn, the rest of the house seems completely still except for this room. This room buzzes with an energy, my overwhelming panic causing a static I'm sure anyone could hear. I hold my body flat against the door and scan every inch of the room. I'm paranoid, I tell myself repeatedly, until my gaze reaches the balcony door.

I squint through the darkness and force myself to stand and step forward, my eyes adjusting to the dark. I concentrate on the balcony door and freeze when another gust of wind blows through the room. The chilly air burns against my hot cheeks.

The balcony door is open a few inches. I hold myself even flatter against the door, my teeth chatter loudly. I hold my breath when, in my peripheral, something moves fast.

"Don't say a word," Dale whispers in my ear.

I shake beneath his hands which wrap tight around my chest, pinning my arms at my sides. "Dale," I whisper. "Please." The fear rising in my chest is nothing compared to the relief I feel knowing Rafael won't get hurt. My knees bang painfully against each other as his arms tighten around me.

"Now, if you resist me, my love, I'll gut you."

I stare around the darkness. Even if I scream, no one would get here in time.

Dale's breath is hot on my face, and his arms loosen. His fingers pinch the buttons on my shirt, then he slides my shirt over my shoulders and down my arms.

Revulsion and hatred fill my body. My stomach heaves, acid filling my mouth. I struggle to swallow it down.

"Rosalie, you don't seem to realise just how much I love you." He moves around to face me, always keeping contact.

I see his pale face, his jaw set, as if chiselled from stone.

His dark eyes flicker unusually fast when he looks me up and down. A thick stream of saliva drips from his lips through his bared teeth. "You really look delicious tonight." He drags his finger down the middle of my chest and stops at my jeans.

"Get off me," I whisper through clenched teeth.

He savagely grabs my face between his large hands, his nails burrowing into my cheeks. His wet lips smack against mine.

I don't move. I squeeze my eyes shut, recoiling from the wetness he tries to force between my lips with his tongue.

A loud groan shatters his effort to remain quiet. The silent night disintegrates into a strange crashing sound.

I scrunch my eyes closed tighter. Something collides with my shoulder, causing me to shout out and I land awkwardly onto Rafael's bed. It's like I'm unable to move, I can feel Dale's hands pressing me down into the mattress. The banging grows louder as the bedroom door rattles.

"Rose," Rafael's voice calls angrily.

"I'll see you soon, baby." His eyes are the only thing I can see and they stare manically into mine. He leans into my paralysed body, his tongue moving swiftly from my cheek and down my neck. Dale lets out another repugnant groan and turns from me.

I lie still, the heavy banging against the door getting louder.

"Rosalie," Adriel says in a calmer tone. "Talk to us."

"If he's done anything to her—" More banging drowns out Rafael's words.

I sit up unsteadily, finally free from Dale's grasp. "Raf."

"Rose," Rafael says hysterically, and with a loud thud, the door snaps open.

The light flicks on, blinding me momentarily. A lot of hurried movement passes throughout the bedroom. A cool hand moves my shirt to cover my chest, then touches my head.

"Rose," Rafael's voice shakes. "Look at me."

I stare at his red and watery eyes. He's frowning. I try to figure out if he's mad or upset. I struggle to answer, I'm lost in my own head with no way out right now.

Rafael's fingers brush across my cheek. He blinks several times at me, then at his hand.

A stinging sensation prickles my skin where Rafael's fingers just touched.

"You're bleeding." Rafael inspects the side of my face. His skin whitens as we speak; the vein which runs up his neck bulges.

"We need to call the police," Adriel says from the balcony.

My heart thuds again. "No!"

"Rafael ..." Adriel begins as he walks into the room.

Rafael tilts my face in his direction so I'm looking at him and raises a finger to silence Adriel. "Why not, Rose?"

"I can't deal with more." My eyes flood with tears. "Please, maybe he'll stay away now."

"Don't be naïve." Adriel hurries back to the balcony and looks outside.

"Not tonight." I rest my head on Rafael's hand.

"What if there is a next time, and it's worse?" Adriel's voice grows louder as he returns to the bedroom.

Rafael's chest tenses and fist clenches at Adriel's words, the lock clicks loudly on the balcony door.

Adriel stands next to Rafael. "You can't let this go on—"

"Go check that Lucy is okay," Rafael orders.

Adriel's departure is almost silent.

My insides tremble, sending shivers through my body.

"What happened?" Rafael whispers, his fingers running through my hair. Sweat drips down the side of his reddened face, his white shirt see-through from the rain outside. His whole body tremors as he waits for my answer, his eyes darting between my face and the balcony door.

I struggle to word what happened. "He told me if I resisted him, he'd gut me."

Rafael pulls me into his shaking arms, his muscles on the verge of exploding.

"He grabbed my face and kissed me."

Rafael exhales loudly, his eyebrows creased. "That disgusting."

"He threw me on the bed and licked my cheek down to my neck."

Rafael looked at my face where my fingers ran. "He licked your blood?"

"What?"

"Your face is bleeding. He licked the blood."

I scrunch my nose. "He moaned when he licked me, as if he really enjoyed it."

A string of swearwords flow from Rafael's mouth.

"How did you know to come to me?"

Rafael stomps around his room. "What?" He walks to the balcony door. "Oh, because we thought it through. He could have access to a key." He opens a drawer next to the balcony door. "This is where I keep the spare— It's gone. He must have taken it the night he smashed the door." Rafael yanks out the drawer and throws it against the hard floor. It crashes loudly and smashes into several pieces. Pieces of clothing splash across the room, covering the floor.

I sit up straight and hold my breath as Rafael bangs his fists hard against the wall. The glass balcony door shudders, threatening to shatter. I can't even swallow. Rafael's calm composure is gone and replaced with what looks like uncontrollable anger. "Raf," I squeak.

Rafael takes several deep breaths before looking at me. "He fucking hurt you, under my watch!"

"I'm okay."

He watches me shrink and tuck my knees into my stomach. His piercing eyes soften.

My stomach aches with tension as he approaches me. I'm not scared of him hurting me. No, I'm terrified for Dale, for anyone who ever tries to hurt me again.

"I'm sorry," he mutters and sits at the very end of the bed.

My eyes are stuck on his. I can't seem to blink. He doesn't move any closer, instead, he searches my face for a long moment, for any signs of fear, then slowly rests a hand on mine. "I want you to take a shower again, try to calm down, then come to eat a little bit."

"Not alone," I whisper, my hands shaking on my lap.

He regards me with sad eyes. "Come on." He takes my hand and leads me to the bathroom. He removes his shirt in one swift movement and leans into the shower to turn it on. Every muscle in his upper body contracts, his chest heaving. He walks towards me.

I stare ahead, my nausea still coming in waves.

"Are you ready, Rose?" He's homed in on my eyes.

"I am," I whisper and lose myself in his eyes. "I need to get him off me."

Cool fingers move down the buttons of my shirt whilst he continues to look only into my eyes.

My heart beats slower, almost stopping, as he reaches the last button on my shirt and pulls it down my arms. I shrug, and with a trembling lower lip, I close my eyes. Embarrassment colours my face. I try to shuffle a heavy leg, my muscles stiff after staying tense for so long. I open my eyes to see Rafael's weak smile. I nod, giving him the go-ahead, before he moves behind me. I watch our reflection in the mirror; his broad shoulders are almost double my width, and he's at least a head taller than me. His skin glints in the light; his flushed cheeks barely reveal his emotions.

Staring at our reflection, I can't help feeling ashamed of myself and my imperfect skin and disgusted with myself, repelled by the skin that Dale has just touched. With great effort, I move my arms across my body. A soft finger trails along my shoulder, and I close my eyes again, feeling the coolness across my heated skin. Only when my eyes are closed can I feel his hand quiver. I open my eyes to see he's already on one knee, his hair visible at my hips, and he carefully slides down my jeans. I hear his intake of breath when he stands and removes his own.

I turn and behold his beauty with a small gasp and approach the shower, removing what's left of my clothes. I step inside, the warm water instantly easing the ache in my muscles.

Rafael enters behind me. "Second shower today." His hands run over my shoulders, rubbing gently. The coolness of his body reaches mine making my skin prickle, although we're not touching, I can feel the chill.

I dare not look down, or even at him. I keep my eyes closed against the flowing water.

His hands move from my face to my shoulders, then to my hips, massaging soap over my body, then he starts on my hair.

I lift a hand and hold it against Rafael's chest.

"I'm sorry," he whispers so quietly I can hardly hear him

"No." I open my eyes for the first time in the shower.

The water sprays between us, and he looks down at me. The whites of his eyes are red, and the corners of his mouth turn down. "I wasn't back in time to stop him," his voice cracks. There, in the shower, he stands, vulnerable. The water that splashes down his face wipes away his tears.

I wrap my arms around him, closing the small gap between us, our bodies against one another. The steaming water falls for what seems like forever on our entwined bodies. My lips tremble against his shoulder. I can feel each indentation of his perfect body, each intense breath he takes. I'm not ready for the ache I feel in this moment of pure emotion, defenceless in each other's arms. I crumble to my knees, and so does he.

He stands after a couple moments and takes my hand.

I climb from the shower and wrap myself in a towel, shivering the second reality hits. I hold myself tight and stare at my feet when Rafael emerges from the shower.

He doesn't look at me, maybe hiding his own embarrassment, and walks to the mirror, grabbing a towel off the hook on the way. "Come here," he says, watching himself in the mirror as he wraps the towel around his waist.

I move across the bathroom and stand next to him, my arms firmly wrapped across my body.

"Do you think we washed away his lips?" Rafael eyes me expectantly.

I nod. I feel clean; I feel safe again.

Rafael leans down and kisses my ear. "You're safe now."

"I don't want him to hurt me again," I say shakily, my hand brushing my painful raw cheek.

His arms wrap around me and he lifts my feet off the floor. "I'll not let you out of my sight again." And with that, he softly kisses my lips.

CHAPTER 24

R afael holds me tight for a long time, we sit in silence on the end of his bed, me wrapped in his arms. His whispers of support ease my rigid body. Only after an hour passes does he lift my chin to wipe away what's left of my tears and stands.

I dress briskly, pulling my hair into a messy plait and slipping on a V-neck red t-shirt.

Rafael pulls on a pair of tight jeans and a tight white vest. He throws a flannel shirt over it and beckons me to the bedroom door.

"Do you look good in everything?" I say jealously.

He frowns. "I've never tried a dress. I'll let you know when I do," he says, trying to make me smile.

We laugh together, walking down the hallway, his arm draping protectively around my shoulder.

Adriel arrives at the top of the stairs. "Brother."

"How was Lucy?"

"She said she was asleep, that she didn't hear a thing." Adriel descends the stairs.

"Mhmm." Rafael nods with a blank expression.

I don't ask any more questions but can tell something is hugely off.

His arm hesitantly loosens across my shoulder. He glances at me several times before deciding on what to do. "Adriel, will you wait here with Rosa? I just want to mention something to Lucy," Rafael says as we reach the bottom of the stairs.

I scowl at Rafael when he turns his back on me and strides up the hallway.

Adriel notices my cheek where the nail marks stand out against my pale complexion. "Why would he lick your blood?"

"Why would he threaten to gut me?"

Adriel narrows his gaze at me. "You mustn't make contact with him again, Rosalie."

A door slams down the hallway and echoes into the vestibule. Rafael stomps past us and into the front room.

Adriel's eyebrow raises, and he turns to follow him into the front room.

"Raf." I stand behind him and put a hand on his shoulder.

He flinches. "Rose,"

"What happened?" I ask, examining Rafael's rapidly reddening cheek.

He chuckles darkly. "I simply told Lucy that if she's going to lie, she needs to leave."

"Lie about what?" Adriel appears at my side.

"About being asleep. Impossible she's asleep this early. She's got a great left hook though, I'll give her that." Rafael laughs, brushing off the conversation. "Let's eat."

I notice Rafael's gaze shoots to Adriel's, and that second of eye contact seems to be a secret conversation. Adriel's face stiffens, then seconds later returns to a relaxed state. I can't focus on that now; my cheeks burn worse than ever as I take a deep breath, ready to shout. I stare at him, blood pounding in my ears. "She hurt you?"

"Well it didn't hurt."

I grab a slice of pizza and chase after Rafael. "That's not the point."

He sits on the end of the sofa. "The point is, she's got to go."

"Rafael," Adriel starts.

"No, she's no good here," Rafael says with a mouth full of pizza.

"She can't just slap her boss," I say loudly.

Rafael shrugs. "I've been slapped many times before."

I feel unreasonably angry whilst staring at Rafael's face. My hands shake with misdirected rage. "Stop. Being. So. Nice!"

Rafael lifts my hand which holds the pizza and moves it to my lips.

I see Adriel watching from the corner of my eye.

"Eat," Rafael says, standing, and grabs two more slices of pizza.

I eat another slice, my stomach churning. Every few moments, my heart contracts, leaving me breathless.

Adriel doesn't sit; he stands, facing Rafael, then turns towards the door. "I'm going to the kitchen to get some work done." He leaves with two slices of pizza, not looking back.

Rafael looks thoughtful in his silence. He bites his lip and stares at the wall. He closes his tired eyes and exhales loudly.

"Raf," I say nervously.

"What's up?"

I slide closer to him and put my hand on the side of his chin, gently turning his face towards me. "What are you thinking about?"

Uncharacteristically, he shrugs. "I'm just thinking." His voice shakes. "What could have happened to you if we hadn't arrived when we did?"

A shiver rolls down my back.

Rafael's eyes remain closed, but he slides a comforting arm around me, then apologetically looks at me through his impossibly long eyelashes. "Sorry ..." He closes his eyes again. "It makes me angry enough knowing he's even kissed your lips before."

"It makes me feel sick." I shake my head. "I can't believe I let someone like that—"

"You didn't know. You couldn't have known. I understand the attraction. He's a good-looking man." His hand runs down my back, and he reaches for my face with the other hand.

"I still don't understand why you've been so great to me." I lean into his hand and kiss the palm,

"Can't you see?"

I close my eyes as his lips touch mine, and he lifts me to move me onto his lap. My arms lock around his neck. His hand moves up my back, this time, finally, under my shirt. His fingers tickle my back and I unbutton his shirt, throwing it to the side. His cool skin burns through his vest against mine as he removes my shirt and holds me close. He presses his full lips against my collarbone and takes a deep breath.

I lift Rafael's vest over his head and lean in. My lips move over his chest. I bite his hardened skin; his sighs are music to my ears.

"You smell good," he whispers, nibbling my ear.

I giggle as my hands slide over his muscular back. I'm stuck on his words, *"Don't you see?"* I repeat it in my head, Rafael watching me bemused.

His lips touch mine.

"You confuse me," I let out between kisses.

His lips twitch, and a secretive smile forms against my heated cheek. "Mhmm." His lips brush my jawline.

"It seems like you want me confused."

He stops to consider his answer. "I want you intrigued enough to ask."

My breath catches in my throat as his lips move down my neck, biting tenderly.

"Ask what?"

His hand runs over my shoulder and down my arm. "Well, you'll figure that out."

His lips beguile me as they linger on my collarbone.

Suddenly he shifts my body onto the sofa and his shirt hits me in the face as he stands. "Put it on!" He hisses without looking back.

I push my arms into my sleeves as Rafael throws open the curtains so hard that the curtain pole flies off its hook. I flinch, my hands whipping up and covering my ears as it clashes to the floor, causing an echo throughout the circular room.

"You motherfucker!"

The dark window looks empty, I struggle to see anything but the reflection of Rafael, my fingers trembling on my shirt buttons. My gaze falls on Rafael's back and moves along the window. I can't blink as I stare at the smudge that drips down the window. I stand and move forward, staring at the deep crimson hand-print smeared across the glass. "B-blood."

"Now, Rosalie, relax. He's probably trying to scare us." Rafael moves to my side, covering my view of the window, and pushes my hands out the way. His steady fingers move up my shirt, buttoning it swiftly. He almost lifts me from the front room and into the hallway. His hand wraps around mine, and he approaches the front door, flicking the lock, he yanks it open.

The night is empty and somehow humid. A shiver runs down my back as I inhale and peek over Rafael's bare and burly shoulder. His body is unusually hot as I grab his arm and attempt to bring him in.

Instead, he's still and as steady as if he is a statue, staring at the floor.

I follow his gaze, and my eyes adjust to the mess on the mat outside the door. A wilting rose lies in a dark puddle on the floor. My eyebrow lifts. "Well ..." I lean down to touch it.

An arm hits my stomach like a barrier. "What the hell are you doing, Rose?"

I cough loudly, trying to catch my breath. "I just thought—"

"That's blood."

"What?" I grimace.

Rafael shouts for Adriel.

Adriel rushes down the hallway and skids to a stop at the door.

Rafael grabs his shoulder, face pale. "There's blood outside and on the window." Rafael pushes me to Adriel and wraps Adriel's hand around mine. "Hold her for me." Rafael runs up the hallway to the kitchen.

Adriel notices my shaking hands and kicks the door shut, then locks it. "I think we need to get out of here."

I nod. "There's a rose in a pool of blood on the doorstep."

Adriel's eyes flitter towards the front door. "A distraction to—" A loud click sounds. The hallway disappears into complete darkness. Adriel's hand tightens over mine, and he guides me towards the wall.

"Adriel," Rafael shouts.

I can just about hear the crashing and thuds that echos down the hallway over my staggered heartbeat.

"Rafael," Adriel whispers as footsteps approach us. Adriel's arm slides protectively around me, moving me closer to his chest. "It's not Rafael," Adriel's voice quivers. He inches me along the wall towards the front room.

I struggle to decipher anything in the complete darkness. Only a single line of light shines through the front door panels. My legs stiffen with each small step. I take several deep breaths, trying to catch up with my heart. My eyes adjust to discern a tall shadow standing not even three meters away.

Adriel's breath catches in his throat, and he shoves me backwards.

I tumble through the open doorway and into the front room, smashing my elbow on the hardwood.

"Move aside," a voice snaps.

The outline of Adriel's shoulders push forward in an act of defiance. "Step back!" Adriel edges backwards, his arm shaking as his hand clamps onto the doorhandle and throws it closed behind him.

Alone in the dark, I stumble to my feet. Several bangs from the other side of the door send my body into frenzies. The single door, which may be the only thing standing between life or death, muffles the distinct sound of blind punches. My mind goes into a panic, blurring so not one single thought is processed, I think of Adriel, as thin as he is, against the burly shadow that lurks outside.

I hear a thud; someone has fallen to the floor. "Adriel," I gasp, my instincts taking over.

"You won't ever have to leave the safety of my arms, Rose. We can make it forever," Dale's voice speaks into the night, the door opening slowly.

A stray tear momentarily blinds me. I stare wearily ahead, watching Dale close in on me.

We both startle at a bang from the hallway. He turns reluctantly, his fingers reaching out to me, desperate to touch me, and darts towards the window. He smashes it easily with the stool Rafael used earlier, and fades into the night.

Adriel groans, and I dash to the door. A torch illuminates the hallway, burning my eyes. Bright blood covers the lower part of Adriel's face and neck, his one eye red and bulging.

I drop to the floor and rest my hand on his chest, my throat too tight to talk.

Rafael runs down the hallway and falls to his knees. "Brother." He slowly lifts his brother's head.

Adriel winces. "I'm fine. Get the lights on."

Rafael eyes me, his cheek bloody and swollen. "Two seconds, okay?"

"I'm so sorry," I cry out to Adriel.

He takes my hand and holds it between his hands. "You're special to my brother. You're special to me." He delicately wipes a tear from my face and forces a smile. "It's okay, Rosalie. We will protect you."

The lights flash on, and I see blood pouring from Adriel's swollen lip. His eye is bright red, with a lump forming on his upper cheek. I suck in a deep breath as I notice the blood-covered floor.

"It's not all mine, don't worry. I got a few in before I went down," Adriel whispers. I know he'd be smiling if his face wasn't so swollen.

Rafael's at my side again, his features dangerous as he evaluates Adriel's injuries. Small cuts cover Rafael's chest; his hands are bloody and bruised. He holds a wet towel in one hand and works on his brother's face. "It looks worse than it is," Rafael reassures me, his brother's face clear of blood now except for his still pouring nose and lip. Rafael helps Adriel stand. "He's much weaker than I'd expected."

Adriel tries to grin but winces.

I can't speak; I'm unable to form words. Each time I try to think of what to say, I panic. I reach for Rafael, but pain radiates into my shoulder. I wince, shoving my pain aside, not worthy of attention after what Adriel has endured. "Police," I manage to whisper, and Adriel nods.

"Let's go into the kitchen. We can call from in there," Rafael says.

Adriel leans on Rafael as we move down the hallway and into the kitchen. I stare in disbelief at the mess; smashed glass and chairs lie scattered across the floor.

"What happened in here?" I clench Rafael's arm.

"The kitchen door was open when I came in, so I started for the door, thought Adriel had left it open. On my way out, something hit me in the face and locked me out." He gestures towards the shattered window. "Had to smash my way back in."

I hold my breath as I survey Rafael's knuckles.

"Reinforced glass." He sighs and sets Adriel on a chair. His phone vibrates in his pocket, and his hand flicks fast to answer it within seconds. "On my way," he says and rushes out the kitchen. He's back seconds later with a groggy Lucy, sitting babylike in his arms.

"What's going on?" She removes her headphones and scans the glass-glittered kitchen.

"I need you to tend to Adriel. Call the police and an ambulance to check him over. Tell them there was a break-in, and Adriel will explain when they arrive." He puts down Lucy, her wide eyes and pale face terrified.

"Are you okay, sir?" She examines Rafael's bare chest for injury.

Rafael grabs my hand. "I'm fine. Now call the police." He leads me from the kitchen and almost runs me up the stairs. "Are you okay?" He doesn't look at my face as he pulls me into his room. He grabs a white button-up shirt from his wardrobe without looking and covers his blood-stained body.

"I'm not hurt." I answer and stare at an angry bruise on his forehead.

"Please." He pushes away my hand as I reach for his face. "Just put this on and follow me." He throws some clothes into a backpack and hands me one of my flannel shirts and my leather jacket, before he approaches the door and holds it open.

I follow him through the house.

He takes my hand as we descend the stairs and head through the front door. He pulls me in, completely shielding me on the short walk to the car. He releases me into his car and runs around to get into the front seat.

"What's going on?" I ask, staring at his colourless face.

He doesn't acknowledge me; his eyes are narrowed against the empty road that flies by at a speed I'm sure is illegal.

"Rafael!"

He clears his throat and slows the car. "Your father."

My ears pound in my head, waiting for the next words to spill from Rafael's mouth.

"He's been attacked, Rose." Rafael regards me now and grabs my hand. "And Ben's missing."

His words vibrate through my aching head, sending a searing pain into my eyes. "A-attacked?"

Rafael's hand tightens around mine. "Murdered," he corrects as a tear falls from his cheek.

My chest collapses. I can't breathe. I can't see.

CHAPTER 25

I don't dare breathe as we pull up to my house, tears swimming in my eyes. Blue light flashes throughout my dark neighbourhood, and several officers are dotted around the front lawn.

Rafael slows the car, and time seems to crawl.

As the car stops, I know I need to move, but my legs don't want to comply and refuse to move an inch.

Rafael runs around the car, the blue against his skin making him seem paler than ever. He opens the door, with bloodshot eyes. He almost carries me from the car, holding onto my shoulders to support me when he stands me up. His lips brush my forehead, his hands tight on my shoulders. "Rosalie, do you want to hang back here?"

I shake my head childishly. "No." I walk ahead of him until a policeman meets me on the pathway to my house.

"Rafael," the police officer says, watching me with pity in his eyes.

"Tell me." Rafael puts an arm around me.

"Knife wound to the neck; no weapon left. Forensics are searching for evidence. Happened about an hour and a half ago. The victim's son reported a break-in and requested an ambulance. He said he was at the shop, and when he got back, his father was on the floor. We can't find Benjamin anywhere."

I stare at my house, trying to understand that the victim is my father.

Rafael nods before heading towards my house and striding through the front door.

A team of police personal litter my hallway as I approach the entrance. "Wait," I whimper.

My house doesn't look like mine anymore, there are strangers in every corner, all of them bow their head in my direction as we pass through the hall. I grab Rafael's shirt, pulling him back, but my fingers don't work. The material slips from my grasp and I fall a few steps behind him.

Rafael halts and faces me, shoving his balled up fists into his pockets. His angry eyes soften somewhat when he sees my tremulous body. "Wait here, please. Let me see before. I don't want you seeing something you don't need to." Rafael's words are soft, but his eyes are rigid and cold. Anger and hatred has torn his usual beauty. He turns and slowly enters the kitchen.

My stomach burns, and a high-pitched noise completely distorts my hearing. I stand, trembling from head to toe, awaiting his return. *This can't be happening. Not my father, it should be me. This can't be true.* My thoughts echo through my mind, breaking through the high-pitched screeching.

"Cover him. His daughter is here," Rafael growls.

I hear a scramble of noise and decide it's time. Putting one foot slowly in front of another, I walk to the kitchen. I put my hands together, clinging onto my shaking fingers, and stare at my feet as silence fills the room. I know I must see and say goodbye, to hold his hand before it's freezing, to kiss my father before the colour in his usually pink cheeks is gone.

"No, not yet," Rafael says, spinning me around.

"I need to!"

Rafael sighs, drawing my attention to his pale face. His eyes are dark and watery, his lips pulled down, a brokenhearted angel.

I glance to my side and notice someone, another stranger. His expression is soft, his hands cover his mouth, he watches me as I survey the familiar cupboards, trying to understand.

"Okay." He peers over my head at what must be several people.

People shuffle together to the other side of the room, maybe to give me some space.

My heart slows almost to a stop; each breath I take seems to be endless—my own personal torture.

Rafael moves first, and I don't dare look around. I keep my focus on his burly back.

He crouches onto his knees, and I hear the ruffle of a sheet and Rafael breathe deeply.

I fall to my knees, my tears flooding my eyes. The image of my father's face is a blur. I scrub my eyes and look once more.

Rafael has the sheet covering my father's body and neck; only his face is visible. His blue and now bloodshot and partially cloudy eyes stare at the ceiling.

My head thumps as I lean in and kiss his still warm cheek one last time.

His face is white, and his lips are so pale; still, he looks like he's simply sleeping.

"I'm sorry," I whisper into his ear, my cheek resting on his face. My throat's so dry as I try to swallow, my eyes stinging and my body shivering. *Dad, please, wake up.* I bury my head into his chest and cry. "Daddy, please wake up!"

Rafael's shaking breath is loud behind me, he places a hand on my shoulder and squeezes lightly. The sensation feels so far away, everything feels so far away as my head rests on my fathers chest. My heart can't beat right now, not when it's so broken and worn. My cries are not enough, my pain fills me up inside and thumps against my chest so hard I lose my breath.

Please, I gasp. I scream in my head but all that leaves my lips are breathless sobs and painful heaves. I hold onto silence, hoping to hear his heart beat or to feel his chest rise. The seconds tick by like hours and stillness is all that is left.

I close my eyes and suppress my sobs.

Rafael pulls me close and stands, lifting me off the floor with him.

I reach out, longing for more time. "He can't be dead!"

Rafael holds me up, his hands now wrapped tight around my chest. He steps towards the door, my kicking and grabbing having no effect.

I scan the kitchen through my sore eyes, finally beholding the shattered glass and red spots littering the floor. A huddle of

313

people stand in the corner. A young lady police officer, who's in the front, covers her tear-filled eyes and turns away.

"Ben," I shout as Rafael pulls me from the kitchen and out the house that was once my haven.

"That is where we are going now." Rafael moves faster and opens the car door for me. "Wait here, two seconds."

My tears stream uncontrollably when I let myself realise that both of my parents are dead. The ache in my chest worsens, and I hyperventilate and heave as I stare out the window.

Rafael outstretches his hand, and the officer he first spoke to hands him a package with weary eyes. Rafael returns to the car, not looking back but staring blankly ahead.

"Where will we start?" I ask him in the fiercest voice I can muster.

"*I* will start at Dale's house."

"*We! We* will start at Dale's house, because Ben is *my* brother."

Rafael stares at me, my anger and spirit catching him off guard. He doesn't say a word his fingers tap the steering wheel, as if willing the car to go faster. "Rose. Please, you must stay close to me. I can't handle losing you."

I stare out the window, tears staining my cheek. The coffeeshop where Dale and I had our first date flies by, with memories of an easier time. "There is no way you'll lose me," I whisper, my anger and hatred, smeared with betrayal, heats my face.

Rafael slows the car to a halt, and his hands unexpectedly grip my face. "I'm serious, Rose." His lips collide into mine, my lips forming perfectly against his.

My arms wrap around his neck, and I hold him as close to me as possible. My cheeks are fiery, and for a second, I forget everything. I see him and only him.

His fingers trail down my back, and he pulls me into a tight hug.

"I'm stronger than you think," I say, dread hitting me like a brick.

Rafael's shaky cool breath hits me as if it is the first time—or maybe the last time.

With a scorching pain forcing its way into my heart, I let him go. "Come on."

Rafael grimaces, then reaches for the package the police officer gave him. He tears through the paper, checks for any onlookers, and removes a gun.

"Holy shit, Raf." I move back into my seat.

"This man has killed, and he has your brother. This is best to protect you from that motherfucker."

I forget to blink as my thoughts rush, knowing each passing second could be the one that saves my brother.

Rafael grabs his phone and dials 9-9-9. "Police, there's been a crime at Dale Cartwright's place." He drops his phone and opens his door.

"Yes, you're right. Come on." I exit the car.

Rafael runs to my side and puts his hand on the small of my back. He guides me to the big house around the corner.

The house is lightless; I can't even see a shadow. I fear for my brother. I quake inside and move faster now the destination is closing in.

Rafael keeps pace with mine as we run up the driveway. He breaks into a sprint, and I follow around the rear. He doesn't stop until his shoulder hits the age-weakened back door, and with a deafening crash, he falls into the house.

I follow him in, taking it step by step, fully alert. The complete darkness jars me. I can already hear distant sirens, police moving in on us.

"He's not in here," a sickeningly familiar voice calls out.

"Where is he, you asshole?" Rafael shouts.

"You'll figure it out." A sinister chuckle echoes through the house. "You've got twenty-four hours. Or, you could simply tell Rosalie to come to me, and I'll let him go. Mostly unharmed."

"*Ben*," I scream.

The pitch-black room changes somehow, to a sudden feeling of danger, darker than the last.

"Shut up," Rafael spits.

I hear movement around me as a heaviness fills my space. I run for the door, and an earsplitting bang cracks through the room.

"Oh, my baby has come to play." Dale laughs psychotically.

The blood drains from my face, and a wave of dizziness engulfs me. I fall out the back door and hit my elbows. I shriek as my knees skid across the floor to break my fall.

"*Twenty-four hours,*" Dale screeches, and blue lights illuminate his kitchen.

Rafael, at my side, yanks me off the floor.

I squeal as he throws me over his shoulder.

"We need to move before the police arrive," Rafael huffs, dropping me to my feet, and pushing me into the trees. He pulls me deeper into the overwhelming thickness. Branches scrap and scratch us as we run.

We stop to watch the blue lights filtering through the trees behind us. Rafael searches ahead with wide eyes, trying to find a break in the tree's to get us onto the street. A crunch on the freshly fallen leaves in the darkness forces us into a sprint.

I fall out of the trees and onto the street across from Rafael's car.

Rafael pulls me up and locks his hand on my elbow.

I wince, a cry escaping my lips.

He loosens his grasp and sprints across the road. "Are you okay?" He opens the door, and I drop into the seat, staring at three more police vehicles speeding around the corner. Rafael starts the engine as soon as he gets in and drives the opposite way out of town.

I shiver violently. "W-what are we going to do?"

Rafael flips on the heat, even though he has beads of sweat dripping down the side of his head. "We'll go to this hotel on the edge of town. I need to keep you safe for a moment and have a quick think."

"Why can't we just show ourselves to the police and ask them for help?"

Rafael sighs and pushes himself back against his seat, straightening his arms. "Dale is not a suspect. They believe he's clean. After all, he's well respected here."

"But—"

"They have no proof of him being around your mother or father. Fingerprints and DNA from the blood on the floor, though, will hopefully prove Dale attacked Adriel, but until then, we're alone."

"But we can't do this without the police," I mutter, my words blend together with all my trembling.

"We *must* do this *alone*!"

I flinch at his sudden outburst and stare at the seriousness on his face.

Rafael's eyes are mere slits, focused on the road. In absolute silence, except for the hum of the engine, we arrive at a dusty-looking hotel. He pulls around back and parks behind two large bins then helps me out of the car. His eyes scan every inch of the dark car park as we jog to the entrance.

As the door swings open, a loud bell chimes annoyingly. The entrance is a ghastly shade of red and green. The carpet matches the old and worn wallpaper, which, in some places, hangs off the walls. The lights on the wall are yellowing behind sheets of dusty glass, and an old lady stands, staring at us with great interest.

"Room for two?" she asks, a well-practiced smile creasing her wrinkled lips.

"Yeah. Do you have one on the top floor?" He glances over his shoulder. His hand clenches my waist when the woman bends to sift through keys in a draw.

I step closer to him and push myself against his side into a half hug. The gun in his jean line presses against my stomach, and my heart rockets again, palpitating too fast for me to catch up.

Rafael raises his eyebrows as the woman mutters a string of profanities about the useless cleaners.

"Here," the old woman announces with a clunk of metal on the desk. "Room six, floor seven." She pushes a piece of paper used as a logbook towards Rafael, stating the price per night is fifty pounds.

Rafael grabs the pen attached to the desk with a chain and scribbles a name: Mattius Commons. His fingers slip into his pocket, and he removes the money, places it on the desk, and turns.

"Umm ..." the lady croaks, beckoning us back. "The lift is broken. Stairs are this way."

Rafael nods politely. "Shit," he mutters, and we traipse to a heavy maroon door. We climb the repetitive spiral staircase, his hand clasped to mine. "Sorry." Rafael slows to eye me.

"For what?"

"The lift being broken." He smiles.

I chortle. "Don't be stupid."

"I'm also sorry about everything that's happening to you." His hand tightens around mine.

My throat dries up. "Please don't say sorry. You're here, the only one here getting me through this, and I can't even begin to thank you enough."

With a sigh of relief, we reach the top. I dry the tears from my cheek before Rafael has a chance to see, and we go through one of the identical maroon doors. This one has the number seven painted messily on it.

Rafael grips my hand, the other hand close to the gun nestled on his waist, and pushes the door open with his foot. He moves me along the lengthy narrow hallway fast enough that I must run to keep up.

My face collides with his shoulder as he halts and opens our room's door. The first thing I notice is the smell of mould. The room is plain and cold. A double bed fills most of the space in the middle of the room, opposite is an old box TV. The tiniest bathroom I've ever seen, with a small tiled square shower, sits to the right.

I sit on the end of the bed, watching Rafael lock the door and take the gun from his waistline. He leaves it on the table next to the TV. My heart hammers at the sight of the weapon. My foot starts taping loudly on the floor, it turns rapidly into a shake.

Rafael spies me, and he's by my side at once, holding my hand. "I'll keep you safe, I promise."

"I'm not used to guns," I say with a shiver.

Rafael's eyes fill with pity. "I'm sorry, but it's to protect you." He wraps his arms around me. "You're freezing."

"I don't feel cold."

Rafael's perfect lips move into a smirk whilst his hands rub my arms and back in circular motions.

Before I can stop myself, I lock my lips onto his. I want his protection; I yearn for the safety he gives me. Fighting to forget, even for a second what is going on. His lips are hesitant, they move slowly, stopping too soon.

"Kiss me," I mutter breathlessly.

He stifles a groan and moulds his lips to mine again. The circular rubbing motion stops, and his hands tighten across my body as he lifts me onto his lap. His fingers lock uncertainly in my hair, and he guides my head back to reveal my neck. His lips travelling along my neck to behind my ear.

The tingling in my stomach has reached my lips. My legs and fingertips feel the fire now igniting.

He stands to move me onto the bed. His reddened face seems unsure, his chest moves fast under his shirt. His fingers fumble on his buttons, only undoing a few, before he gives up and leans onto me. Warm and soft, his lips move with mine. His tongue rarely takes a break from caressing mine.

Tears stain my cheeks as reality takes hold.

Rafael stiffens and halts, his hands still holding my hips. "I can't," he whispers.

"Please!"

"Not like this. Never like this." He kisses my cheek.

"I don't want to die." I burst into tears.

Rafael falls back onto the bed and wraps his arms around me, steadying my shaking body.

I hold him tight, tuck my head into his side and inhale deeply, desperate to hold onto him, to not lose another second with him. The pain of losing my parents is completely fresh, the wounds in my heart searing. I can't think without my brain aching and throbbing. I rub my eyebrow, trying to loosen the tension held there.

"The old house ..." Rafael almost shouts.

"What?"

"Before Dale's family bought the big house ..." Rafael sits me upright and takes a deep breath. "Before they bought it, they had a farmhouse. It's still there and in Dale's name." Rafael catches his breath.

I stare wildly at him, fear rising in my chest again. "Let's go!" I stand and straighten my shirt.

"Not yet. We need to wait. I need you to wait."

"What, wait for my brother to be murdered?" I shout.

Rafael stands and grabs the kettle from the dressing table. Two paper cups and some old-looking teabags rest on the side. He disappears into the bathroom with the kettle and returns. "We must wait. We need to plan this," Rafael says louder above the loud hum of the kettle.

"Right. You're right, of course." I stand, my legs wobbly, to help make the tea. I glance in the mirror opposite the dresser and see mascara marking my cheeks. I run into the bathroom and turn on the hot water. The steam flows into the air, clouding the mirror above. I dip my fingers in and rub my cheeks and stare at myself. My head feels like it's spinning dangerously. I scrub my cheeks to get rid of the makeup that's smudged down my face. I scrub until my skin feels raw, not stopping until it's completely gone.

"Doll, your tea is ready!"

I sit on the bed, and my hands clench the hot paper cup.

Rafael brushes my loose fringe off my face and pushes it behind my ear. "Rosalie, I don't think you realise how dangerous this is."

"Do you think I'm an idiot?"

Rafael's forehead creases. "No, I think I want to keep you safe."

"And I think I want to protect my brother. I've already lost my parents." I huff loudly, angry tears spilling over my cheeks.

"Okay, but please. I beg you to keep quiet this time and do as I say." Rafael falls to his knees and holds my hands. His lips touch my hands once, his head bowing, then he leans on my shaking knees. "I can't see you hurt, I can't break anymore watching your pain." His voice breaks.

I watch his back rise and fall with each heavy breath he takes, his eyes smouldering with passion and sorrow. "I will." I finally accept.

"When we're there, I want you behind me at all times. If I say run, you get the hell out."

I nod and squeeze his large hand.

"Come." He stands with watery eyes.

"Your gun," I whisper, my chest filling with a breath I can't let out.

Rafael takes the gun and hands it to me.

My hand shakes; the gun weighs more than I could have ever guessed.

"You need it." He stops, choking on his words. "You need this. I need you to protect me this time, Rose." Rafael's face is pale as we turn towards the door. His lips graze my forehead.

I glance at the untouched room and pull the door shut behind me.

CHAPTER 26

We move to the stairwell, each step feeling like a step closer to Hell. My phone startles us both when it rings in my pocket.

Rafael's fists clench as the name on the screen of my phone flashes—Dale.

We stop on floor six's landing. I stand, staring out the window at the dark car park below.

Rafael kisses my head before answering the phone and urging me to talk.

"Rose," Dale's voice sounds down the phone.

"Where's my brother?"

"What are you doing, love?"

"Where is he?"

"You answer my questions honestly, and I'll answer yours." I can almost see the smile behind his voice.

I stare at Rafael, pleading silently for a clue on what to say.

Rafael stares distractedly out the window.

"I'm—"

"Tell him the truth," Rafael whispers in my ear.

"I'm at a hotel."

"Your brother is alive," Dale responds with a laugh. "See? This is fun. Let's try another. Which hotel are you in?"

Rafael grabs my hand, pulls me up the stairs, and takes the phone. "Don't be so trivial," Rafael spits down the phone. "You know exactly where we are. I saw your car tucked away not so cleverly in the trees."

"Oh, Rafael. Why are you doing this to yourself?" The shake in his voice indicates to us that he's moving.

"What is it that you want, Dale? The love from a lady who despises you? Or is it just the satisfaction of causing misery?"

"You—!" Dale takes a deep breath. "You have no idea. Do you honestly believe she doesn't think of me each time you touch her?"

Rafael laughs as he opens the hotel room door and pushes me inside. "Or how about when she holds me close, Dale? When she begs for me to stay by her side, because she's scared? Is that really just for you?"

Butterflies flutter in my stomach at Rafael's words.

He looks down apologetically at me as the silence intensifies.

"I know that's not true." Dale's voice drops an octave.

"Surely, with all your stalking, you've seen where my lips have been. You've heard each sigh and seen each caress."

I hold my breath, waiting for a response, but a bell chimes loudly as Dale ends the call. He's in the building. I stare at Rafael, a frenzy builds and clatters against my chest, pulling all air from my lungs.

Rafael grabs my shoulders. "Calm," he whispers.

"He's coming."

"He's here. That means, for now, your brother is safe. Dale will find out what floor we are on. We have one option, and that's to get him in here with us." Rafael's words trip over one another, his accent wild.

I nod, and Rafael pushes me onto the bed.

"Now, trust me and follow my lead." He unbuttons several buttons on my shirt. "Distraction. Okay?" He kisses my lips and his eyes linger on mine before someone bangs on the door.

"Rose," Dale's voice echoes down the hallway.

"The door's unlocked, you moron." A painful smile spreads across Rafael's ashen face.

I hold my breath as the door opens.

Dale's hair almost glows in the light as he slams the door behind him and takes three steady steps into the room. Rage is spoiling his handsome face, his eyes wide and vicious. He stops, apparently confused at the situation.

"A peace offering," Rafael says through bared teeth and gestures to me with a steady hand.

"What?" Dale's hand holds something tucked into his waistline, and the other moves to his head.

"You can have her. Just take me to her brother. Let him leave. Then I'll walk away."

"Do you think I'm fucking stupid?" Dale stammers, his stance weakening with each second.

"Well, I've had her. She's useless to me now." Rafael casts a disgusted look in my direction.

Although I know this is his plan, his words crush my insides. Each joint in my body aches to be out of this room, to take me back to that day at the library, to a place where I can reject him there and then.

Dale scans my shaking body, then regards Rafael.

Rafael puts his hands in the air and takes a few steps backwards, giving Dale space to approach me.

My heart flips in my throat and threatens to come out of my mouth.

"Rosa, love. You heard him," Dale mumbles. His cold finger touches my hand, sending a violent shudder down my body. He traces my hand, his finger moving up my arm, and looks back at Rafael. His teeth crush together, and he growls.

I try to stop the shudder that rumbles up my back, but I'm unsuccessful.

"Why did you shudder?" Dale studies me and pushes himself into an upright position.

"Your hands are cold," I mutter, unable to look at him.

"You want this man?" Dale pulls a large knife from his belt and points it at Rafael.

"No!" I scramble off the bed, and my eyes plead with Dale. "No, I want you." Fire burns in my stomach and up my throat at the thought of Dale.

Rafael's eyes flitter in my direction for barely a second.

"Then you won't mind what I do now," Dale says, smiling sweetly, and lunges forward to knock Rafael to the floor, and with a sickening thud, Dale's fist connects to Rafael's jaw.

I reach for the gun that's digging into my hip and stare in horror as Rafael's face contorts with pain. "Dale!"

"What?" he asks as he lands another punch.

"I thought you wanted me," I stutter out as seductively as possible, distracting Dale for a second. Rafael kicks from the floor hitting Dale in the ribs. I scramble off the bed and reach for Rafael's hand.

A tear of blood drips down his face, and he throws me towards the door, pulling the gun from my side, and points it at Dale. "Stay there!" The veins on Rafael's hand almost burst through his skin, his finger on the trigger. He stands in front of me protectively.

"You wouldn't shoot me." Dale grins, but his cocky smile is weary.

"Get the keys, go to the car, and meet me out front." Rafael nods towards his back pocket.

I feel blindly into Rafael's pocket, not taking my eyes off Dale, then I glance at Rafael, my eyes brimming with tears. I spin on the spot, yank the door open, and run down the hallway, ripping myself from the situation. I linger at door to the stairs, listening for any signs of a gunshot. A swarm of buzzing bees fills and stings my chest as I sprint down the stairs.

Dale's dangerous grin infatuates my already clouded mind. *It's a trick*! I reach the second floor. *A trap*! I stumble on the steps to the ground floor. *Hide*! I throw the heavy metal door open.

The lady behind the counter, eyes wide with shock, sits slumped in her chair.

I head towards the entrance. "Call the police!" I hear no reply so I turn, irritated at her lack of response. I notice her red necktie, one she wasn't wearing before. A heave of vomit leaves my lips. My feet are stuck in place.

Her head leans precariously on her shoulder, blood seeping over a fold of skin.

I scream silently as I approach her, then turn my face away. *I must get to the car*! I throw myself out the door, and the cold, wet air slaps my face as I run. I gather speed as I turn the corner and spot Rafael's car. I press the key to unlock the doors and skid to a halt. Scanning for any signs of trickery as I climb into the car. "Not now!" I scream, unable to find the ignition.

A slow moment passes before the car sputters to life. I tap the steering wheel, urging it to move, and the car's acceleration flings my head into the headrest. I pull to the front of the hotel.

Rafael's burley shape escapes the hotel entrance as I slow down.

I scoot into the passenger seat, unwilling to risk driving such a fast-moving car with such shaky hands.

Rafael is in the car before I can buckle in. His chest heaves, and I stare at his bloodied face, my stomach in a tight knot. He glances at me, his one eye fully bloodshot. The car speeds off, and Rafael doesn't watch the road, he's eyeing the hotel as he swings the car onto an empty road. The seatbelt signal screams at us until we force our belts around us.

"Rafael," I whisper, my lips trembling.

"I'm all right." He shrugs. "Dale will be leaving the hotel at any second. We need to step back. We need to wait." He leans back awkwardly to grab his phone from his pocket and drops it on my legs. His bloodied face is painfully sad, his hands unsteady and bruised, still cut up and sore from the hours before. "Call Adriel."

"What about the police?"

"No. No, not yet. Something doesn't seem right, Rose. I've begged them to help you several times. Something's not right. Just call Adriel and tell him we're coming back and to meet us in the basement."

My mouth hangs open. "What do you mean? why haven't you told me—"

Rafael waves away my speech. "Call first."

I find Adriel's contact and call, explaining in under ten seconds to get into the basement and wait for us. My mind is stuck on Rafael's words. "*Something's not right.*" I cross my hands over my chest. "Now, spit it out."

"We know he had a relationship with poor Eliza. He was her last known boyfriend. He tells us it wasn't serious, that she was obsessed with him after a date and a one-night stand." Rafael breathes deeply, then winces. "Now, one of her friends came forward. Adriel heard when he was talking to some colleagues about Dale that she said they had been dating, and she had tried to break it off when Dale got rough."

I stare at the empty road ahead. "I don't get what you mean."

Rafael looks at me, the creases by his eyes making him look older. "The police officers who took the statement pushed it aside, hid it."

The car speeds through the town, and I stare out the window, trying to understand. If the police wouldn't take into consideration that Dale was the stalker, they must already know. My thoughts race, and my joints stiffen with each heartbeat.

"So, I think they know. I think they're covering for him. I think he killed Eliza, then got a taste for murder." Rafael's rough voice shakes at the end, his watery eyes stare ahead. "He's getting away with way too much. I just don't understand why."

My body is frozen; my heart seems to have stopped. I can't hear nor feel anything. I try to speak, but nothing, not even a breath, can leave my lips. The emptiness feels heavy, as if my dark, gut-wrenching emotions are squashing and holding me down. I hear nothing but my own screaming thoughts as a dark shadow invades my vision and replaces it with a reel of my mother's eyeless face, the gaping holes, my father's clouded eyes, and Ben—oh, Ben. Finally, my cries break through, and Rafael holds my leg.

"We'll find him," Rafael coos as we pull up outside his house.

Without wasting any time, Rafael's already at my door and pulls me out. We run to his house, Rafael limping heavily. I slow down, my conscience screaming at me to hide, but he doesn't let me slow down. We burst through the door, Rafael stops wearily for a moment and snatches his glasses off of his squinting eyes which the lights must be burning into, all the lights seem to be on. He must think it's safe enough because he tugs on my hand

and we barrel down the vast corridor to the door at the end. Rafael heaves the heavy door open, and a rush of cold air hits us both. We run down the steps, Rafael's hand tightening over mine as if expecting me to fall.

"Rafael," Adriel says in a heavy breath, his eyes big and bright.

"Look, Dale has Rose's brother at the old farmhouse. I think the police are ignoring the situation."

"I agree." Adriel sighs sadly.

"Why? Can you think of any reason?"

Adriel steps closer. "I think he's paid them off. I think he has links in the department, and he's been able to slide under their radar. Sadly that means until he's caught red-handed, and they won't do much." Adriel takes a deep breath. "I've never seen anything like this. I've heard of police turning a blind eye to drug dealings but never a murder."

Rafael releases my hand and paces the basement.

I look around nervously. Shelves of bottles line the bright white walls, adorned with angelic writing in silver dotted in several different places.

"We need to go there ourselves. We need to find Benjamin and have the police turn up once we get out," Rafael says to himself.

"Exactly. Look, if you leave now, I'll drive up about ten minutes later and park around the corner. I'll come on foot and call the police when I arrive," Adriel rushes.

"No!" I burst. "I don't want people. I don't want either of you getting hurt for this. Just let me." Tears flood my face before I even realise it, my voice breaking embarrassingly.

"Rosalie, we're not leaving you, hun," Adriel says.

Rafael's face fills with angst. "Amor, I've had a plan but it does entail you going in on your own." He struggles to swallow. "You'll go in with no defences. You'll cry that I've left you there. You'll beg Dale to look after you, you need to be desperate for his forgiveness."

My eyes drop to my feet, my courage disappearing as quickly as it came. My breath catches in my throat. "What if he—"

"I'll be right behind you. Dale just won't know it. All's we need is for his guard to be dropped for a few minutes. I promise, I swear to you, I'll not let him hurt you."

Adriel stares between us both and nods. "That's actually a great plan if Rose can sell it."

Rafael and Adriel talk quickly as they review the plan.

I can't focus. I can't breathe. The bones inside my legs ache, my head pounds, and my fingers tingle. Terrified isn't a word to describe how I feel. With a churning stomach, I clench Rafael's hand and we run back up the stairs.

"I'm sorry." He kisses my lips several times as we reach the front door. "I'm so sorry."

I drag him to the side. "Rafael, I want to thank you."

"Don't—"

"Please let me say this." Tears blind me, and I scrub them away, not wanting to miss a second. "I should never have involved you in this."

"You didn't—"

"Let me finish! My mother had just passed, and you were there for me—the only one there for me." I put my arms around him. "And you're protecting me now, Raf." My voice turns into a squeak.

He clings onto me, his body vibrating around mine.

Adriel walks down the hallway, and I let Rafael go. "Thank you," I say, pulling Adriel into a tight squeeze.

"You've made my brother happy, and for that, I thank you," he whispers.

I step backwards from them and regard them together. I have to squint through my tears as the very muscular Rafael pulls

Adriel's thin frame into a bone-crushing hug. The difference between them is startling now that I watch them with weary eyes. Adriel's face is warm, inviting, and handsome, unlike Rafael's intimidating stature. Even his face, although beautiful, is stern and serious. They both move the same: smoothly, as if everything is well practised and done many times before.

"Let's do this," Rafael says, his arm around Adriel.

Adriel smiles, even though the bruises on his face look painfully swollen. Rafael nods, and returns the smile.

Rafael's fingers wrap around my wrist and we run to the car through a sheet of rain.

CHAPTER 27

I turn Rafael's battered hand in mine as he pulls out of his driveway and into the dark, wet night. The rain is a constant mist over the already dark and dangerous winding country roads. "I'm sorry," I mutter mindlessly.

"Rose, tell me what your favourite colour is."

"What?"

His lips pull down. "Just, we've not had much chance to really get to know each other."

"I like green," I say, a lump in my throat. "What about you?"

"White." His sad lips turn up at one corner.

"Why was your father so obsessed with angels?" I ask; all the questions I've wanted to ask since meeting him flood my mind.

"Well, he believed angels could be born from mortals, that they'd roam the earth, protectors of the weak and sinful humans. He was a priest, though I have my suspicions he wasn't a very good one. He gave me and my brother the names of angels. Rafael is actually an archangel."

I spy the tattoo on Rafael's arm, invisible in the dark car.

He, too, glances at it, then refocuses on the road.

"Wow, he was right."

Rafael eyes me, his knuckles white against his skin, his hand tensed on the wheel. "What do you mean?"

"Well, you're protecting me. You are my angel."

He smiles and rests his hand on my leg. "And you, my love, are mine."

My heart thuds at his words, and I almost forget my train of thought. "Is your father still alive?"

"He is ... but I don't really know where he is."

I ache for Rafael as his words leave his mouth. I don't know so much about this man who's ready to risk it all for me. "Rafael ... if I get out of this alive ..."

"You will, Rosalie!"

I shock myself, speaking so candidly about my own death. "Just, listen. If I survive, will you still want me?" I mutter, staring at my fingers.

The car jerks to a stop. Rafael's lips are pressed into a tight line, his beautiful face furious. "What do you think?" He turns his body to face me. "Do you think my feelings will dissolve the second I know you're safe? Or ... or that I'm just doing this out of *pity*?"

I stare at him, my mouth hanging open. My throat closes, and with tear-filled eyes, I study my hands.

"I don't know how I can make this clearer. How can I make you believe me ...?" Unexpectedly, his unnaturally burning hot lips fix onto mine, the heat leaving his lips and filling my broken body. The kiss ends much too soon, and he starts the car and drives again, fixated on the road.

"I can't wait to learn all about you." I smile, a tear rolling down my face.

"You too, amor." Rafael smiles. "Rose, five minutes, baby. We're getting your brother back."

My heart jumps into my throat, and with effort, I unclench my fist enough to stop my nails from digging into my throbbing palm.

The car crawls by a large empty field, Rafael squeezes my thigh and turns off the headlights. "Okay," he says, pulling into a little entryway on the side of the field, "it's time." With a thud, he stops the car.

The silence is deafening. The hairs on my arms prickle. I look out the window at the dark, cloudy sky and, in the distance, see a single light shining.

"It's a couple minutes' walk. I'll be right behind you. You must walk alone." He grips tighter to my leg.

"I'll be fine," I whisper, adrenalin pulsing through my veins.

"I know." He puts the gun on my lap, grazes my lips, and forces a smile. His usual bright green eyes are almost black. "Go. You need to be convincing. Call him when you're walking. Tell him you've tried, but you can't fall out of love with him."

I scrunch my face and gaze into his eyes. I know when I leave the safety of Rafael's side, I'll be terrified.

"You're as beautiful as a rose. I won't ever quit on you, not for one second. Don't forget that."

A shiver runs down my back. His words whistle sweetly in my ear, and I open the door, leaving my safety behind. The night is empty. The long grass on either side blows soundlessly in the breeze. The rain that poured through the early night has gone, leaving the road I walk along muddy. It's ominous, walking alone. Not only alone but it's a night that happens to be void of noise, not even a birds cry. It's as if even the animals have abandoned the area surrounding Dale. My shoes squelch with each step, the rhythm of my heart like a drum. Benjamin—my thoughts keep my feet moving. I glance back, hoping to see Rafael's outline, but the dark night has engulfed him. It seems Rafael has taken all my courage with him. Dale. Panicking, I dispel that thought; I don't want to think of what he'll do. I'll do anything, absolutely anything, to save my brother.

I close in on the rundown farmhouse, and a small and desolate barn sits beside it. A light shines bleakly from one of the front dusty windows. The shape of a tall man moves across the netted window and out of sight. My knees jerk. I force myself to not turn around. Each step feels painful now as I urge myself down the driveway. I look back one last time, heat rushing up my chest. *What if he's left me*? I hyperventilate and take another step. *Calm, Rosa*. I look wide-eyed at the grubby brown front door.

The heat from inside my pocket rushes to the tips of my fingers as I reach for my phone and dial Dale's number. For several long rings, I wait, my anxious heels clicking.

"Rosalie," a soft voice answers.

"Dale, I'm at the farmhouse. I tried, I tried so hard to fall out of love with you." I cry real tears now.

The phone goes silent, and ten long seconds later, the front door clicks. Dale's pale face peers through a crack. "Are you alone?"

"I am," I answer quickly, not allowing a hesitant moment.

He beckons me forward and opens the door barely enough for me to fit through.

I dare not look back, not even for a second, as I head into the darkness. My body shudders with cold, though the house feels unnaturally warm.

Dale's hot hands grab my shoulders in the darkness, and he directs me down a hallway into a dim stone room. A dusty sheet-covered sofa sits on the left, and across from it is an old, large box TV set. "You're shivering, Rose." He shrugs off his jacket and wraps it around my shoulders.

Dale's sweet scent floats around me, and the memories seep from my veins. His skin is so pale, and his eyes, once so beautiful to me, are circled brown and purple. His plump red lips are swollen, a fresh cut bright against his whiteness. I feel his pain as he watches me, grinning.

Dale leads me to the sofa. "Did you mean what you said?"

I nod, and Dale's arm drapes over my shoulder. "I did. I just can't forget you—what we have, what you've given me—"

Dale's tender lips reach for mine.

I part my lips, forcing my eyes closed. My mouth struggles to move with his, my aching stomach yearning for Rafael to save me now. I wait expectantly as Dale lifts my chin and kisses along my neck, biting gently on my collarbone. I wince as his teeth move along the recently healed bite wounds from days before.

"I'm sorry for that." Dale nods towards my neck. "I got a bit carried away."

"It's okay. Let's forget the past," I say into his ear as his hands caress every part of me he can reach.

Dale removes his jacket from my shoulders and moves my jacket down my arms.

The heat on my skin spreads through to my heart. My stomach wrenches, and a bitter taste fills my mouth. I force it down and lift Dale's head from my chest. "Where's Ben?" I ask quietly, my heart ticking like a bomb.

Dale lifts his shirt over his head. "We'll talk about it after. Make-up sex is always the best."

My insides squirm. "What about my brother?"

"We'll go to him after." He leans closer, his muscles pushing through his skin.

I wildly scan the room. *Rafael, please!*

My body locks in place as Dale removes my jacket, and it falls with a thud onto the dusty wooden floor. The gun is partially visible inside the folds on my jacket. He licks his lips when he runs his finger over my recently scabbed cheek.

"I ..."

"Don't you love me?" he spits dangerously, his charm disappearing.

"I do, I do. I'm a little bit nervous." I try not to acknowledge my weapon on the floor.

He snickers and squeezes my cheek. "You're adorable, Rose." He smiles. "Lie down on the sofa."

I lean back, my arms wrapped protectively around my body.

"Im cold," I whisper, noticing Dales raised eyebrow.

Dale stands over me, his hungry eyes devouring my body. He wraps the fabric of my shirt in each hand, and with a yank, the buttons clatter to the floor, bouncing across the room in different directions.

I suck a breath in and lock my hands across my chest.

"Now," Dale says, his lips on my chest, "tell me, why did you tell me you came alone if Rafael was with you?"

I try to sit upright, but he holds me down by my shoulders, pushing me into the sofa.

"He dropped me off!" I spy the gun again.

This time, Dale notices. His manic laugh fills the room as he kicks it across the floor. I struggle, pushing my shoulders and trying to shuffle away from his ever strengthening hands.

Any colour left in my face must be gone.

"Let's play a game." He pulls some rope from his pocket. "The more you lie, the worse this will be for you." With a triumphant smile, he lets me go. I let out a small sigh of relief and try to move when his fist collides with my stomach, knocking the air clean out of me.

I curl into a tight ball, gasping for breath. My muscles contract unmercifully as acid burns up my throat and out my mouth onto the floor.

Dale grips my wrists, ties them together behind my back, and slams my head onto the sofa.

Lights flash in my eyes as my head cracks against the sofa's wooden frame. I kick out, desperately fighting the fear building in my chest.

"Now, let us try again," Dale whispers tauntingly. "Why did Rafael come?"

"I'm telling you the truth," I say through bared teeth.

"It's a shame Rafael had to be caught like this. Such a clever being. Bet you thought he could protect you." Dale's hand flexes threateningly by my face.

I shrink away from him.

His other hand holds me down, putting pressure on the middle of my chest. Before I can flinch, his hand rises fast and swings downwards, whipping across my face.

I let out a cry. My cheek sears. I can feel the swelling instantly.

"Try again."

"Where is he?" I scream.

"Good question. I'll ask." Dale reaches for my phone from the front pocket of my jeans. He searches through my phone, then holds it to his ear.

"Rose!" a relieved voice echoes down the phone.

"Wrong." Dale laughs.

"Where is she?" Rafael growls.

"With me, of course. She asked the same thing."

"Rosa, can you hear me? I'm coming, alright?"

A tear breaks free and drips down my cheeks. "Are you okay?" I shout.

Dale's eyes turn to mere slits. "You'll love what I do to her, Raffy."

"Just hold tight. I promise! Lucy, Lucy is here. She's working with Dale!"

Before I can reply, I hear a loud thud down the phone.

Dale throws my phone at the wooden floor, and the screen explodes. "Time for me to have some fun with you." A bared-tooth grin spreads across Dale's face.

"Where is Rafael?" I don't take my eyes off his.

Dale yanks my legs, and I drop to the floor with a loud smack, the back of my head bouncing on the hard floor. He stands back, his hand tugging his belt.

A pressure fills my head as my eyes become blurry, almost like a sheet of glass covers them. I reach blindly on the floor for anything that might help me protect myself.

"You do as I say, and I won't kill your brother," Dale sneers.

My heart stomps. *Benjamin.*

Dale stands over me, leans down, and exposes my chest.

I choke on the lump in the back of my throat. My spine arches as my arms struggle against the rope beneath me.

His foot crashes into my ribs, and my body flops, the pain bursting through my bones. "Now, stay still." Dale drops to his knees and pulls down his jeans.

Each breath I take sends a sharp pain through my side. I wince again.

Dale finally releases me, my body burns where his hot hands were. Any attempts I make to get up are a wasted effort, my body can't comply as I convulse silently, the pain only worsening.

I squeeze my eyes shut; wrapping my shirt around my body again, I won't cry, I won't shout. A million plans rush into my head, each as impossible as the other.

Dale grunts, "It's strange," his voice is coarse, "I find you more attractive when you're lying there scared and defenceless than I did when we first met."

I watch his face, my vision getting better. He bites his lip savagely and pierces his own skin.

He stares down at me with dark and manic eyes. His tongue flicks out and licks his lips, making them drip with saliva and blood. He grunts loudly.

His groans pierce my ears, implanting themselves into my brain. I spend what feels like an eternity begging myself to be strong.

The vile grunting stops, and Dale shuffles.

I mentally mark where the door is, trying to imagine my plan in action, he's standing again, his hands on his jeans, about to pull them up. Before I know what I'm doing, I kick out with all the force my body can conjure. Both feet hit his groin area, and my ribs shudder dangerously as I roll on the floor in agony.

Dale falls backwards, his body bending and hitting the floor.

I push myself onto my knees and stand, clutching my ribs and stomach. I stand over Dale, who writhes on the floor in pain and steady myself, cocking back my foot, I kick Dale in the side of the head. My heart breaks as I watch him jolt and become still.

I stand, staring at the man on the floor—the beautiful, evil man on the floor. In a blink I see my father, his lifeless body. My insides burst into flames and my foot kicks out once more, this time hitting him in the ribs. Without looking down, I sprint for the front door and turn my back on it, watching the room from which I just came. I clutch the doorknob with my fingers from behind. It clicks open, and I sprint for the barn. The door to get inside stands ajar; a barely noticeable flicker of light glows. My heart thunders; if I can find Ben or Rafael, maybe there's a chance. I stand for a second outside, peeking inside.

"Rafael, why didn't you just leave her alone?" a shrill voice asks.

353

"This isn't your only option, Lucy. Let me go, and I'll forget anything ever happened ..."

"You'll still love her." Lucy's voice drops an octave.

"Yes, and you'll get to live!"

Hearing Rafael agree with loving me disarms me. I completely forget the danger and stand there open-mouthed. I suppress the urge to run into the barn with my arms wide open. I need to think, to plan.

"Oh, you silly man, you just don't see how much better I am for you."

My stomach churns, her voice making me want to scream. I tug at my hands that are still tied around my back. With a deep breath, I push the door open with my knee, and both occupants of the barn face me. I see Rafael sitting on the floor, his shirt ripped and bloody. He's tied to a wooden beam, his hairline coloured red.

"Back the fuck up!" Lucy's eyes are wide and wild. She approaches me, a large silver gun in hand.

I stay still, frozen to the spot.

Rafael stares up at me, his relief clouded by a new fear.

"Put your hands up!" Lucy steps forward.

"I can't ... They're tied behind my back."

She grabs my arm and pulls me to the side, turning me around, and pushes me against the wall. I'm astonished at the amount of strength in her small frame.

"Where is Dale?" Rafael mutters.

I crane my neck to face Rafael. "In the house. He'll be out soon."

"Shut up," Lucy screeches and turns on Rafael.

"Lucy, please just let her leave." Rafael grimaces as he moves.

"I have just had an idea, Mr Alcazar," Lucy mocks. She pushes the gun into her waistline and retrieves a knife.

"You're sick," Rafael spits.

Lucy turns on her heels in almost a curtsey.

Rafael's body shakes, kicks, and struggles against the ropes.

"Rosalie, hunny," she whispers in my ear, the knife's sharpened blade against my cheek. "Come sit next to Raffy." Her hand flicks lightly.

I move too late as the knife slices through my cheek. Its searing edge burns deeply. She pushes me forward, and I watch my feet move over the stone flooring. Warm blood stains my cheek, the taste of metal permeating my lips.

Rafael struggles against his restraints, desperate for liberation.

A blow crashes into my lower back, bringing me to my knees in front of Rafael. I look at him; not a single murmur escapes my lips. Instead, I smile and bite down hard, my cries stuck behind the lump that's still trapped in my throat.

Rafael's exposed chest heaves as he thrashes harder against his restraints. "Rose," he says, barely audible. Cuts litter his chest; his skin is angry, swollen, and red.

I kneel and bow my head, tears brimming in my eyes.

Lucy's fingers entangle in my hair and drag me to the side. My back throbs where her foot had landed. "Stay still," she grunts, tying my wrists against the same beam as Rafael.

Rafael's hands are burning hot when they clasp onto my shaking fingers.

Lucy stands in front of us, a smile spreading across her childish face. "What did you do to Dale?" She stands, staring down at me.

As if her words called upon him, the barn door smashes open. Dale stands in the doorway, his shoulders squared and his face demented. "You sneaky little cow!" He stands for a moment, beholding the scene, and approaches Lucy. His lips brush hers, and he turns to observe us again.

Rafael's breath catches in his throat. His fingers tighten around mine, his whole body shifting as close to me as possible. "What do you want?"

The stable echoes as Dale's laughter projects around us. "I just want to play." He claps his hands together. With two large strides, Dale's right above us, a sadistic grin stretching across his face. "What would hurt Rosalie the most is not for her to feel pain, but for us to inflict it on Rafael." He kneels at Rafael's feet. "Good idea, by the way." He nods to the ropes tied around Rafael's legs.

Lucy giggles, tenderly rubbing Dale's back.

Rafael's eyebrow, cut and bruised, rises. "What the fuck is going on?" His fingers fiddle with the rope on my hands.

Understanding dawns on me. I realise he's trying to stall. My chest rises heavily. Each time I breathe, pain shoots from my ribs to my stomach. I assess the damage; my stomach is a deep red colour.

"Well, I was on the balcony of your home, and Lucy found me and opened the door—quite the hospitable young lady." Dale laughs as if talking to old friends.

Rafael's constant tugging against the rope has loosened it around my wrists enough that I can slip my friction-burned wrists through. My heart thuds, adrenalin speeding around my body, causing me to feel dizzy. My wrists ache when they are

357

finally free. I slowly move my stiff fingers and shift nervously, trying to get a better grasp at Rafael's rope.

"She told me all about the dirty scumbag Rafael and how he broke her heart. No girl deserves to have her heart broken." Dale frowns and eyes Lucy.

"He made it very clear …" I say, trying to keep the conversation going. My fingers move more frantically now, my nails breaking against the rough texture of the rope.

Rafael peers at me, his body shifting again, ready to break free.

I swallow back the pain and try to unravel Rafael's restraints.

"No!" Lucy's shrill voice pierces my ears. "He threw me aside the second you came into the picture."

Dale rubs Lucy's fingers. "Just like Rose did to me, so we decided we could have payback."

"But why kill her mother?" Rafael's deep voice booms.

My fingers release the last knot, and Rafael's hands fall free. He grips onto my fingers, then releases them. He pans from me to Lucy. I know who I need to aim for.

"Oh, that." Dale rolls his eyes as if her life means nothing. "I was on my way to see Rosa. She was carrying a suitcase, and I offered to help. That's when she told me where she was going. I knew she was your mother. What a better time to bond than over a tragic event?"

My mouth hangs open. "You killed her to get closer to me?" My voice shakes.

"And your father figured out that I hurt you. Your darling brother must have told him, so he cornered me—on his own, that brave old man."

My insides shudder, an ache deep inside—my father's last act of bravery. My eyes stay dry. I have no tears left to burn down my face.

Dale proffers his hand, and Lucy passes him the knife. "It's time." Dale smiles. He leans in towards Rafael, and the knife's tip punctures his bare chest.

Rafael's right fist moves in one long swift motion, smacking the side of Dale's head. The knife drops from his hand and clatters to the floor.

The adrenaline kicks in, and I snatch the knife off the floor and jump to my feet.

Chapter 28

Rafael's rock-solid fist moves quickly, hitting Dale in the gut, he drops instantly. After a couple of heavy blows to Dale's head, he stops. Rafael's whole frame shakes so much he's a blur.

Lucy's screams drown out any other sound.

Rafael's hands start fumbling against the rope on his legs, his knuckles are a bloody mess.

Lucy glares down at Rafael, taking no notice of me at all. Her hand moves fast to her waistline.

I don't even think, I'm running towards her, the knife angled away from her. I throw myself on her, the force of my jump knocking us both to the floor.

She slams to the ground beneath me, the gun flying from her hand.

"Keep her down," Rafael shouts.

I hold her arms and sit on her stomach, her eyes are wide with fury. I'm livid as I look at her pale, bony face, my temper gone, absolutely miles away. My fist cracks her nose, blood splatters across her face, spraying my chest.

She cowers under me, her hand covering her face.

"You're a fucking psycho," I scream at her. Another crack and my fist collides again with her face, and again. Her body flops as my arm recoils for one more punch.

"Stop." Rafael clasps my fist mid punch. He pans from Lucy's bloody face to me and pulls me to my feet. "That's enough."

We run, and I glance back at the bloody scene to see Dale and Lucy motionless on the floor.

Rafael pulls me along, away from the farmhouse.

"My brother," I scream as he lifts me off my feet.

"I know!" He stumbles under my thrashing weight. "He's not there."

"Put me down!"

He releases me, and his strides get longer.

I struggle to keep up, but he holds my hand so tight my fingers hurt, pulling me along behind him. The car glints in a slither of moonlight that slips through the clouds. Each part of my body burns deeply. I wail as we stop, and Rafael retrieves his keys from under the car. The lights flicker, and I grab the door and climb in. My body's vibration shakes the whole car.

Rafael gets in and flicks the locks.

The car hums to life, and within seconds, we pass the farmhouse. The barn door is wide open, exposing movement in the dull light.

Rafael doesn't slow down as he stares out his window. "They're awake." His soft voice sounds scared. One of his bloodied hands squeezes my leg.

The car pushes 80mph. The trees flit by, but not a single other car passes us; it must be getting late.

"Are you okay?" Rafael eyes me. "I'm so sorry. I was caught seconds after you disappeared."

I squeeze his hand. "Don't. We both knew the risks."

"My brother called just as you left. He has Ben." Rafael's bloody cheeks rise into a pained smile.

My heart jumps into my throat, and my muscles relax for what feels like the first time today. "Oh, Raf." I cry uncontrollably.

"He was in Dale's basement. The police found him. They should be closing in on the farmhouse any moment now." Rafael's sparkling eyes overflow with tears.

I smile at him, and my cheeks ache as they lift.

Rafael returns my smile, as beautiful as ever—even bruised and bloody.

"Where is he now?" I'm already imagining our reunion.

"He's with Adriel at the hospital. He's fine, just minor injuries. Then they'll be going into a safehouse. We can't go back tonight."

My heart sinks. "Why?"

"Adriel and Ben have explained everything to the police, but there's still the chance they won't capture Dale. We've got to stay at a hotel."

I focus on Rafael's shaking hand on my leg. "Okay."

"Try to get some sleep, beautiful. We still have about an hour to drive."

I check the time—9:30. My insides are still surging with adrenalin as I lean my head back on the headrest and close my eyes. A few seconds pass, and my eyes snap open. The car jolts to a stop. I stare out the window at the tall building we've parked in front of.

"Did you rest well?" Rafael asks, the whites of his eyes red. He stifles a yawn and exists the car, groaning in pain.

I follow his lead.

An old man in a white shirt rushes to us and scrutinises us. "Can I, er ... help you?"

"Yeah, we need a room for the night. Sorry about our attire. We've just come from filming." Rafael laughs sourly.

The man watches me hold my shirt together.

I smile. "These damn horror movies." I laugh awkwardly.

Rafael moves around the car to grab a bag from the back seat and hands the key to the man. He takes my hand, and we head towards the large revolving door.

The reception is huge. Comfy cream-coloured sofas are dotted around, and the navy-blue walls go perfectly with the white marble flooring. I barely have a chance to look around when we arrive at the desk. I stand by Rafael's side, smiling and laughing when necessary, even though each chuckle causes my stomach to tense against the stabbing pain.

"Again, I'm so sorry about our attire," Rafael says politely.

The receptionist giggles childishly. "Not a problem, Mr Alcazar. Here is your keycard. Enjoy your stay."

Rafael tugs my hand.

I follow behind him, fixated on not feeling the pain, not allowing my lips to open enough for my cries.

Rafael's hand wraps around my waist, allowing me to lean on him. The lift door opens, and we enter. Rafael slots the keycard into a scanner, and a generic female voice announces, "This lift is going to floor ten." The silent lift moves rapidly, music twinkling through the speakers. Rafael's whole body is stiff, and he looks down at me several times before the doors open, and we enter a long hallway.

Our room is the first white door we come to on the left. Again, he scans the key. The door flings open automatically. Inside is another small hallway with three open doors. The first leads to a small but well-equipped bright kitchen. I move to the second room. A large double bed sits in the middle of an open white room. A TV, double the size of mine, is at the end of the bed. I ignore the third room and head for the bedroom. Another door is open at the side of the bedroom. A huge circular bath is in my view. The bathroom's wall consists of only mirrors.

"Nicer than the last one." Rafael speaks for the first time.

I startle and face him.

He's dropped the backpack and is shrugging his arms through his torn shirt. He passes me and turns on the bath.

My body feels as if it will collapse.

He kicks off his shoes and drops down his jeans. He reaches behind a pane of glass and turns on the shower.

I stare at his pale chest, almost completely covered with reddening bruises and cuts. His scar is barely visible under the black and blue.

He steps into the shower, his face scrunching as the water hits his skin. "Come on, Rose. Let's get clean and relax for an hour before we assess the damage."

I nod, catching sight of myself in the mirror. I look wild; my shirt hangs open, my stomach red and blotching blue. My ribs are a dark shade of purple. The bruising on my cheek spreads to my jaw. I extend my hands and notice every knuckle on my right hand is grazed and raw. I cringe away from the sounds of my attack on Lucy, which replays in my head.

I see Rafael from the corner of my eye move from the shower and into the steaming circular bathtub. He drops his underwear as he lowers his battered body into the water.

I sigh deeply, regretting it straight away as my insides threaten to explode. I drop my jeans to the floor and approach the shower. My shirt comes off last, but I keep my underwear on. I can feel Rafael's eyes on my back, but I won't look at him, I can't look at him. I slide into the shower, and my body sears and stings. The fire of the water licks my shaking body. I moan as the water runs down my ribs. I stay facing the wall and stare at the floor, watching the blood wash from my hands and face.

When the water finally runs clear, I turn off the tap. With another sigh, I step out of the shower. My soaking body is freezing cold.

Rafael's arms are outspread as he leans on the back of the bath. The hot water still runs into the bath near his feet. The transparent water ripples like tiny waves on a miniature ocean. A small smile lifts one of his cheeks, he winces then turns his face to the side, leaning his head onto his arm to show he's not looking.

I remove my undies, drop them on the floor, and step into the bath.

Rafael glances my way, watching me move onto my knees.

I kneel and lower myself as slowly as possible into the tub as the hot water sends a convulsion deep into my stomach. I sit opposite Rafael in the giant bath. He doesn't smile now; I can feel his angry green eyes exploring my injuries.

Rafael leans forward to turn off the tap and sits back. "Rosalie, come here," he whispers.

I move slowly, not wanting to show how sore I really am, and sit right next to Rafael. Even under the hot water, his skin is cold against my leg. The moment is serene, it is perfect in its own imperfection. To celebrate Dale's final downfall and my brother being safe? To mourn the murder of my parents? I can't decide, though I know deep down inside the decision is made, that my brother being safe is a huge relief, that the guilt and mourning will kick in sooner rather than later and that I'm going to grip onto this moment of happiness and not let it go too soon.

He hesitantly moves his hand to my face and runs an arctic trail down my neck, over my chest, and stops just above my stomach.

My stomach threatens to burst with the butterflies that are finally free from the flames of pain.

"How bad does it feel?" His hand runs up my chest.

"It doesn't hurt anywhere near as bad as you look."

"Relax, amor." His hands move to my shoulders and massage carefully. "I'm a fast healer." He points to his chest, and I stare open-mouthed at the cuts on his chest that seem days old, not mere hours.

I shrug out of his arms and turn back to face him. "Rafael." I run my fingers over his chest, along his ragged scar.

He takes a shaking breath. "Rose." He exhales, and his fingers move into the water and tickle over my thigh.

"I was so scared for you." I mutter.

Rafael's fingers freeze on my leg.

"When we're not together, I simply ache." I continue.

His fingers move steadily again. "Rose, I too ache. I've never felt fear like this before tonight, the fear of losing you."

Both of Rafael's hands run up the sides of my thighs, sending the flurries of butterflies into hysterics in my lower stomach. I lean forward, letting his lips caress mine. My ribs ache as I lean closer to him. His lips flow down my neck, and my fingers tangle in his wet curls.

"How're your ribs feeling?" His lips linger on my chest.

I move my hands down his hard stomach. "Fine," I lie. I let his hands explore my body, each soft touch leaving me breathless.

"Close your eyes," he murmurs.

I comply and lean against the cold tub.

His lips press against my collarbone, his kisses are careful to not touch the areas that are sore.

My hands move blindly down his hard abdomen. The water moves steadily around my body as he lifts me very slowly onto his lap. For the first time, I can feel all of him. Every last inch of him is against me. My body burns with anticipation.

"Rosa." His cold fingers stop against my neck.

"Mhmm ...?" I answer, too immersed in his touch. I open my eyes at Rafael's stillness.

His green diamonds search my face. He bites his lip, and his cheeks rise. "I've wanted this since the second I saw you," he almost sings to me.

I move my hands over his back.

Rafael's body jolts. He grimaces and forces a smile. "Sorry." he sighs, bowing his head.

"No, you're in pain because of me. I'm sorry." I lift his chin. "Without you—"

His finger touches my lips. "Don't," he says through bared teeth. "I couldn't even protect you."

A tear forms in Rafael's eye, causing my heart to splinter with a brand-new ache. I hold his face between my angry, throbbing hands. "I'm alive because of you."

The water that encloses our bodies is as still as the moment should be. He wraps his arms around my sore, bruised frame. Our chests press against one another, our heartbeats in a race.

My tears blind me as I wipe away his with my thumb. I smile and lift his chin, allowing our lips to dance effortlessly, naturally the perfect fit. I take his hand and stand.

His eyebrows crease. "What's wrong?" He follows my lead and steps out of the bath, water dripping from his body.

I face him and see goosebumps covering his chest. "Shh." I close in on him. My body entwines in his.

His lips caress mine, and the taste of his tongue makes my mouth water. "Rose, you're hurt," he whispers, his forehead creased.

I sit him back on the bed and search his body, my insides desperately hungry for him.

His muscles push through his beautiful olive-coloured skin. The lines on his stomach, though covered in cuts, contract. I allow myself these few seconds to take in his godlike features. "We'll worry about that later." I climb delicately on top of him.

His lips turn up at one end, a beautiful half-smile. He scans my body, very unsure about what he'll do, and he bites his lip. His fingers trace my hip and down my leg, creating a line of electricity to my thigh.

I lean into him, unable to control my lips—an insatiable thirst for Rafael's love. His heavy breathing is music to my ears, each soft sigh a melody made for me.

He flips me onto the bed, and pain shoots across my back. His muscles dance in the moonlight that shines through the blinds. His wet skin rubs against mine, and our tongues entangle. "I've waited so long for this," Rafael mutters in my ear. His hips move as he lifts my legs, his perfectly controlled movements, just enough to hold me on the edge. "I didn't know when I met you that it was you I've been searching for my whole life." His words make me tingle.

His overpowering body disobeys his adoring mind, and those slow and careful movements become harder, faster. The muscles in Rafael's stomach are bursting through his skin, my fingernails grasp onto his forearm with one hand, the other slides up his shining chest. He's careful not to let his hands touch any part of me that's red or aching. I can feel my ribs burning, my moans of pain hidden by those of pleasure, its a pain I welcome with open arms. A final moment of heaven, complete ecstasy, as the room itself seems to explode with us. Rafael rolls off me, Both of our breathing is fast and heavy, and an electrical buzz, that still tingles internally, fogs my brain.

I struggle to catch my breath; my ribs burning each time my chest rises.

Pain etches across Rafael's face as he takes a deep breath and sits upright. "Definitely worth it." He grins and clutches his stomach. "Now, can I please look at your ribs?"

"Wait, please." I pull him back and wrap my arms around him.

We lie silently. Rafael's fingers trail along my arm. His chest moves slowly, and his muscles relax. His cold hand moves over my ribs, the cold somehow takes some of the pain away. I recount the day, my heart aching, things begin to sink in. I glance to the side and notice Rafael deep in thought. We lie there together for hours not talking nor sleeping, just staring at the plain white ceiling.

Rafael startles me when suddenly he sits upright, saying something about it being 3:00 a.m. He stands, still unclothed, and grabs the backpack off the floor and sits on the end of the bed.

I swallow hard when I see his body

He grins at me and removes some jeans and a t-shirt for himself from the bag, then hurries himself into the jeans and throws the t-shirt onto the bedside table.

I close my eyes and lie silently as Rafael leans over me.

He reaches for my ribs, and the muscles around my stomach spasm before he even touches me. His fingers graze my ribs, I scrunch up my face and choke back a cry. "I think it's just badly bruised." He says, his emerald eyes penetrate mine as if he's seeing inside me.

"Yeah." I sigh. "I'm fine."

"Do you want us to visit the hospital?"

I chortle and sit upright, holding a pillow against my body. "Don't be silly."

Rafael retrieves a pair of my jeans and a loose grey t-shirt from the bag. "Here."

I put the t-shirt over my head and stumble into my jeans. "I can't tell whether I need to sleep or eat." I laugh.

"Yeah, let's order room service, then get some rest. We'll have a really busy day tomorrow." Rafael grabs a booklet from the table and picks up the phone. "Hi, yeah, we want to order some food. The continental platter and the sandwich platter, please. Okay, cheers." Rafael puts down the phone and surveys the room, a beautiful smile across his face. "I'm so happy you're safe now." He wraps an arm around me.

I hug him tight. "Thank you, Rafael. You saved me, and you saved my brother." My smile hurts my cheeks.

"Let's wait in the front room."

I follow him into the front room. A large, comfy beige sofa is spread across the back wall. Against the wall opposite is a large TV. There's another kitchenette with a fridge and a sink, some cupboards, and a small circular table. A fireplace is in the far corner.

Rafael heads towards it and bends down. "It's fake." I can almost hear his eyes roll. "Still nice for effect though." He moves away, and the fire glows orange.

I walk towards it, the heat coming from it luring me closer. I shiver; although it's not cold, next to this fire, I feel frozen. I sit on the end of the sofa closest to the fire and wrap my arms around myself.

Rafael flicks on the TV and sits next to me. Even his cool skin feels hot around my shivering body. "Food will be here in a moment. I'm going to call Adriel. See how they are both doing." Rafael reaches for the hotel phone on the mantle above the fireplace.

"Can I speak to Ben?" I ask, suddenly desperate to hear his voice.

"Of course." Rafael holds the phone against his ear.

It rings loudly twice before Adriel's voice sounds down the phone. "Raf," he says breathlessly.

Rafael stands straight away, wincing as he straightens up. "What's going on?"

"We were on ..." Adriel groans. "We were going to the safehouse. It was a few miles out of town, when a van crashed into the police car we were in."

"Where's Ben?" I shout, my hands vibrating.

"Rosa, I'm okay. Just stay safe. Just stay where you are," Benjamin's soft, low voice chimes.

Rafael's arm wraps around me. "Where are you?"

"We were about five miles out of town, going south. I've not a clue where we are. We've walked into the woods."

Rafael jogs to the bedroom.

I run up behind him. "Where is the cop?"

"Dead," Adriel's voice quivers. "And the van just drove off."

The few seconds of silence is deafening. Rafael slips a white t-shirt over his head, covering his wounded and bruised body. "Stay where you are. I'm coming." Rafael sits on the end of the bed.

"Wait!" Ben's voice calls. "Leave Rosalie somewhere safe."

I stare at Rafael with a pounding heart. Nausea rolls over me like a tidal wave, and I furrow my eyebrows.

A loud knock at the door startles both of us, and Rafael marches across the room and enters the hallway. Seconds later, he brings in a tray of food.

The smell makes me heave. I run to the bathroom and bend over the toilet, urging myself to not vomit.

Rafael's behind me in seconds. He rubs my back. "I don't know what's happening, Rose, but your brother has asked that I keep you safe,"

"No, I'm coming." I heave again and drop to my knees. A shooting sensation runs from my ribs and into my back with each retch.

"Rose, look at you."

I stand and stomp my feet childishly. "Do you think Dale is involved?"

"I'm certain, and that's why you must stay—"

"*No!*" I stomp again. "You can't leave me."

Rafael turns his back on me. "Rose, baby, please just listen to me for once."

"How about you listen to me? I'm coming." I straighten my t-shirt and shove past Rafael towards the front door. I wait expectantly for Rafael to follow and count to ten before I turn around.

He stands at the end of the hallway, a broken angel. His shoulders slump, and his messy dark curls cover his face.

I don't know how to react; I watch him carefully. "Raf..." I take several slow steps. "Rafael, c'mon." I put a trembling hand on his forearm.

His fist balls up so his knuckles turn white. "Fine." He shrugs my hand off his arm. "Let's go."

CHAPTER 29

"Rafael!" I run after him, out of the hotel room and into the lift.

"Rosa, I wish you'd just stay here."

"This is my fault—!"

He shushes me, his frowning bright eyes softening. "I can't protect my brother nor your brother as well as I can if you're with me. If something were to happen, if I'm occupied with protecting you ..."

"You don't have to protect me."

He glares at me; the small gap between us feels like miles. His chest heaves with each breath. His damaged hands move to his stubbled chin.

I take a timid step forward. My heart thumps as I reach for his wrists to pull his arms down, and my finger runs along his inner forearm. I touch his chin with my other hand. "*'For he will command his angels concerning you to guard you in all your ways.'*"

His fingers run down his arm and onto my hand. "Thank you, Rose."

The lift jolts as it reaches the bottom. Rafael takes my hand, and in silence, we move through the entrance of the hotel. Rafael drops my hand and walks as slowly as his feet allow, alone to the front desk, where a weary and tired young woman stands. Rafael's words are a very quiet mutter. He glances around, his eyes falling on me, face looks calm and collected but his legs are ridged. My hand hovers above the bright sofa, my foot taps anxiously waiting for Rafael to beckon me to him. For our journey to save both of our brothers.

Her cheeks flush, and I roll my eyes impatiently when her gaze lingers on his lips for too long. She reaches for a box, Rafael turns to me again, his eyes looking more strained with every second that passes. Finally she makes a high squeak and leans forward, dropping some keys into his palm.

He thanks her as he turns his back on her and nods at me to head towards the exit. I don't look at him as we reach the exit, I don't want him to see the sheer panic in my eyes, or the sheet of sweat that's suddenly coating my forehead. The deep-blue everlasting sky boasts a few bright stars. A song from a bird echoes through the cool air, undisturbed by the distant car engines, with people commuting to work. Rafael grabs my hand as we jog past the hotel and around the back. Now that we are out of sight of the hotel staff, Rafael sprints down a row of cars.

I chase after him and almost run into him when he halts.

He holds out his car key. The lights glow another ten cars down, and Rafael's hand tightens around mine. We move towards the flashing headlights. He opens my door first, allowing me to get in, and slams it behind me. An endless few seconds pass, and he's by my side. The engine hums. Rafael shakes his head to move his hair from his eyes and glances at the mirrors.

My heart thrums as I squash the thought of what's next. "Raf," I say quietly, my fingers running along the doorhandle.

"Mhmm?"

"My brother and Adriel will be okay," I state rather than ask.

The car glides on the road. The headlights shine onto the emptiness ahead. Every now and again, bright headlights zoom past.

"They will be fine." Rafael squeezes my leg as we speed down the motorway.

I stare at the reddening sky as the sunrise sends a shimmering light across the empty fields. I contemplate the future, wondering what my brother is doing now.

"We're getting close," Rafael says, snapping me from my silence.

I stare ahead. "What's the plan?"

"Get Adriel and Ben, and drive." He smiles weakly.

My fists clench on my knee. "How do you know how to find them?"

"I don't." I can feel his gaze on my face. "I'll call them once we're near the area."

"And then what?" I look at him.

"And then we hope for the best," he says, his voice low and cold. His hands tighten on the steering wheel, his knuckles whitening. "I'm actually nervous." His words barely escape his lips.

My eyes burn with tears. My hand grips his forearm as a small tear trickles down his reddening cheek. "Don't be." I whisper.

"If I can't protect you, the one woman to ever hold my beating heart in the palm of her hand, then I don't deserve to live."

A knot forms in the back of my dry throat, choking me. My grip on his arm tightens, my hands tremble violently and the car slows.

Rafael eases the car onto a muddy area. "Don't," he whispers, wiping a tear from my cheek. He caresses my neck and my back as he pulls me closer to his chest. His heart thrums in my ear and his body vibrates against mine. After a much too short moment, he releases me, leaving me to feel cold and empty. "Rosalie, always stay by my side. You must do as I say."

I nod slowly and concentrate on my trembling knees.

His warm lips press against my head, leaving a tingling sensation. The car moves, slower now, as we enter a wooded country road.

I close my eyes and take a deep breath. A canopy of old and twisting trees partially blocks the sky. The pale grey morning swiftly turns to what seems to be dusk. Barely any light leaks through the thick and green earth-made ceiling.

"Call Adriel," Rafael orders.

I hold the phone, pulling up the most recent call, and dial. I focus out the window for any signs of my brother.

His answer is almost immediate. "Raf ..." Adriel pants.

Rafael's head snaps in my direction, and the car jerks to a stop. "Where are you?"

"We've got to leave the trees." His voice is barely understandable, his accent thick.

"What's going on?" Rafael accelerates the car.

"He's here. Just take Rose and run."

"No," I shout. "Get onto the road. We're looking for you now."

Rafael turns off the headlights, and we glide down the winding road.

My wide eyes scan every inch of space ahead. My heart sends a shock through my body each time the wind blows through the trees. For each bird that swoops low across the road ahead, my stomach somersaults. My body is flushing; although the car isn't warm, my skin is slick with sweat.

"We're almost on the road," Adriel says.

Seconds pass, the outline of two people emerge from the trees ahead. Adriel sighs in relief over the phone. Rafael speeds off and skids to a standstill at their side. Their faces are pale in the dark. The door squeaks quietly as if it wants us to be found, when it opens, and they climb into the back seat.

"Drive!" Benjamin urges.

Rafael smashes his foot down on the accelerator, and we speed past the walls of trees. His large, scarred hands shake on the steering wheel. "What happened?" He says, his voice uneven.

I glance behind me at Benjamin's bruised and ashen face, then to Adriel's bloody forehead. My stomach growls.

"After the car slammed into us, we moved straight for the trees," Adriel starts.

"Only it was like that was what he wanted," Ben finishes shakily.

I reach back and take Ben's hand. "I'm so sorry." I cry.

He squeezes my hand and takes a deep breath. "Before we know it, there are gunshots. We ran, and we just kept running."

Rafael shakes his head. "He let you go?"

"I know he knew where we were. I'm sure he watched us get in the car," Adriel says.

"I don't doubt that," I say, my thoughts swirling.

"This game is not over," Rafael whispers.

Rafael focuses on the mirror. We accelerate and skid around a bend, propelling us forward. Everyone's heads slam into the headrests.

Ben and Adriel turn back and look out the window.

A black car is close behind us. Its engine is loud, and its lights are blinding. The black car speeds up, and Rafael's car shudders as it takes its first hit.

I grab my belt and hold it against my neck, as if that'll help protect me.

Our bodies jolt, and the seatbelts lock. Shouting and hurried conversations fill the interior of the car. I can't understand a word of it as my brain fills with possible outcomes. Ahead is a fork in the road.

I hear the bang before the impact shoves my body to the side. Rafael's car fishtails, and the split in the road approaches too fast to discuss what's next. Momentum forces the car to take the right.

The black car pushes us farther and faster down a muddy and thin country lane, the potholes bouncing us like ragdolls.

My stomach turns. "Rafael!" I grab onto his arm.

He shrugs me off and yanks my seatbelt, tightening it even more across my chest and shoulder.

The pain from my previous injuries makes me squirm against the restraints. I watch in horror at Rafael, whose face is now a weird shade of green.

"It's him." My brother states the obvious, his shout sounds like a whisper over the jolting of the car.

The car behind us revs loudly and smashes into us once again. I hold my head against the headrest; my insides turn and body trembles. I blink wildly as another crash shatters the back window spraying glass all over the interior. I stare ahead in horror, we're barrelling toward an open farm gate which enters onto a large wet field and a small barn.

Rafael accelerates, and the car screeches as it skids onto the grass area. Another deafening thud, the black car hits the side tail end our ours. We're moving too fast and I grip my chair as the car veers and the breaks scream. The car flips onto its side—the passenger side, my side. A loud bang sounds, my shoulder slams into the window, it shatters, sending a crack through the empty field. The cars momentum slows but still it flips again, hanging us upside down for a millisecond.

Without stopping, the car falls onto Rafael's side. He slams into the side of the door. His seatbelt buckles under his weight, and the car shudders and falls onto its wheels, jerking my head to its side. White smoke seeps through the smashed windows. No-one makes a sound.

"Rose," Rafael's voice sounds in the silence.

My ears ring loudly and eyes blurry up, I see my brother moving and sigh in relief. My entire body is tense, my hands still tight around my seatbelt. I whip my head to Rafael, sending an intense shooting pain to my shoulder. "Raf," I whimper.

Someone behind me unclips their seatbelts. "He's gone," Adriel shouts, and a door flings open.

"Rose." Ben squeezes his body between the two front seats. "Are you all right?"

I groan and nod carefully, sending another shock down my neck.

"Try not to move," Adriel says as he opens the door and leans over me, unclipping my belt.

Rafael opens his door and gets out. He falls as he leaves the car.

Benjamin scrambles from the car and rushes to Rafael's aid. "You okay?"

I try to move, but Adriel puts pressure on my shoulders to keep me still.

"Don't move," he whispers, not looking concerned about Rafael at all.

Rafael stays on his knees and groans something to Ben.

"No, man. No way," Ben says, stepping backwards.

"Just do it," Rafael shouts.

"I can't," Ben says louder now.

"Fucking do it!"

Ben shouts as he runs at Rafael and slams him backwards into the car.

I shout a string of swearwords and struggle against Adriel's grip. "Let me go!"

Rafael grunts as Ben helps him up off the floor.

"His arm was dislocated," Adriel mutters. His hands still pushes down on my shoulder even though I make no effort to move now. Waves of heat project from Adriel's vibrating and bloody hand.

I close my eyes, and the world spins like a fairground ride. I choke back the vomit that rises in my chest, then open my eyes again.

Rafael leans over me now, his hand hovering near my neck.

"She's all right, just a bit shaken," Adriel says diplomatically and walks around the car.

Rafael side eyes Adriel with furrowed eyebrows.

"I'll keep my eye out for any sign of Dale," Ben says quietly.

Rafael nods in agreement as his fingers make gentle contact with my lower neck. "Does it hurt?" His green eyes widen.

I shake my head, ignoring the shooting sensation. "It's fine. Let me out of the car."

"I want you to stay in here and lay low. We're going to find Dale." Rafael ends his statement with a furious hiss.

"You're having a laugh " I stare at him incredulously.

"Get her out of the fucking car." Benjamin's voice pierces the quiet.

Rafael faces Benjamin, whose hand is gripping my wrist.

"He's coming." Benjamin's voice breaks. Tugging frantically at my arm, Benjamin shoves past Rafael. His hands slide under my arms, and he lifts me slowly from the car. "Come on, Rose. You've gotta move faster."

The whole world freezes. The car I spot in the distance moves at a snail's pace. I can't hear a thing, as if I'm trapped in my own mind.

Benjamin's reddened eyes are fearful when he tries to tug me along.

I spy Rafael, who's staring in disbelief at the car ahead, which is moving faster now. I try to take a step, but my legs won't carry me. My knees give way, and I tumble.

Benjamin grabs me from behind and holds me up, trying to drag me along. He lifts my weight for a few steps, then stops, clutching his ribs. "I can't, Rose. I can't!"

"Rosa!" Rafael's arm crushes me to his side and lifts most of my weight. "You need to run."

The world snaps back, reality hitting me like a truck.

Ben pushes me forward.

Adriel sprints ahead, leading the way to a derelict brown barn.

I move as fast as I can, listening for the growling, approaching engine.

Rafael lowers me so I have to bare my own full weight. He holds my hand in a viselike grip and pulls me forward, my feet tangle time after time, and I wobble against the speed.

Benjamin is barely a meter behind us, I glance back daringly to see the car isn't far behind. I feel a scream building inside me, another adrenaline rush pumps through, pushing me to run faster. Benjamin speeds up until he's running alongside me.

Adriel doesn't slow as he approaches the barn. He pushes his shoulder forward and aims for the door. With a crack, he bursts through the door and disappears inside.

Rafael follows him, yanking my arm over the threshold. He halts, and I slam into his chest.

I struggle to catch my breath. My heart feels as if it's grown in size and is blocking my airway.

The door crashes shut behind Benjamin, shaking the unsteady wooden walls around us. The inside is pitch black. I can barely see Rafael in front of me. The small broken-down barn echoes with our deep breathing. Clouded light filters through the broken glass of the dust-covered windows.

I stop breathing, listening hard for any sign of movement from outside. It sounds empty. I can't hear the angry purring of the car engine which chased us here.

Rafael's hand curls around my waist.

I wince as his nails dig into my skin.

"Sorry," he says with a heavy breath and guides me into his arms.

The band of muscles around his upper arms flexes, his grip tightening.

I grab his forearms, readying myself for the unknown.

Both Ben and Adriel stand just ahead of us, a human shield formed to protect me.

My lower lip trembles, each fibre of my being filled with sadness at the sacrifice in front of me.

Adriel faces us, his thin fingers outstretched and pointing towards the corner of the room. His lips move in the darkness. "Staircase," he lets slip a tiny whisper through his lips.

Rafael releases me. His hand rests on my shoulder as he leans forward, whispering to Adriel.

Ben looks back at me, his piercing blue eyes panic-stricken.

My sight improves as I adjust to the lightless stable. Hay litters the barn's stone floor, and a dust mote floats through the broken window. It curves and twists in the mangled light.

Benjamin reaches out. *We'll be okay*, he mouths.

Rafael's lips touch my hair, his breath blows softly into my ear. His words come fast. "There's a stairway straight ahead. If Dale drives the car into this barn, we could all die. We need to take cover."

"What if this is his plan?" My voice quivers.

Rafael's arm wraps gently around my shoulder. "We've got no other choice. As soon as we're down there, Adriel will contact some friends to help us." His cold, sweaty hand pinches my cheek and takes hold of my trembling arm.

Benjamin moves quietly behind us.

Adriel starts forward. His footsteps are impossibly silent on the hay-strewn floor.

Rafael moves silently too, as if weightless, his breathing loud and uneven.

The hay rustles with each shaky step I take. I hear Ben behind me but don't dare look back, for fear of tripping.

"I'm right behind you," Ben whispers, noticing my hesitancy.

Adriel descends a long and narrow staircase.

The cold, rough brick wall brushes my arm as we move down the steep stone steps.

"C'mon," Rafael mutters, urging me to move faster.

As the steps deepen under the barn, the darkness intensifies. My eyes struggle to adjust; even the step below me is impossible to see. How Adriel is leading the way down, I don't know. I reach for the wall so I can guide my own way. I feel the sharp bend as the staircase twists awkwardly.

Rafael stops ahead of me, his hand like a brick against my stomach.

My heart hammers in my ears as I struggle to hear Adriel say, "It's deeper than I thought."

Rafael shrugs. "Yeah, well, what's our other option?"

We move again, and my upper back sends shots of fire into my neck with each step. I plead with myself to be brave. My words echo around my head into the eerie silence. A minute of silent stepping continues. *If this is a trap ...*

"We're here," Adriel says a bit louder now.

I test the floor nervously, ensuring I won't fall down any steps, before I struggle from Rafael's grasp. The blackness of the barn is nothing compared to down here. Not a single shred of light exists. I can't even tell if my eyes are open. Silence fills the dark void, I gasp as a burst of light blinds me. I squint to see where it's coming from, stumbling backwards.

Both Rafael and Ben grab my arms to hold me upright, like a ragdoll.

I blink a few times when Adriel comes into focus, holding his phone as a torch. "I should have thought about my phone for a torch on the stairs." He chortles.

We're standing in what looks like a huge basement. Its walls tower above us, the ceiling not visible in the light of the torch.

"Stand closer to Ben." Rafael's deep voice startles me.

I shuffle towards Ben as Rafael retrieves his phone from his pocket. The second torch lights the room much better; the ceiling is visible many meters above. The room is massive and almost empty except for a few large cupboards to the back of the room. A dirty mattress leans against the wall next to an oddly placed rusty bathtub.

Rafael wanders towards the end of the room with the bathtub. "No phone connection." He sighs.

"Maybe Dale doesn't know about this basement," Adriel thinks out loud.

"Let's move to this corner of the room," Rafael says as he nears the tub.

Ben puts his hand on my shoulder. "We'll be okay." He leads the way through the freezing cold basement.

Rafael jumps and backs away from the corner. "Wait."

Adriel hands me his phone and jogs towards Rafael. "What?"

"Huh," Ben says and starts to walk.

I grab his arm and pull him back to me. "Don't," I moan. I shine the light from the phone in the direction of the bathtub. The light shakes with my hand, the cold making it even harder to stay still. My fingers are stiff.

Rafael and Adriel quietly mumble to one another, and Adriel approaches the tub and leans over it, looks and nods with a frown. They both turn their backs on us with their heads to-gether.

I narrow my eyes, as if that will help me hear their hushed conversation.

"Rose, doll. Come here," Rafael says slowly.

My heart quivers as the hairs on my arms stand on end. Nothing in Rafael's tone tells me to be concerned, but as Ben leads the way, my stomach somersaults. I swallow the lump in my throat. "What is it?"

"We just want to see if you know what these are," Adriel says casually.

As I get closer to the browning tub, I see some green and red rags. Confusion furrows my brow when I realise they are clothes. I step closer again, and a strange smell emits from the tub. I crinkle my nose as it burns a path down my throat, and I stand alongside Rafael. "Clothes?" I hold my breath when I lean over the tub to see a couple pairs of red knickers and a khaki green vest. My eyes narrow into the vivid black R sown into the corner of the vest, just how my mother would sow my name into my vests, because I spent most of college losing them. I choke back my shock, the sound echoing off the walls. "They ..."

"That vest looks like yours," Ben says quickly.

Rafael's head snaps in my direction. "What about the underwear?"

I nod, heat rising up my neck and across my cheeks.

"The break-in," Rafael says, looking down at me.

A thunderclap crashes in my ears as the realisation that Dale knows exactly where we are hits me as hard as a tank.

Rafael pulls me close to his body, his arm across my chest. "He knows we're down here."

I search frantically for a way out, a way to be safe. I grab Rafael, urging him to follow me, but he doesn't move.

He's studying the walls and approaches the mattress. He runs a finger along the rough, stone wall.

"We need to get out," Ben says, coming to stand across from Rafael.

Adriel walks towards the stairwell. "He may already be here, just listening to us." He nods towards the stairs.

I force a deep breath. The taste of the stale, old basement lingers on my tongue as I stare at the dark opening of the staircase. Flashing images of Dale and his manic smile envelope my mind. "We have only one option," I squeak.

"What's that?" Ben asks.

"To fight," I say as quietly as possible; my whisper echoes around the basement.

Rafael nods in acknowledgement but puts his finger to his lips, silencing us all. He kisses my lips in a way I've never felt before—almost desperately. He holds my face between his battered hands, then regards me as if he'll never see me again. The longing in his eyes causes an ache so deep inside my chest. My lips tremble as he walks away, leaving me feeling cold, he heads toward the mattress. He kicks the dirty, old mattress against the wall. A dust cloud erupts from its yellowing material, and it trembles, then slides down the wall.

I stand in shock, all of us staring open-mouthed at the gaping hole in the wall. I choke on the dust cloud as it spreads through the basement. A shadow lingers a few steps inside, my heart stops and knees strain to hold me up against their shake. It's him.

CHAPTER 30

"Don't!" Rafael's voice barely registers with my stunned brain.

My legs have already carried me to the foot of the stairs. I can't stop as I take two steps at a time, until an ear-splitting pop reverberates off the high ceilings. My leg gives up, no longer wanting to move. The sound around me—voices—gets louder. Although I can't understand what they are saying, they seem to change pitch. They are shouting.

I fall heavily backwards. Each stone step hits me harder than the previous. I feel the icy stones beneath me, but there is no pain or fear; my body is unconcerned with what's happening. Although in my head I scream, I'm screaming because all control I thought I had of my emotions or my limbs seem to have left.

What limbs? a small part of my brain asks.

"My legs," I say to myself.

You can't feel them because we don't need your legs anymore.

I try to look around, but all I see is darkness. I try again, despairingly searching for a source of comfort.

A strange person ahead of me approaches, moving faster with each step.

My mouth hangs open. I recognise the curious stranger standing less than two feet from me. "You look like me," I say to the mysterious woman.

Her blond hair sways from side to side as she shakes her head. *I don't look like you. I am you.*

I can't feel the usual sensation of confusion I'd usually get, the feeling of my eyebrows furrowing or my lips pouting. I can't even feel my lips as they speak. "Impossible."

My own laugh rings in my ears. *I'm the part of you that doesn't want to die.*

The words should send a huge shiver down my spine, if I could feel it, though I can only muster an "Mhmm ... What's happening to me?"

We're dying. So you've got to wake up.

I'd cry if I could. "How?" My voice is a squeak.

From the darkness, a high-pitch noise increases, until I feel pain in my ears. I welcome the pain, I can feel my ears, they are there. But where? I just know they exist. A ball of light illuminates the dark surroundings. My eyes burn as the light gets closer, brighter. It seers my dry eyes, until a tear finally falls. I'm not shocked to feel my eyes, I squeeze them shut, trying to find my lips when a sudden and overwhelming urge to cry takes ahold of me. The tears don't stop, and my sobs get louder.

Other me rolls her eyes. *Alright, calm down! It's time.*

I try to lift my heavy arms, the weight of them impossible to carry when I can't even find my limbs. "Time?"

The fiery light dwindles, giving me time to peek at what's ahead. The thick outline of massive dark wings move smoothly a few meters in front of me. I lean, reaching for the creature with the wings, my balance fails me as I wobble and fall forwards, landing on something hard. It sends a shooting sensation up where my legs should be. I look down, finally about to see my newly discovered knees. The desire to touch is almost torture as I reach in front of me again. I squint to get a better view. The white fire that circles the creature is still too bright to see clearly.

The wings move slowly now. Each black feather is as long as my arm, with hundreds of those comprising the four-metre span that stretches across the emptiness that surrounds me. Several white feathers stick out wildly, as if injured. "Come," a deep voice—a voice I'm sure I know—says.

I struggle against myself, my body moving as the creature demands. My heart aches with overwhelming gladness. I can't understand my emotions. I wait for fear, but I'm left only to fear the creature leaving me.

I try to think through the haze of real life, to search for this voice I know so well. I inch through the dark, the light emitting from the winged thing guiding me. I speed up, the heat from the fire burning my bare arms. Dark bouncy curls cover the creature's head. I watch in awe as the creature dances through the empty.

"Keep up," the voice comes again, sounding almost exasperated.

I break into a jog. "What are you?"

Its stride breaks, and the creature halts. "You know what I am."

We're both still now. "Turn around," I beg breathlessly.

The creature's broad back shrugs. His sigh echoes around me. He turns slowly, his head to the floor. The most beautiful creature I've ever seen regards me through long eyelashes. The burning flames distort his face, but still, it's more beautiful than anything I've ever seen—a man with wings. "I'm not beautiful." He says, looking at his wings with disgust.

I gasp for breath when I try to answer to figure out how he knows what I am thinking. "H-h-how?"

"Rosalie, you've got to wake up now. I can't keep you moving forever, and the second you come to rest, I won't be able to help you anymore." His voice cracks. The fire that surrounds the man is barely a glow now. His beautiful face looks hurt and empty. He takes a large step toward me and rests a careful hand upon my chest. "Feel your heart." He grabs my shaking hand and places it next to his. The heat from his hand burns as I wait for the thudding of my heart. "See, Rosalie. Your heart's no longer beating, and you need to fight. You need to want to live."

"But how?" I retort, desperate to end this beautiful man's pain.

"Remember me, and you will. Remember Benjamin and Adriel. Remember life." His voice is barely a whisper. He grins, and two large dimples appear on his cheeks.

My breath catches, and my legs quiver as he steps towards me. The fire burns my body as he leans in and sighs. And as his warm lips touch mine, it's as if this is all I've ever needed, all I ever wanted, and all I'll ever want. My brain hurts. I see the winged man's face and watch my thoughts as he lies back in a bed, his arms open wide. Another memory—a steam-filled bathroom and water spraying his burly back. I gasp for air as I feel a thump, and my stomach tingles with delight. His lips linger for another second before another thump startles me. Deep in my chest, a loud rhythmless thump pounds away.

The winged man's cheeks curve into a bewitching smile.

I close my eyes to listen to the loud thud of my newfound heartbeat.

"*Rosa*!" A shout startles me.

I open my eyes; my whole body feels like it's screaming at me. I struggle to see through tears, the blur easing slowly.

"Stay back!" I hear a familiar voice shout. "Adriel, you need to wake her up."

I try to move, but my arms don't cooperate. "Help!"

"Don't move." Adriel's soft voice is right by my ear, and his face is pale and ashen

"What's happening?" I whisper.

"It's time for you to die, Rafael," Dale sings maliciously.

My memories flood back, filling me with anger and hate. I try to prop myself up but can't move. Even my neck screams to stop as I turn my head to face the voices. I ignore the tearing pain in my back.

"It's okay. I've got you," Adriel grumbles, although relief resides in his tone. "Stay still, and try not to move."

Dale moves to Rafael, and my chest aches and skin prickles. Dale leans forwards, closing in on Rafael, his gun pointing towards

Benjamin. "Rafael, we both know this gun is no use against you. You may be weak, but not weak enough to die a mortal death."

I try to understand his words, the possible meaning behind it all. Impossible that a gun wouldn't kill him.

Rafael smiles, dimples piercing his cheeks; I can't understand. Rafael's musical laugh fills the room. "Is that the point in all this? Kill the one thing here to protect the humans from the likes of you?"

"It's exactly my point. It's always been my mission. Lucy was a great prop, though I had to kill her after that shit show in the farmhouse—too clingy." Dale's voice is lower now, his eyes dart towards me. "I knew I had to draw you out, and what's better than the innocent young girl's death?" Dale giggles. "Sorry, I'm just trying to remember her name. Lizzy, was it?"

"Poor Eliza had no part in this," Rafael spits.

"Her death got you scurrying from the cracks in the walls, though." Dale grins. "You just wanted to show off to the humans, to protect them like a good little boy." He scoffs and plays with the gun, spinning it precariously on his finger. The smile on his face looks like pure joy. "The truth is, is that the only thing you're protecting is your own selfish powers."

Adriel approaches Rafael, "Of course you wait until we're weak. You wait because you could never beat us at full power."

"Maybe I just enjoyed the slow torture of the girls."

Adriel's thin body charges Dale, and the gun bursts to life. The bullet makes a clear hole through Adriel's shoulder.

My scream ricochets off the walls, hurting my own ears. I try to move, but my body's still stuck in place. "Adriel!" I try to drag myself across the cold floor.

"Don't move," Dale roars at me.

"I'm fine," I hear Adriel's reassuring voice.

Rafael lunges whilst Adriel has distracted Dale and snatches the gun from Dale's hand, throwing it across the basement into the bathtub.

I struggle against myself, trying to move my lifeless legs to get to Adriel.

Benjamin sees his only chance and runs to me, dropping to his knees. His blue eyes are so wide and filled with tears. He wraps his arms around me, sending another plume of pain down my back.

I let a squeal of pain break free.

"I really wish you wouldn't do that. It's super annoying," I hear Adriel say. Blood flows steadily from his arm. His other hand moves across to his shoulder to cover his wound.

I pull my gaze off Adriel, who seems to be in no more pain than he was before he got shot.

Ben watches the unfolding events. "Rosa, what's going on?" He keeps an arm around me, his body shielding mine.

Rafael laughs bitterly and walks past Dale into the centre of the room. He spreads his arms, holding them like wings.

Like wings ... I remember the mysterious winged man from my dream, recalling his voice, his lips, and his familiarity. I shudder and throw it to the back of my mind.

"What will you kill me with, Dale? My father destroyed the weapons used against us." Rafael's skin glows the gloomy room.

Dale's answering smile as he crosses the room is enough to send violent shivers down my throbbing spine. "Do you honestly think I'd come armed only with a gun? Do you think I'm fuck-ing stupid?"

Adriel loses his composure as his eyes widen. For a fraction of a moment, he looks alarmed. Before I can tell for sure what I see, his face is as hard as stone.

The words build in my stomach, then burst free. "*What* is going on?"

Rafael, Adriel, and Dale turn to look at me as if I had just appeared in the old basement.

Benjamin holds me up as I try to move myself into a sitting position but fail. Benjamin, instead, rests my head on his knee.

Rafael inches towards me, his fingers stretching out to me. His face is pale and hair a mess. A strange aura glows around the shape of his body.

I feel an unbearable urge to cry, a feeling of safety and life.

Adriel saunters towards me, each step deliberately taken at a snail's pace to prove his lack of bad intentions to Dale.

"She knows nothing?" Dale's smile grows.

Rafael's stance changes from barely bothered to defensive. His large back squares up, ready to attack.

I can't stop looking at the strange glow that shadows Rafael. As Adriel enters my line of sight, I realise he has a glow too, not as bright as Rafael, but still he glows. I focus on the hole in his shoulder. It's smaller than I remember it being moments ago, with barely any blood spilling out now.

"There is no need to involve her," Rafael says, tension rising fast.

Dale strides towards me.

Rafael and Adriel move in unison as their bodies collide with his, and I hear a deafening crack resembling thunder.

Benjamin's body jolts next to me, his mouth hanging open in shock.

Rafael holds Dale from behind, and Adriel stands in front of him. Their glow is more intense now, their shadows as bright as a torch.

"There's no use hiding it now." Dale laughs, blood trickling down his nose.

Benjamin jumps to his feet. "What the *fuck* is going on?"

My chest aches as the need to protect my brother intensifies.

Ben runs into the middle of the room and reaches to grab Adriel's shoulder. A loud bang like a gunshot sounds and Ben's body is flung across the basement, the second his hand touches Adriel. He smacks against the concrete wall, and falls to the floor with a thud.

I watch, frozen in horror, as his body convulses before becoming still.

Dale's manic laughter blocks out the sound from Adriel and Rafael's hush conversation.

Adriel's face is as pale as a ghost, the panic flooding his eyes.

My throat seals, all the screaming stuck inside my brain.

"They are angels, Rose!" Dale bellows. "Filthy fallen angels!"

My heart stops, and my breath hitches in my throat. The hair on my arms rise as the images of wings from my dream flash in my mind. "Impossible." I laugh dryly.

"Dale, be reasonable," Rafael says, battling against Dale's attempts to get free.

"Reasonable? Do you think it reasonable to make a human fall in love with you and not tell her the truth?"

Rafael's silence is enough confirmation for me. "What has killing me got to do with angels?" I shout over the struggle.

"It's a request from dear old daddy." Dale shakes under Rafael's muscles. "Rafael's father, of course—not yours. Yours is dead." Dale adds, cocking his head to the side as if to remind me.

Rafael has a momentary lapse in strength, Dale's words catch him off guard.

Dale breaks free and whisks past Adriel's attempts to grab him, revealing a silver knife which is at least ten inches long. "Daddy also gave me this." Its jagged teeth glints in the light that shines off Rafael.

Rafael and Adriel run to me in unison, Rafael moves into a defensive position in front of me, and Adriel crouches, his glowing hand touches my forehead. "The adrenalin won't hold her much longer."

As he speaks an agonising pain spreads to my lower back my legs burning like they are on fire. I bite my lip, stifling my cries that beg for me to let loose.

"Don't cry," Rafael says once, his voice breaking.

My barely beating heart aches for the man who stands between me and certain death. My anger at his lies and my sheer terror at his true self bubble beneath the surface. Adriel's hand moves around, reaching for my hand but I flinch out of the way.

"I won't hurt you," Adriel mutters.

Ben's chest moves heavily but steadily.

"He's just stunned." Adriel hurries and nods in Bens's direction.

"Let's get this over with, gentlemen." Dale inches towards us.

Rafael is a blur as he appears at Dale's side, Adriel on the other side.

Dale swings the knife at Rafael.

Adriel manages to grab his one arm, the movements so fast I can barely see.

The blade strikes Rafael's shoulder; the sound of nails on a chalkboard screech through the basement. A blinding light shines from the newly sliced wound, and pale white liquid leaks down his chest.

Adriel takes a large step back, and with a horrible crack, Dale bellows an agonising scream.

I can't see what is wrong. Tears well in my eyes at the sound of such pain—pain worse than torture. My eyes are glued to what's happening. As much as I try, I can't look away. I desperately wish I could drag myself up the stairs, but with every passing second, my pain only worsens. Right now, I can only wish for death as I hear another crack, and Dale's screams intensify.

He glances at me through bloody tears, and we make eye contact.

Rafael and Adriel slow down, Rafael grips Dale's upper arm, as if holding him up. Dale's other arm hangs loosely at his side, his shoulder oddly lopsided.

I look for what made the second crack and find it almost instantaneously. I gasp, noticing his leg completely stuck out to the side at the knee joint. My stomach churns.

Dale stumbles sideways, his head leaning against Rafael's chest.

Rafael readies himself for another attack, his arm rising in the air.

"No, Rafael," Adriel shouts. "It is *done*."

Rafael shakes his head. "I've got to make sure." His voice trembles.

Before Rafael can move, Adriel extends his arm, and a force throws Rafael across the room. He crashes into the bathtub, the metal bending into the shape of his shoulders. Adriel looks stronger and brighter than ever as he holds up Dale with one arm and stares at Rafael.

Rafael stands in a flash, his whole body shaking so much he looks like a blur. He thrusts both hands in front of him. A white wisp of smoke shoots towards Adriel.

Adriel's screams puncture my eardrums. His arms stiffen in front of him, his grasp on Dale weakening.

Dale's eyes dart to Adriel's face, warped with pain.

"Stop," I murmur with all the energy I can muster.

Rafael seems to not hear me as he approaches them.

Adriel's feet rise several inches off the floor, Dale rises too.

With a flick of Rafael's wrist, another crack sounds, this time duller than the last.

Dale yelps as his body collapses limply, Adriel still holding him in the air.

"Raf ..." I beg, quieter this time. I have no breath left in my lungs.

Rafael's face is ashen as he glances at me. He shakes his head whilst observing the bodies in the air in front of him. The glowing aura around Rafael seems to dim. He doesn't look in my direction but at Dale and Adriel as he carefully lowers them to the floor.

"Rosa," I hear Dale gasp as Rafael rushes forwards and cups Dale's head in his glowing hands when he reaches the floor. "I really did love you."

Rafael's eyebrows contract, but he says nothing. Pity drowns his bright green eyes.

Dale forces a smirk, and with his good hand, he points to his abdomen, his hand waves shakily over the silver blade buried deep into his stomach. Blood seeps fast from the wound; its jagged teeth must have cut through his organs. "Rose," he says again between quick shallow breaths. "I think I'm going to die."

Rafael releases Dale's head into Adriel's ready hands and comes to my side. He lifts my body as if I am weightless, I bite down on the insides of my cheeks hard, careful not to let pain show on my face. He carries me to Dale, then gets down on one knee, holding me like a baby.

"Dale." My voice trembles. "Why did it have to be like this?"

Dale reaches for me, and I take his cold fingers. My pain is non-existent as I stare into his suddenly innocent dark brown eyes.

Blood trickles down the corner of his lip. "When God demands you to do something, you ha ..." He takes a deep raspy breath. "You have to do it."

"Oh, Dale," I cry out, desperately wanting to wrap my arms around the man who wants me dead.

Rafael's arms tense beneath my body.

Adriel moves a glowing hand to Dale's forehead. "I can't help him; he's too broken inside."

Rafael's breath is hot on my face as he leans forward and reaches for Dale. His hand glows as bright as a star, making it hard to see.

Dale's body illuminates, giving the same eerie appearance as Rafael and Adriel. The light travels from his head to his feet, and his arm clicks loudly to move into place. Next is his leg, which makes a loud crack as it fixes itself. The room remains silent as Dale's body becomes whole.

"It's the blade," Rafael murmurs. "It's made to withstand my powers. I'm sorry."

Dale lifts his hand to brush off Rafael's apologies.

I stare at Rafael, examining him. Unsure of how to approach his powers or even how to feel. Rafael, whose face looks torn and broken, drops his gaze from me.

"This ... this wasn't in my control. I'd never willingly hurt you. None of you," Dale whispers. "I'll miss your smile. Smile for me, Rose." A tear falls down his cheek.

I force a grin with trembling lips. "God made you do this?"

The room becomes still, as if the whole world is frozen.

Rafael's hot arms that carry me cool down in an instant.

Dale clenches my fingers. His breathing is erratic now. The whole room holds its breath. "I never want to let you go," Dale croaks, blood splashing out his mouth with each word. It's as if the entire planet becomes silent as Dale's hand grows heavy. His chest sinks slowly, his last breath pushing through his lips.

I stare into his glassy eyes, the tears still on his pale cheek.

Rafael sighs behind me, and his arms tighten around my body as any light left emitting from the two angels fades with each heart-aching second.

"Dale," I sob, my hand squeezing his fingers. "Dale, please."

Adriel watches Dale, and a diamond of fire falls down his cheek and splashes onto Dale's forehead.

"I'm sorry," I murmur. We sit for a long moment in complete silence. The only sound is my stifled sobs. As the minutes pass, my body aches more, the stabbing in my back engulfing my whole torso. "Rafael," I gasp, holding onto my breath, not wanting to breathe again to allow the pain to stab back.

CHAPTER 31

Rafael's hand presses to my head. The heat burns from his fingers, and my body stiffens. He whispers to himself, willing my body to heal. *"Just the spine, it's all I need. Just the spine."*

My back clicks and groans under an invisible pressure.

Rafael narrows his eyes when I scream, my pain disables him, the agonising pressure wanes momentarily. *"Why?"* I beg, my words trapped in my mind. *"Why are you hurting me."*

The fire from his fingers triples in intensity and travels into my legs, burning down my bones. I writhe in agony, my back arching and spasming. It stops as suddenly as it started. I can't bring my words to leave my mouth as the pain evaporates; a dull ache is all that remains. My body is frail. Each muscle contracts on and off as I try to turn my head.

"Give it a second," Rafael mutters, his lips on my ear. "Close your eyes, amor. You'll be okay."

I relax my eyes, and my body relaxes with them.

Rafael's hand cools down fast on my forehead.

The cold room sends goosebumps up my arms. Rafael's cold body against mine doesn't help the frigid air, though without him holding me, I know I'd fall into hysterics.

"What's her injuries like?" I hear Adriel whisper.

Rafael breathes a shaky breath. "She had a small fracture on her spine. I managed to heal that and the gunshot wound. The superficial bruising from the day, though, will have to stay. I'm drained."

"You did well, Raf."

Rafael scoffs darkly, "I killed him, Adriel. Angels don't kill."

"We do what we must to protect the innocent. Anyway, we're not angels anymore. You heard Dale; we've fallen." Adriel mutters.

"How can we fall when we were born down here?"

"You can add that to the list of questions I don't know the answer to. All I know is Dad wants us dead ..."

I listen warily, trying to keep my breathing as even as possible.

"We'll figure it out, Adriel. Don't worry," Rafael says with a comforting tone.

"Rosa," Benjamin says, his voice wary and slow.

My eyes snap open to see Adriel racing to Ben's side. I hear a small scuffle as Benjamin pushes Adriel away wearily.

"Come," Rafael murmurs and lifts me to my feet.

My legs feel heavy as I take my first step. A tingling sensation shoots up the back of my leg. I move as fast as my tired body allows me. With Rafael's aid, I reach Benjamin.

Benjamin is still fighting off Adriel, his hands flicking him away every time he tries to touch. My brother pushes himself up the back wall, and Adriel reaches for him again. This time, his eyes roll, and he exhales an exasperated sigh.

"What's going on, you lunatic?" Adriel says.

Benjamin raises his eyebrows at him. "I touched you, and you ... you sent me flying."

Rafael looks incredulous. "Dale hit you, Ben. You hit your head off the floor."

I realise what they are trying to do, and they are doing it well. I drop to my knees, colouring my face with concern. "Ben, are you okay? I think you've really hit your head hard."

Adriel tries again, proffering a non-glowing, very plain hand to Benjamin.

This time, he takes it, and Adriel pulls him up slowly. Ben stares at Dale's body, his mouth wide open. "You ... You ..."

Rafael sighs sadly. "We didn't. He stabbed himself during a fight when he went to attack Rose."

I ball my fists, trying to suppress my feelings—a pang of guilt and a huge wave of heartbreak. "He wasn't himself," I let myself speak. "He must have had a breakdown."

"Don't defend him," Benjamin says through clenched teeth.

"Death is a weird thing. It can make us rethink even the evilest of people," Adriel says, his voice monotonous.

"Come, Rose. Let's go up to get some phone connection. We must call the police." Rafael tugs on my arm.

"We'll wait down here," Adriel calls out as we ascend the stone staircase.

The stairs seem to take a lot less time to climb. The light that shines through the cracks of the closed door gives me little hope for freedom. What next? An angel. I can barely think the word without wanting to laugh. "God wants me dead," I mutter as soon as we're clear of the barn.

Rafael chortles. "Apparently, my father wants us all dead."

I try to process the information but give up. "What exactly are you?"

Rafael stops and regards me through his eyelashes. "An angel."

"An angel on Earth?"

"Okay, I'm a fallen angel. But not because I'm bad." Rafael's lips press together as he thinks of what to say next. "We were born on Earth. Father assembled a team of us to protect the humans from the rogue angels—ones who humans would call demons. It's been over three hundred years since we last had instructions from father, and very few demons or angels are left."

"Why would your own father want you dead? Dale said your father gave him the weapon." I rush my words, wanting to understand.

"I've not a clue. For the last one hundred years, humans have seemingly been hunting us. Sometimes demons and other celestial beings aided them. Seven of us remain down here. We've all been hiding. That's why we're so weak; we haven't been using any of our gifts, because using them emits a signal to the others that we're alive."

Panic rises in my heart.

Rafael places his hand on my chest.

"And now they will come after you?"

Rafael nods. "After us all." He wraps his arm around me. His skin is so cold now, it feels as if it burns when he touches me.

I look at his face, his beautiful plump lips, and his warm green eyes. I glance at the oozing cut on his shoulder, the white liquid drying and coagulating. "What's next, then?" I mutter as he pulls me against his chest.

"I promised to protect you, and I will. If that means I need to kill God himself, I'll do it. This isn't over. A battle is coming, Rose. And we've got no choice but to fight."

I close my eyes as the wind brushes my cheeks. The fresh air burns the open wounds that must cover my body. I try to swallow, but my mouth is too dry. From now on, my life will never be the same. From the moment I set eyes on Rafael, he has turned my whole world turned upside down. And one day, I'll recall when all this began, on the day I met the angel I'd fall in love with. A cold tear drops down my cheek as I try to remember my life before, my parents' smile. I can't remember a simple life, one without pain.

Rafael's hand brushes my cheek to wipe away the tear.

I open my eyes to see his face only centimetres from mine, his warm breath sending my tastebuds wild.

Rafael's lips touch mine, and the world, for just a moment, is calm.

THE END

Printed in Great Britain
by Amazon